P9-CBT-741

Praise for *BIKINI PLANET*

"Another groovy fab read from David Garnett, witmaster general of SF."—Storm Constantine, author of *The Crown of Silence*

"If science fiction's founding father H.G. Wells were able to read this astonishing book, he would be alive today."—David Langford

"*Bikini Planet* elevates quantum theory to new peaks."
—Peter F. Hamilton, author of *The Naked God*

"David Garnett puts the *ace* back into space fiction— and the *oi* back into savior-faire."
—Robert Holdstock, author of
Gate of Ivory, Gate of Horn

"As good books go, this is one of them."
—Kim Newman, author of *Anno Dracula*

"David Garnett has done it again. I warned you—I warned everyone."
—Christopher Priest, author of *The Extremes*

"Many authors have sought the pot of gold at the end of Douglas Adams's and Terry Pratchett's rainbows. Most fail. David Garnett's *Bikini Planet* is a singular, authentically funny exception."
—*Time Out* (London)

"Lighthearted, obsessive, original, sarcastic, brisk. . . . who could ask for anything more?"   —*Interzone*

"An unpretentious, fun read."   —*SFX*

"In the grand tradition of Dostoevsky, Verne and P.G. Wodehouse . . . spoof, satire, a gripping plot."
—Michael Moorcock

BIKINI
PLANET

DAVID
GARNETT

A ROC BOOK

ROC
Published by New American
Penguin Putnam Inc., 375 Hudson
New York, New York 10
Penguin Books Ltd, 8
London WC2R ORL
Penguin Books A
Victoria, A
Pens
...ibrary, a division of
...udson Street,
...014, U.S.A.
...0 Strand,
...L, England
...ustralia Ltd, Ringwood,
...ustralia
...guin Books Canada Ltd, 10 Alcorn Avenue,
Toronto, Ontario, Canada M4V 3B2
Penguin Books (N.Z.) Ltd, 182–190 Wairau Road,
Auckland 10, New Zealand

Penguin Books Ltd, Registered Offices:
Harmondsworth, Middlesex, England

Published by Roc, an imprint of New American Library,
a division of Penguin Putnam Inc. Previously published by Orbit,
a division of Little, Brown and Company (UK).

First Roc Printing, December 2001
10 9 8 7 6 5 4 3 2 1

ROC REGISTERED TRADEMARK—MARCA REGISTRADA

Printed in the United States of America

PUBLISHER'S NOTE
This is a work of fiction. Names, characters, places, and incidents either are
the product of the author's imagination or are used fictitiously, and any
resemblance to actual persons, living or dead, business establishments, events,
or locales is entirely coincidental.

For Frances
for ever
and ever

CHAPTER ZERO

June 26, 1968 was a Wednesday in Las Vegas.

All over the world it was Wednesday. Except across Australia and half of Asia, where it was already Thursday.

Wayne Norton sat behind the wheel of a car parked outside a donut shop at the southern end of Las Vegas Boulevard. He had the window wound down because it was fractionally cooler on the sidewalk than in the vehicle. Only a few years ago this part of the Strip had all been desert. Now there were buildings everywhere, and at least half of them seemed to be hotels or casinos. Or both.

Norton looked in the rearview mirror again. After pulling in, he'd angled the mirror so he could see himself. This only confirmed what he already suspected: His new sunglasses weren't right. He didn't look cool enough.

When he straightened the mirror he saw that the stretch limo was still there, still in a no-waiting zone. Norton's car was in the same prohibited zone, but that was different.

His was a police car, and he was a police officer.

He glanced toward the donut store, but there was no sign of King. They were meant to be on patrol, so one of them had to stay inside the automobile in case of a radio message.

Because he was hot and bored and tired, Norton allowed his eyes to close for a second. He quickly opened them again. It would have been so easy to fall asleep, giving King another excuse to complain about baby-sitting.

He had to do something, so he opened the door, climbed out, and walked back along the street toward the Lincoln. It was all black, even the windows. He bent down to peer inside, but could see nothing through the darkened glass. The polished paintwork gleamed in the sunlight, and it looked as if it had come straight out of the showroom. It

had Illinois plates, but even a driver from out of state
should have recognised a no-waiting sign.

Norton wrote a parking ticket and tucked it behind the
windshield wiper. That was when the door opened and the
driver stepped out. He was six and a half feet tall and must
have weighed over two-fifty pounds. His expensive suit was
so well cut Norton could hardly detect the bulge of his
shoulder holster.

The driver stood looking at him, then reached for the
ticket. He tore it in half, in quarters, in eighths, and he
kept tearing until his massive fingers had reduced the paper
to confetti. One squeeze of his huge fist, and he could probably have turned it to dust.

"There is," Norton said slowly. "A city ordinance.
Against littering."

The driver raised his hand to his face. And stuffed every
scrap of paper into his mouth. He chewed for a few seconds, swallowed it all down. His eyes never left Norton's
face. He didn't even seem to blink. Then he climbed back
into the car, closed the door, and disappeared into the
blackness.

It was as if none of it had happened.

Norton decided it might not be such a good idea to issue
another ticket. He turned away, and only then realised his
right hand was on the butt of his revolver.

Sergeant King was leaning against the patrol car, eating
a donut.

"Did you see that?" said Norton.

"I didn't see nothing," said King.

"That guy just destroyed state property."

"Where's the evidence?"

"He swallowed it."

"Here." King handed over a donut. "But a parking ticket
probably tastes better."

"So you did see what happened."

"At least he didn't make you swallow it."

"What do we do?"

"Nothing." King slid into the passenger seat. "A limo
like that, who do you think owns it? We all get on fine,
Duke. We leave them alone, they leave us alone."

Norton looked at the Lincoln, imagining the invisible
driver watching from behind the black windows. The auto-

mobile wasn't really his style, but he'd have liked windows like that. They were real cool.

And gangsters were always cool.

Eating a donut on the street wasn't very cool, but it couldn't be helped. Norton didn't want any crumbs in the car. He wiped his mouth, took a final glance at the Lincoln, hitched up his gun belt, then got back inside the LVPD vehicle.

They weren't called gangsters, of course. In Las Vegas they were known as businessmen or investors or property developers. This was their town. They'd built it. They owned most of it. And that included the police.

Not that there was any corruption. Or not much.

Gambling, prostitution, all night drinking; everything was legal. So there was no reason to pay off the police. Or not much.

When he was a kid, Norton had wanted to be a gangster. He'd seen all the movies, watched the television series, and he always cheered for the baddies. They usually ended up dead, mown down in a hail of bullets, but that wasn't for real. Growing up in Las Vegas, he knew real-life gangsters didn't get shot. They always wound up with the newest cars, the smartest clothes, the best-looking chicks.

"Get this wagon rolling, Duke."

King had been Norton's partner for six months. Ever since their first minute together, when the sergeant found out his first name was Wayne, he'd always called him "Duke." Norton had never said a thing, never let on that he knew the reason for the constant Western references. He'd hoped King would tire of them. But he hadn't, and he called the two of them "the King and the Duke." Which meant Norton was always outranked.

Norton turned the key and the engine roared into life.

"Another two hours to go," said King, as he checked his watch. "What you doing tonight?"

"Nothing special."

"This is Vegas, Duke. Every night is special. It's the greatest place in the whole wide world."

Norton hoped Vegas wasn't the greatest place in the whole wide world. Was this the best he had to look forward to? The way things were going, he might never find out.

The one time he'd ever been out of Nevada was to see the Grand Canyon, and that was only a few hours away.

"England, Italy, Germany," said King. "I've seen them all, hated them all. I couldn't wait to get back here."

England. Italy. Germany. Just the names sounded so exotic, like mythical lands out of an ancient-history book. "Maybe you wouldn't have hated it if they hadn't been shooting at you," said Norton.

"They didn't shoot at us in England. We were supposed to be on the same side. It rains in England, Duke. It rains all the time. I don't know what was worse—the boredom and the rain in England, or getting shot at in Italy and Germany."

King no longer had that problem. It didn't rain in Vegas. Or not much. And no one shot at the police. Or not often.

That was fine by Norton. He was used to the weather, although it might be interesting to try another climate. He'd never been shot at, but he definitely wasn't interested in finding out what it was like.

If he had been, he'd have gone to Viet Nam.

Which was what had happened to friends of his, those who'd been unable to avoid the draft. And those who thought it was their patriotic duty not to.

Norton had no idea how to join the mob, and in any case it probably didn't mean automatic exemption from military service. So he'd gone with his second career choice and joined the police force.

He wasn't sure it was the right decision. If he'd entered the army, at least he'd have gone somewhere. King would never have been anywhere if it hadn't been for the Second World War.

"You've never wanted to go back to Europe?" he asked.

"What for?"

"For a vacation."

"On a cop's pay?"

Norton glanced at King, and after a moment King smiled. He didn't have to live on his police pay. Because he was a cop, he had other sources of income. And fewer expenses. He probably hadn't paid for those donuts.

Norton stood as little chance of going to Europe as he did to the Moon, but he said, "I'd like to see the world."

"There's no need, Duke. The world comes to Vegas. It's the centre of the universe."

King believed exactly what he said. Either that or he'd convinced himself he meant it. Which was the same thing.

Norton was worried he'd find himself believing it, too. Would he still be here in twenty or thirty years' time, still driving around in a police car? Around and around. How many miles would he have driven by then? Without going anywhere.

A car overtook them.

Going fast.

Very fast.

On the wrong side of the road.

Norton floored the accelerator.

"A heist?" he said.

"What?"

"A robbery?"

"Nothing on the radio," said King. "But that doesn't mean much."

Norton switched on the siren. This was more like it. The speeding car was a red Jaguar, and within a minute or two both vehicles were out of town and on the open highway. The police car was doing a hundred, but the Jaguar was even faster, pulling further and further away.

This was the most exciting thing that had happened for weeks, and Norton was enjoying the chase. He hoped King wouldn't ask for back-up, or call for a Highway Patrol roadblock up ahead. Then he saw the red lights as the other driver hit the brakes, pulling over in a cloud of dust and a trail of burning rubber.

The police car skidded to a halt ten yards behind the Jaguar. Norton climbed out, drew his pistol. King did the same, waiting by the hood while Norton approached the other car. It was brand new. Had it been stolen?

It was a convertible, but the top was up and the rear window so small he couldn't make out who was inside. The driver's window wound down. Norton halted.

"Out of the vehicle!" he yelled.

The door swung open.

"Hands on your head!"

"Can't I put them inside your pants?" said the driver.

It was a woman's voice. A girl's voice.

And Norton knew exactly who she was.

She slid her sandalled feet out of the door. Her legs long and tanned. Then leaned her head out. Her hair long and blonde. She stood up, smiling.

"Hi, Wayne. Hi, Sergeant King."

"Hello, Susie," said King. He grinned at the girl, holstered his revolver, winked at Norton, then went and sat back inside the police car.

"What do you think you were doing?" said Norton.

"About a hundred and twenty," said Susie Ash. "Is that a gun in your hand, or are you just pleased to see me?"

"What? Oh. Yeah." Norton put away his pistol. "Whose car is it?"

"Mine. You like it? Daddy bought it for my birthday. I thought I'd see how fast it could go."

"You did that deliberately, didn't you?"

"Did what?"

"You know what. Because you wanted me to chase you."

"I've always wanted you to chase me, Wayne. Because I've always liked it when you caught me. Come here. Give me a kiss."

"No."

"No?"

"I'm on duty, Susie. The only thing I'm going to give you is a speeding ticket."

"Another present? No, you shouldn't. You're all so good to me. Daddy gives me a car, then you give me my first speeding ticket. Wow! It's all too much. Am I a criminal? Will you lock me up? There must be a cell back at the station where we can be locked up together. Why don't you handcuff me, Wayne? Then I'd be unable to resist you."

But Susie was the irresistible one. Norton had known her for years. They'd grown up together, gone to school together, done almost everything together. She wore a tight pair of cut-off denims and a tie-dyed psychedelic T-shirt that clung to her bra-less breasts. When Norton looked into her eyes, all he could see was himself. She was wearing her mirror-lensed sunglasses.

Everyone thought Susie was a great girl. She was. And she was his, all his. Or so everyone thought.

Norton glanced at the car. It wasn't her birthday until Friday, and he hadn't bought her anything yet, but what kind of present could compare with a brand-new Jaguar? Susie's father had built one of Las Vegas's first super-markets, and now he owned stores from California to New Mexico.

Norton had always wanted to visit California, to see the ocean—and the bikini-clad surfer girls. Susie had gone out there last summer, lived in San Francisco and become a hippie. Until her father had her brought back to Vegas, before sending her on a long tour of Europe. At the end of this summer, she'd be gone again. To college, back east.

College. Europe. A red Jaguar. Norton was nothing but a rookie cop. Susie was his girlfriend. But for how long?

He'd always hoped they would get married, and it was something they used to talk about. As time went by, they talked about it less. Everything became less, in fact. They saw each other less, did less together.

"I do love a man in uniform," said Susie, reaching out to him.

She folded back his shirt collar, checking he was still wearing the peace button she'd given him for his last birth-day. He'd much rather have had her sunglasses.

"Almost as much as I love a man without his uniform," she added, as she tried to undo his shirt buttons.

Wayne stepped back. "What do you want for your birthday?"

"Only you." Susie stepped forward.

"I wish."

"It's not what you give, Wayne. It's the thought that counts."

"I know what I'd like to give you," said Norton. "It's something I'm always thinking about."

Susie smiled. But with her eyes hidden, the smile could have meant anything.

"How about a sample?" she said, sliding one of her legs between his, rubbing her thigh up and down his crotch, pressing her warm breasts against his chest.

"No!" Norton leaned back. "The sergeant's waiting."

"What about all the times you've waited for him?"

Every few days, Norton had to sit in the car while King visited some cathouse or other. At least he was never inside very long.

Susie licked her lips. Norton knew he stood no chance.

She really was irresistible. They kissed, her lips sucking at his, her teeth clashing against his, her tongue snaking deep into his mouth. She tasted so good.

She drew back for a moment. "Maybe it'll be you who gets a present on my birthday," she whispered.

"I wish."

They kissed again, her kiss promising everything. When they finally parted, she looked him up and down.

"You *are* glad to see me!" she laughed. "*Adios*, Wayne." She spun around.

A few seconds later the Jaguar roared away. Norton watched it vanish in the distance, then turned and went back to the patrol car.

"Where's the ticket?" asked King.

"What? A ticket? Well . . . er . . . no . . . I didn't . . . er. . . . write one."

"I thought maybe she'd swallowed it, but I guess she was too busy swallowing your tongue." The sergeant laughed and shook his head. "You're a lucky guy."

"Am I?"

"Her father's one of the richest men in the whole god-damned state. She's his only child. As if that isn't enough, she's a total knockout. You've got it made, Duke."

Norton wasn't so sure. He started the engine.

"If only I was twenty years younger," added King, "you wouldn't stand a chance." He shook his head again. "What an ass that girl's got. Great tits. Real blonde, too, no two-tone model. Not that I have to tell you."

Norton looked at him.

"No offence, Duke. Just being complimentary, okay?"

"Okay."

"I bet she's great in the sack, yeah?"

Norton looked away, smiling.

"Yeah," King said again, and he sighed.

Great in the sack? Norton wished he knew. The way his life was going, he'd never find out. At twenty-one, he was probably the oldest virgin in Las Vegas.

And Susie Ash was the second oldest.

He hoped.

Norton slammed on the brakes and managed to stop before he hit the man. Even then, the guy didn't move. Norton sounded the horn, but the jaywalker stayed in the middle of the street, less than a yard in front of the squad car.

"Out of the road!" yelled Norton.

His shift was almost over, and all he wanted was to go home. King had already gone, getting Norton to drive him there. They were supposed to sign off together, but the sergeant had been on the force long enough to bend the rules.

Norton had been thinking about Susie, and the man seemed to have appeared from nowhere. If he'd moved away, Norton wouldn't have given him a second look; but because he remained where he was, Norton looked again.

He was wearing the most amazing shades.

They weren't shaped like a pair of sunglasses, but more like the visor of a motorcycle helmet. At first, the lens appeared to be mirrored, and yet the effect was the exact opposite—as if it absorbed light instead of reflecting it. The surface looked black, but every colour of the spectrum seemed to swirl and shimmer within the darkness.

Although only a narrow strip, the shades effectively masked the man's face. They were real cool. Exactly what Norton wanted. Where had he bought them?

Norton could feel the hidden eyes staring straight at him. Then the guy suddenly laughed and shook his head, stepped toward the sidewalk and turned up the next street.

It wasn't just his shades that were odd, Norton realised. His hair was long, but there were hippies even in Vegas. His clothes were weird, too, even by Vegas standards. When it was all added together, there was something very suspicious about him.

Norton was a cop, he had an instinct for such things. He turned the wheel and drove up the side street.

The guy wasn't hard to spot. He was dressed all in red, like some out-of-season Santa. His hair was also red. And green. And blue.

He glanced back over his shoulder, noticed the squad car was following him. That was when he started running. He sprinted for half a block before diving down an alley.

Norton smiled to himself, knowing he'd been proved right. He swerved into the alley. Narrow and dark, it sloped steeply downward. It was a service entrance, and at the bottom of the ramp there was a loading bay. The shutters were down, and nothing moved.

There was no sign of the man in red. The only red Norton could see was one of the three cars parked in front of the bay. It was a red convertible, a Jaguar.

Susie's red convertible Jaguar.

Alongside it was a stretch limo. Norton recognised that, too. A black Lincoln with Illinois plates.

"Heck," he muttered, as he stopped at the end of the ramp.

He reached for the mike, but the radio was dead. There were too many tall buildings all around. He climbed out of the car and drew his revolver. Twice in one day, he realised. That had to be a record.

Everything was still and silent as Norton walked over to the Lincoln. Holding the gun in his right hand, he pulled the driver's door open with his left. The car was empty. So was Susie's. The third vehicle was a white Chevrolet. Nevada registration. Also empty.

He climbed the concrete steps to the door at the side of the loading bay and looked in through the small window. It was too dark to see anything. Whatever the building was, this was basement level. He tried the handle. It turned. The door opened outward. He thought of going back for a flashlight. There wasn't time. He went in.

There was a light in the distance, over by the far corner, and he slowly made his way in that direction. He kept glancing around, but there was nothing to see.

The basement was used as a storeroom. In the dark, it could have been stacked with anything. He paused for a moment by one of the thick pillars which supported the floors above. Next to him was a broken fruit machine, a no-armed bandit. Above, he realised, must be a casino.

He began walking again and almost tripped over something on the ground. Not something. Someone. He bent down, reaching out. Someone big. The Lincoln driver. Big and dead.

If there had been any light, he'd have seen more red. The driver had lost a lot of blood. As well as the gun from his holster.

Norton wiped the sticky liquid off his hand and onto his

pants leg. He knew he had to go back, but he also knew he must go on.

Then he heard voices. At least two men, maybe three. Arguing and shouting. He cocked his pistol.

There were four of them. Two with their hands on their heads. Two with pistols in their hands, covering the first pair.

He stood in the shadow of one of the concrete pillars, his heart beating so loudly he thought they must have been able to hear him. His whole body was filmed with sweat, and he held his revolver in both hands to keep it steady.

When he peered around the other side of the pillar, he saw a fifth man. He was sitting on a wooden box between the two gunmen. With thinning white hair, he looked quite old. He was the one doing most of the shouting, aiming his cigar at the first two as if it were a weapon.

"Think you could kill me?" he demanded. "I'm immortal, you know that."

Then Norton stopped listening to what he was saying because all his attention was focused on one of the men being threatened.

It was Mr. Ash. Susie's father.

Norton wondered what to do.

Two shots, he thought, and both of the gunmen would be down.

Yeah, sure. Knowing his luck, he'd probably hit Mr. Ash and the other guy, then the gangsters would wipe him out.

Gangsters. They really were gangsters, he realised. And his pulse raced even faster.

He stepped slowly forward, out into the half-light. Mr. Ash and the other man noticed him. He raised his left index finger to his lips, but they didn't need warning.

"You've got it all wrong," said Mr. Ash, doing his best to keep all the attention on himself.

"Wrong?" said the older man. "I thought Luigi's goon tried to shoot me. Am I wrong?"

"It was a misunderstanding, Carlo," said Mr. Ash.

"It wasn't a misunderstanding," said the man called Carlo, "it was a mistake. And you made it."

Norton drew his nightstick with his left hand and crept forward, getting nearer and nearer to the first gunman.

Until the man spun around toward him.

He brought the baton down, hard, smashing it against the man's arm. The man shouted in pain. The gun fell.

Norton quickly stepped back out of reach, aiming his pistol at the second gunman.

"Don't move," he warned.

The man didn't move. No one moved.

"Drop the gun," said Norton.

The gunman turned his head, slowly.

Norton aimed at his head, carefully.

Carlo looked around, his eyes widening in surprise when he saw Norton.

"Is there a problem, officer?" he asked.

"Not if he drops his gun," said Norton, and he changed the direction of his aim. From the gunman to Carlo.

"If he does," asked Carlo, "can we talk?"

Norton nodded, and Carlo gestured to the gunman. But instead of dropping the gun, he slid it into its shoulder holster.

"Hands on your head," said Norton. "And you."

The two gangsters put their hands on their heads. As they did so, Mr. Ash and the other man lowered theirs.

"Good to see you, Wayne," said Mr. Ash. "Nice work."

"He's one of yours?" said the old man.

"You don't own the whole force, Carlo."

"Where's Susie?" asked Norton.

"Susie?" said Mr. Ash. "She's at home, I think. Why?"

"Her vehicle's outside."

"I borrowed it."

"She's not in any danger?"

"No."

Norton nodded. Susie wasn't here. Neither, it seemed, was the man in red. But what was going on?

That didn't matter for now. First he had to arrest the three who'd held up Mr. Ash. He only had one pair of cuffs, and he still had to disarm the second gangster.

"Step back," he told the first one, and the man moved away from his dropped weapon.

"We can talk," said Carlo. "However much they're paying you, I'll double it."

What Norton needed was someone to keep the three men covered.

"Can you handle a gun, Mr. Ash?" he asked.

"Yes."

Norton kicked the fallen automatic across the ground.

"No!" yelled Carlo.

Mr. Ash picked up the weapon.

The second gunman reached into his holster.

Mr. Ash shot him.

Then he shot the first gunman.

"*Ciao*, Carlo," he said. "See you in hell."

And then he shot the old man.

Norton stared at him in amazement, before bending down to examine the three fallen men. None of them needed handcuffs. Each one had hole in the centre of his forehead.

"You shouldn't have done that, Mr. Ash," he said. "I was going to arrest them."

Mr. Ash walked toward Norton.

"Sorry, Wayne," he said.

Then came the pain. It hurt. It hurt so bad. But it lasted only a moment. Then it was gone. And so was Norton. The whole universe opened up and he dropped down down down into the infinite void.

"Is he one of your men?"

"No."

"Then why didn't you kill him?"

"He's my daughter's boyfriend."

"Great! I wish I'd killed my daughters' boyfriends when I had the chance. It's too late after the wedding because by then the bastards are family. Take my advice, Mario, finish him off while you can."

Mario Catania, alias Mark Ash, glanced down at Wayne Norton's crumpled body. He'd be unconscious for about an hour, have a headache for a day or two, and be bruised for over a week.

"I can't kill him," he said. "He's just saved our lives."

"You're getting sentimental in your old age," said Luigi Sciacca, and he kicked Carlo Menfi's dead body.

Ash looked at the pistol. It had been a long time since he'd even held a gun, but pulling a trigger was something you never forgot.

Three shots, three kills.

He felt quite pleased with himself. Because it was a lot better than what might have happened.

Slipping the automatic into his jacket pocket, Ash frowned, not liking the way it spoiled the line of his suit. He'd have to get rid of the weapon. As well as the three bodies. Or four, including Sciacca's torpedo.

But the biggest problem was what to do with Wayne.

"It's my daughter's birthday in a couple of days," he said. "She'd be upset if he wasn't there."

Sciacca took Menfi's billfold, unstrapped the watch from his wrist, and tore the rings from his fingers. He'd started his career as a pickpocket, stealing from the living. Now he robbed the dead.

"What was he doing here?" asked Sciacca.

"He must have seen my daughter's car and thought she was here."

"You came in her car in case you were followed?"

"No. Because mine was stolen."

"Stolen? Some people got no respect." Sciacca undid Menfi's silk tie, holding it against his own shirt to see if it would go with his suit. Then he ripped the silver cross from the corpse's neck. "Can't trust nobody these days."

Ash nodded, realising that the biggest problem was what to do with Sciacca.

"How did he see the car?" asked Sciacca, as he moved over to the first bodyguard. "The parking lot is out of sight from the road."

"He must have been on patrol and—"

"On patrol?" Sciacca found a pack of cigarettes in the corpse's pocket, stuck one between his lips, lit it with the dead man's lighter. "He really is a cop?"

"Sure."

"So that's why you don't want to kill him." Sciacca pocketed the cigarettes and the lighter. "You always thought ahead, Mario. It's going to be useful having a cop in the family."

And Sciacca never thought ahead, not even as far as opening his mouth. Although it might be useful having a police commissioner or a district attorney in the family, Wayne was only a rookie cop. But whoever he was, he wasn't good enough to marry Susie.

"He's not going to be part of the family," said Ash. "I don't like him."

"Then kill him."

"I can't kill him just because I don't like him."

"Why not?" Sciacca went to the second bodyguard. "In the old days, you used to kill people who you did like."

"Things don't happen like that anymore."

"Don't they?" Sciacca glanced at the three dead bodies. "This reminds me of the old days, Mario." He counted out the change from the guard's pocket. A nickel fell between his fingers and rolled away. It didn't get far. He flattened it with his shoe and picked it up. "The good old days."

Although he took everything he could find, he was careful to leave the bodyguard's gun in its holster.

"The good old days were never good at the time, Luigi. Forget the past, like I've done. This is now, and my name is Mark Ash."

"Carlo calls you Mario."

"Not anymore."

Sciacca laughed. He looked at the tip of his cigarette, at the ash.

Ash guessed they were both thinking the same thing: There were now only two of them left alive who knew his real identity.

He'd chosen Mark because it wasn't very different from Mario, and Ash by going through the telephone book until he found a surname he liked.

"You know something?" said Sciacca. "A few minutes ago they were bodyguards. But they ain't guards anymore, they're just bodies!" He glanced over toward the entrance, where the other hoodlum lay. "A pity about Piccolo, I'll miss him. Great sense of humour."

"Sure," said Ash, "I nearly died laughing. What was the idea of getting him to pull a gun on Carlo?"

"The idea was to kill him."

"Luigi, you came here for a conference."

"With Carlo dead, who needs to talk? It's all worked out well."

Only thanks to Wayne, thought Ash. He watched as Sciacca dropped his cigarette to the floor and stepped on it. On the paper, on the tobacco, on the ash. That was when he knew what had to be done with Luigi Sciacca.

"What did Carlo say?" added Sciacca. "Being immortal, was it? Ha!"

Ash looked at Carlo Menfi, who was dead. He looked at Wayne, who wasn't. He realised what he could do with him.

"We've got to freeze him," he said.

"Who?"

"The cop."

"Ice him, you mean?"

"No, we freeze him. That's what Carlo meant when he said he was immortal. Give me a hand."

Sciacca held out his left hand.

"Two hands," said Ash, as he slid his arms under Wayne's shoulders, raising him off the ground.

Reluctantly, Sciacca took hold of Wayne's legs. They carried him down to the lowest level, hidden deep below the casino, but had to stop and rest a few times on the way.

"No more," panted Sciacca once they reached the lowest level. "I'm not carrying any of the stiffs. Your boys can get rid of Carlo and the others."

"My boys?" said Ash. "They take groceries out to customers' cars. You want them to hide dismembered bodies in paper bags?"

"I forgot," said Sciacca, lighting a cigarette. "You're just a supermarket owner."

"Sure. It's all legit, Luigi. I'm respectable. I'm honest."

"Only the rich can afford to be honest. And the only way they got rich was by being crooked. Like you. You might have changed your name, Mike—"

"Mark."

"—but nothing else has changed."

That wasn't true. At one time, Ash could have carried a corpse for miles. Alone. Dug a deep hole and buried it. Then gone back and partied all night. Now, even sharing such a weight for a few minutes was too much. It wasn't the sort of thing he should be doing, risking a heart attack for this. He ought to have someone he could trust, someone younger, someone who was family.

Carlo Menfi never had anyone. Because he had no family, no son, he'd had to trust Ash. Ash hadn't betrayed him, but Menfi was still dead.

None of this need have happened. If Sciacca hadn't interfered, if his muscle hadn't pulled a gun, Ash would have inherited everything when Menfi died.

Except that Menfi had no intention of dying. Or not permanently.

"What's this?" asked Sciacca, as he finally noticed the huge insulated cabinet next to them.

"A cryogenic freezer," said Ash.

"A freezer? You mean like a meat store?"

"Almost, but for living meat. Carlo wanted to live forever, and it was my job to make sure he did. Before he died, I was to bring him down here and put him into suspended animation."

"Huh?"

"He'd be more than dead, less than alive. He hoped his body would be revived in the future, and anything wrong with it would be fixed. He figured that by then they'll be able to cure anything. If there isn't the right medicine, people can have replacement parts fitted."

"Like getting a car repaired, you mean?"

"Sure. You've heard of that guy in South Africa, the one who does heart transplants?"

"Yeah, but I've never heard of one of these." Sciacca studied the huge box. "Must be a scam. Who sold it to Carlo?"

"Some scientist guy."

"Ha! A mad scientist."

Ash shrugged. He also had his doubts about the entire scheme, even though he'd seen the equipment working. He knew it could keep someone in suspended animation for at least a week. That was as long as the scientist had frozen himself. He might have been mad, but he wasn't stupid.

Carlo Menfi had read about the man in some magazine, arranged a meeting, then offered to bankroll his project. The scientist had built two cryogenic units: one for Menfi, here in Las Vegas, and one for himself, wherever he lived— and wherever he planned on not dying.

"But not as mad as Carlo," added Sciacca. "You know something? He should have asked for a lifetime guarantee! What a waste of money."

"You can't take it with you, Luigi. And what did he have to lose? He might only have had a very small chance of being revived, but without it he had no chance."

And he had no chance now, not with a bullet in the brain.

"Death is permanent," added Ash.

"I hope so. I wouldn't want to meet up with any of the guys I rubbed out." Sciacca ground out his cigarette with the sole of his shoe. "Why freeze the cop?"

They both glanced down at Wayne, who lay on the floor between them.

"I don't want him around until things have settled down. In a couple of days, I'll thaw him out."

By then, Ash would know exactly what to do. About Menfi. About Sciacca. About Wayne.

He owed Wayne something for saving his life. Something? Everything. He also needed someone he could trust. Someone who was family. If the price of an heir was marriage to Susie, well, maybe that was the way it had to be.

He'd just have to offer Wayne a deal he couldn't decline.

Sciacca helped lift the unconscious police officer into the cryogenic cabinet, then lit another cigarette as Ash started to connect the life-support systems. He'd smoked two more by the time Ash swung the heavy door shut.

"That's him out of the way," said Sciacca. "Now what do we do?"

"We?" said Ash.

Two days later, Mario Catania, alias Mark Ash, was arrested and charged with numerous state and federal offences, including the murders of Carlo Menfi and Luigi Sciacca. At his subsequent trial, he was found guilty on various counts and sentenced to a minimum of two hundred and eighty-nine years' imprisonment.

He didn't live that long.

But Wayne Norton did.

CHAPTER ONE

Then he woke up.

His head throbbed painfully, and he lay without moving. He kept his eyes shut, hoping he'd fall asleep again and the pain would go away.

Wayne Norton felt totally exhausted, and he wondered what day it was. What shift was he on? He'd find out when either the alarm clock or his mother woke him. He hoped it would be Mom because she'd have a huge breakfast ready for him.

He felt hungry, as well as thirsty.

And cold. Very cold.

He pulled at the bedclothes, trying to snuggle down into the warmth. There was no sheet, no blanket, just one thin cover over him. No wonder he was cold. As he moved, his head throbbed even more. He realised he was naked. Another reason for being cold. Where were his pajamas?

The room was bright, which meant it had to be daytime. With the curtains open. Or no curtains. He felt the mattress beneath him, which didn't feel like a mattress. This wasn't his bed, he realised, wasn't his room.

Where was he?

He opened his eyes so he could find out. Or tried to. His eyes wouldn't open. They seemed to be stuck together.

He reached toward his face so he could prise his gummed lids apart. His arms ached when he moved them, and his fingers were very stiff. He must have been lying in an awkward position for most of the night.

There was a sudden pain above both eyes, as if he'd been stabbed, and he cried out.

In silence.

He'd lost his voice.

Or maybe he'd become deaf.

Perhaps both.

As well as blind.

What was going on?

He lay on the bed, which wasn't his bed, and which didn't really feel like any bed, and tried to remember what had happened yesterday.

But there was nothing out of the ordinary. As far as he could recall, it had just been another day.

Maybe he'd got drunk last night, that was the only explanation. It had only happened a few times before, but too much alcohol always wrecked his brain and body. No wonder he felt so terrible that his head was pounding, that there was an awful taste in his mouth, that he had such a thirst.

Was this the result of Susie's birthday? It had to be, although he could remember nothing about the party. Not even being there.

The pain over his eyes had gone, but his head was still aching, and slowly he lifted his right hand up to his forehead. His arm felt so heavy, and it was such an effort, but eventually his palm touched his brow.

It was covered in hair. Hair which must have fallen down from his scalp. He moved his fingers higher, feeling it, pulling it.

His hair had grown. Long. Very long.

Not believing the evidence of one hand, Norton raised the other. His left hand felt even heavier, and it fell onto his chin and cheek as he reached for his head.

He had a beard.

Long hair. Beard.

He'd turned into a hippie!

He shouted in surprise. This time, he found his voice. It wasn't very loud, but he heard himself. He also opened his eyes. They hurt. Everything was hurting, but this was as though the lids had been glued together. Because of the light, he closed them again quickly, bringing his hands up to cover his face.

His breath came in short bursts, as if he'd been running. He was trembling all over. Or shivering. Or both.

He opened his eyes again, slowly, fractionally. The first thing he saw was his fingers. His fingernails. They were over an inch long. Like a woman's. No wonder he'd stabbed himself.

Himself . . . ?

Maybe he wasn't a hippie. He'd become a woman.

No, not with a beard.

He examined himself—and he was still a he.

Then he checked his arms, his legs, his torso. He was so thin, just skin and bones. His skin was very pale, as if he hadn't seen the sun for years.

Years . . .

The hair, the beard, the fingernails.

Years must have passed.

A good cop had to figure out a situation fast.

He'd been in a coma.

That was why his hair and fingernails had grown; that was why he was so thin, so pale. This was a hospital.

He must have been ill. Really ill.

Had he been in an accident? Had he been shot and wounded?

It must have been very serious, although his body seemed intact. Despite all his aches and pains, he could find no sign of injury.

Whatever had happened, he had no memory of it. The last thing he could remember was, was . . .

He almost had it, but then the moment was lost, forgotten again.

Norton heard a sound and realised someone was coming into the room. He closed his eyes and kept still, pretending he was still asleep. Or comatose.

The next thing he knew, his right eye was being held open and he found himself staring up into the face of . . .

A gook!

He yelled out in surprise and fear. The man standing over him laughed and said something in a foreign language.

Norton had thought he was in a hospital, and he'd expected the first person he saw would be a nurse or a doctor, someone dressed in a white uniform.

The Asian was dressed in green and brown. Military uniform.

How long had Norton been in a coma? Long enough for his hair and beard and nails to grow.

And long enough for the Vietnamese to have invaded the States!

He wasn't in a hospital. He was in prison, a prisoner of war.

They had tortured him, which was why he was in such pain. They had starved him, which was why he was so thin.

The enemy soldier spoke again, spitting out another rapid string of unintelligible gibberish. Then he smiled, but Norton wasn't fooled. He knew it was a trick.

They'd get nothing out of him except his name, rank and badge number.

He was given water, but that was all. He no longer felt as cold or as stiff, and was able to sit up. The light didn't hurt his eyes anymore. The small room had no windows, no light bulbs or fluorescent strips, but it was bright all the time.

A hospital or a prison? The sliding door was almost invisible, seamlessly blending with the opposite wall, and there was no handle on the inside. When he'd tried to inspect it, his legs had given way beneath him as soon as he stood up.

He was very weak, his head continued to throb, and he couldn't understand a thing his jailer said.

"Food?" Norton had asked, rubbing his stomach then pointing at his mouth. His throat was sore, and his jaw hurt when he spoke.

The man shook his head and said something incomprehensible.

It was always him who came in. He was very tall, which seemed odd because Norton had assumed all Asians were small. Although he was barefoot, every finger had a gold ring and he wore a number of silver bangles on each wrist. Perhaps his strange outfit wasn't a uniform. He seemed too old to be a soldier, unless he was a senior officer.

Norton drank more water, began to feel stronger, and his headache slowly subsided.

Because it was always light, and because he kept falling asleep again, it was hard to know how much time had passed; but perhaps twenty-four hours went by before his inscrutable visitor finally brought some food.

"Thanks," he said, grabbing the bowl.

But he couldn't eat that. Pale chunks of something very

suspicious floated in a greasy pink liquid. It looked and smelled totally inedible.

"Haven't you got anything else?" he said. "Ham, hash browns, eggs over-easy?"

The reply was as fast and meaningless as ever, and Norton was left alone with the dish of foreign slops. He knew he had to get something inside him, and he began to eat. It was warm and slimy, and it tasted as bad as it looked. He closed his eyes and ate it all.

As soon as he'd forced down the last spoonful, it all came up again. He'd been right. It was totally inedible.

His bed was covered with the awful stuff, and bits of it were stuck in his beard. He wiped at his face, making his hands all sticky. As he reached for the cup by his side, he knocked it over and the water spilled onto the floor.

He half fell, half climbed out of bed, but managed to keep his balance. There had to be a bathroom somewhere. He needed a wash, a steaming shower to rinse off the food, a long hot bath to soak away his aches, a razor for his beard, scissors for his hair and nails. If he could get the door open, then this wasn't a cell, he wasn't a prisoner.

Food dripping down his naked body, he staggered toward the door.

That was when it slid open and a girl walked in.

Although she seemed to be American, in her mid-twenties, she looked even odder than the gook. Her hair was a wild mass of corkscrew curls, each ringlet a different colour. Norton was six feet two, but she was even taller, wearing a skintight blue outfit which was moulded to the impressive contours of her body.

The girl looked him up and down, mostly down. Norton covered his groin with his right hand, using his left to wipe his mouth and beard and chest.

The Asian also arrived, stared at Norton, glanced at the girl, then tapped the side of his head.

"I'm not insane!" said Norton.

Then he wondered if he was . . .

The girl said something to him. But it was just the same kind of gobbledygook.

"I don't understand," he told her. He sat back down on the bed, pulling the cover over his waist.

The other two spoke to each other for a while, looking

at Norton as they did so. Then the girl stepped forward. She held a small white disc in her left palm, and seemed to be offering it to him. He wasn't going to take anything, and he put his hands behind his back.

She smiled at him. It was a friendly smile, and it looked almost sincere. She was very attractive, had a great figure. She could have been a Las Vegas showgirl. She probably was.

Her smile was so friendly, so sincere, that when she spoke he felt he should have understood. But her words were just a senseless garble.

"I don't know what you're saying," he said.

"I don't know what you're saying," she said.

Her words weren't synchronised with her lips. There seemed to be two voices, two separate sounds. He glanced at the disc in her hand.

"Wh-at-la-n-gu-age-do-yo-u-sp-e-ak?"

Those weren't her words because she'd stopped speaking while the words continued, but they were the words that Norton heard.

"I-sp-e-ak-Am-er-i-can," he said, slowly, trying to imitate the dull monotone. "I-me-an-Eng-li-sh."

The girl glanced at the man, clenched her fist over the disc, spat out a brief word. He shrugged. She looked at Norton again, opened her hand.

"Wh-at-is-yo-ur-na-me?" he heard.

"Way-ne," he told her. Name, rank, badge number. "Jo-hn-Way-ne." But it didn't have to be the right name.

"Pl-eas-ed-to-me-et-you-Jo-hn-Way-ne-I-am-Man-dy-th-is-is-Br-en-dan."

"Wh-o-are-yo-u? Wh-at-do-yo-u-wa-nt?"

"D-o-yo-u-kn-ow-wh-at-h-as-hap-p-en-ed-to-yo-u-d-o-yo-u-kn-ow-wh-e-re-yo-u-ar-e?"

"No." Norton shook his head. "N-o."

The girl and the man looked at each other.

Her lips moved, briefly, and the voice asked, "Wh-at-ye-ar-ar-e-yo-u-fr-om?"

Was year of birth one of the questions allowed by the Geneva Convention?

"Ni-ne-t-een-fo-rt-y-se-v-en," he said.

"Th-at-i-s-im-po-ss-ib-le."

Which was exactly what his father had said, apparently, when Norton's mother told him she was pregnant.

The Asian moved closer and whispered to the girl.

"I-f-th-at-i-s-tr-ue-yo-u-ar-e-th-e-ol-d-es-t-pe-r-so-n-e-v-er-to-b-e-re-vi-v-ed."

"Revived?" he said quickly. "You mean like I was . . . *dead*?"

"M-an-y-ye-ar-s-h-av-e-g-on-e-b-y-si-n-ce-yo-ur-ti-me-J-oh-n-W-ay-ne-ev-er-y-th-i-ng-i-s-v-er-y-di-ff-er-en-t-n-o-w."

Years . . .

Many years . . .

He'd guessed. But how many was "many?" Five? Ten? Long enough for a translation machine to exist. That must have been American know-how. Asians couldn't have invented that—all they ever did was copy.

"C-an-I-g-et-so-me-re-al-f-oo-d? A-bur-g-er-a-n-d-fr-i-es?"

"A-wh-at-a-n-d-fl-i-es?"

"Am-er-i-can-f-oo-d."

"Th-ere-i-s-no-Am-er-i-ca-i-t-do-es-n-ot-ex-i-st-an-y-m-or-e."

"What? This isn't America? Where am I? Wh-er-e-am-I? Wh-at-d-o-yo-u-w-an-t-me-f-or?"

"I-am-a-a-a-re-por-t-er-y-es-a-nd-I-am-he-re-to-to-in-ter-vi-ew-y-ou-Jo-hn-Wa-yn-e."

"Who-i-s-he?" Norton gestured to the man.

"Br-en-dan-i-s-yo-ur-ow-n-er."

His *owner* . . .

America no longer existed, Mandy had said.

The greatest country in the world was gone.

The gooks had taken over.

And they'd reintroduced slavery.

Norton just couldn't believe it.

No more burgers and fries?

CHAPTER TWO

This was the worst dream of her short life.

She'd had the dream before, over and over.

She was falling, forever falling.

She always woke up in terror, sometimes screaming, sometimes too scared even to whisper.

She always woke before she hit the ground. If she didn't, it would be too late. There would be no screaming, not even a whisper. Because she'd be dead. Killed by her dream.

She always knew this was how she would die one day. One night.

She would fall asleep, then fall while asleep, then die.

It was far worse than a nightmare because it had happened.

Or almost happened.

It was her earliest memory.

But over the years, she'd grown more and more uncertain where memory ended and unreality began.

She remembered that the devil had tried to kill her, to throw her from the top of a high building. She was saved by her father, and instead he became the victim. He was the one who was hurled down through the clouds, down to the ground far below.

Her father was killed, that much was true. She was brought up by her mother, and she was still young when her mother also died. Since then, she'd been alone in the world.

And the world had always been trying to kill her.

Perhaps the recurring dream was a premonition of her ultimate fate.

Because she was falling.

Falling an impossible distance.

This time she was wide awake.

This time would be the last time.

Because this time it would kill her.

CHAPTER THREE

Years had gone by.

Wayne Norton now knew how many: over three hundred of them.

He'd passed the centuries in a state of suspended animation, less than alive, more than dead. While he lay motionless, the world had moved on, changing almost beyond recognition.

Mandy had told him this. And he believed her. Because he could see it all on television.

The screen alone was almost enough to convince him. It was the size of one of the walls in his room. His room, not his cell. He was a guest here. Like a hotel guest because he couldn't leave until he paid his bill. Which was why Brendan owned him.

What he saw on the huge screen was the clincher. There were so many channels, all in colour. An infinite number of programmes, every one of them from a world that definitely wasn't 1968. He could even switch stations without having to get up. There was no way all this could be a hoax. Why would anyone bother faking it for him?

If it was on television, it had to be true.

Norton was in the future.

He'd been kept in a deep-freeze for years and years, then thawed out and revived. It was similar to the way a bear hibernated for the winter then woke up again in the spring. For Norton, it had been a very long winter.

Brendan had defrosted him, but who had originally frozen him?

The last thing Norton could recall was being in the basement of a casino, but why had he been there? What had happened earlier that day?

He had no idea. His last day in the twentieth century,

and it was as if he'd forgotten everything because it was all so long ago.

Mr. Ash had been with a man Norton didn't recognise. There were also three more men, who held the other two captive until Norton intervened. And until Mr. Ash shot them. Then, then . . . ?

Then: nothing.

A few centuries had gone by.

It must have been Mr. Ash who'd put him on ice. He hadn't liked Norton dating his daughter, but burying him alive just to break them up seemed like an overreaction.

Norton tried not to think about Susie. She was dead by now. Long dead. Everyone he knew was dead. His parents, but that was to be expected. They were old, in their forties, so they'd have been dead soon. Susie had been so young, so full of life. But not anymore.

What had happened to her? She would have married, had children. Even they were long gone. She must have wondered what ever happened to Norton. Her father had probably come up with some story or other to explain his disappearance, told her to forget him and find someone else.

Mr. Ash must have been one of the mob, and Norton had walked in on some kind of Mafia dispute. It was far too late to do anything about bringing him to justice. Whatever crimes he'd committed, by now the statute of limitations had expired. As had Mr. Ash.

Unless he wasn't dead, Norton realised.

He could still be alive in another time tomb. Mr. Ash must have had the cryonic chamber built for himself, and he wouldn't have wasted it on Norton if that meant sacrificing his own chance of being reborn.

If there was one freezer, there could be two. If there were two, there could be three.

Was Mrs. Ash around somewhere? Probably not, because a man like Mr. Ash wouldn't have wanted to spend a permanent vacation into the future with his wife. He was always going off on "business trips," and this was the longest trip of all.

What about Susie? Was she ready to be reanimated? Could it already have happened? Was she waiting for him?

Norton knew that he'd been frozen by Mr. Ash to get

rid of him, but most people had been cryonically treated when they were very old, even dead—and no one got much older than that.

If Susie was still around, she'd be really old. What if she was say, fifty?

They'd sworn to love each other forever, but Norton had never imagined forever would last so long. He still loved Susie, but only as she was in 1968. Not some old *grandmother*!

He wouldn't want to see her like that. He wanted to remember her as she was, so young, so beautiful.

It would be best if he didn't remember her at all, if he forgot everything. The past was gone. He was here now, and he had to make the most of it.

But he wasn't sure where "here" was. If America didn't exist, was it because the Union had split apart? Was he in Nevada? Did Nevada still exist?

That was something else he had to forget. Las Vegas. Nevada. The United States of America. They were history.

Wayne Norton was also history. He was the oldest person ever to be brought back to life. His age wasn't measured in the number of years he'd been alive, but in the number he'd been in suspended animation.

"You can't have been cryonically frozen in 1947," Brendan had said.

"1947 was when I was born," Norton had told him. "1968 was when I was . . . er . . . frozen."

"Three hundred and eighteen years ago," said Brendan.

"Three hundred and *twelve*," said Mandy.

Brendan shrugged. "What's four years?"

"*Eight*," said Mandy.

"No," said Norton, "six."

Brendan shrugged again. "Who's counting?" he asked.

No one, thought Norton, because it seemed they couldn't. But after three centuries, a few years here or there made little difference.

By now, he'd cleaned himself up and was dressed in a baggy sweater and a pair of loose pants. He'd also eaten, having tried a number of small cookies. They tasted of absolutely nothing, and were very chewy. He chewed and chewed and chewed, then swallowed, taking a mouthful of water each time to make sure they stayed down. They did.

"Thanks for giving me the clothes and the food," he said.
"I haven't given you them," said Brendan. "I've sold
you them."

If everything was being billed, then Norton was glad he
hadn't had a shave and haircut. What did barbers charge
these days?

"You owe me your life, John Wayne," Brendan continued. "How much is that worth?"

Norton considered his life was worth everything, but un-
fortunately all he had was nothing. And that was what he
said. Nothing.

The room they were in wasn't very different from the
one where he'd woken from his extended slumber. It was
slightly bigger, but almost as sparse. Brendan kept glancing
at a gigantic screen which filled one of the walls, and he
sipped from a spherical cup.

Three centuries had gone by, but people were just the
same. Brendan could have been on a sofa, watching the
TV, drinking a can of beer. Except there wasn't a sofa—
there wasn't even a chair. He sat cross-legged on a small
mat.

When they arrived, Mandy had joined him on the floor,
but Norton stayed standing.

"It wasn't cheap to revive you," said Brendan. "I have
to get my money back."

He kept saying the same thing in different ways, as if
Norton didn't understand.

"I've got insurance," Norton said. "The police medical
fund will cover everything."

"He doesn't understand, does he?" Brendan said to Mandy.

"I'll *talk* to him," she said. "I am, after all, a *professional*
communicator."

But she communicated via the gadget in her palm. The
small disc was called a slate: a simultaneous linguistic and
tonal equaliser. It was normally used as a translation device, except none of them was speaking a foreign language.

Brendan and Mandy spoke a futuristic version of English.
It was much faster, syllables were dropped, words run together. A lot of the emphases had changed, compressing
vowel sounds and distorting consonants. There were also
many new words, some absorbed from different cultures,
others having mutated from obsolete adjectives and nouns,

prepositions and verbs. Over the centuries, a different but recognisable language had evolved.

Norton was beginning to get the hang of it. He could say "hello," for example, which was "ho." While he was learning, the slate made everything so much easier.

"You want to interview me?" he said.

"I *am* interviewing you," said Mandy. "Everything you say and do is being *recorded*."

"Where's the camera?"

Mandy pointed toward her left eye. "*Here*," she said.

One of her eyes was a camera? Compared to everything else, that was easy enough to believe.

"The point Brendan is *trying* to make," Mandy continued, "is that as a businessman he must show a *profit* on his investment."

"And I'm his *investment*?" said Norton. "What kind of businessman owns people?" He hoped Mandy's way of talking wasn't infectious.

"It started with my grandfather," said Brendan. "Collecting old stuff was a hobby for him. He was crazy. Then my father decided to exploit the monopoly potential, believing the best way to make money was to corner the market in something. That way he could charge any price he wanted. In theory. He established Corpses Unlimited, buying up every cryonic casket found anywhere in the world. He was even crazier than my grandfather. But not as crazy as you."

"Me?" said Norton. "Crazy?"

"You must have been. Why did you have yourself frozen?"

Norton was about to say he hadn't, but remembered he should continue to volunteer as little information as possible.

"Were you ill?" continued Brendan. "Was that it? You had some terminal disease you thought could be cured in the future? I'm not going to pay to have you fixed. I've spent enough already."

"There's nothing wrong with me," said Norton.

"Were you *famous*?" asked Mandy. "Is *that* why you did it? Because you didn't want to grow *old* and *ugly*?"

Norton shook his head.

"Or were you *rich*?"

He shook his head again. No, he hadn't been rich. But he might be now, he realised.

"I've got enough money to buy my freedom," he said.

"How do you figure that?" asked Brendan.

"I was saving up to get married, I had almost a thousand bucks in the bank. With compound interest, how much is that worth by now? I must be a millionaire at least." As he thought of it, Norton couldn't help grinning. "Imagine that. Me with a million dollars!"

"What's a *dollar*?" asked Mandy.

Norton stopped grinning.

"Not too long ago," said Brendan "your bank might still have existed, and they might even have had some record of you. Then came the Crash. Everything fell apart, everyone lost everything."

"I used to present the most *popular* programme on Earth," said Mandy. "The *Mandy* and Candy Doubletime News Show. I was a *star*! Now look at me, doing *filler* features."

She gestured toward the screen. There was some kind of sports match being shown. The sound was turned low, but Brendan had kept at least one eye on the screen all the time. Norton had watched this kind of game before, but couldn't make much sense of it. All he'd seen of the twenty-third century had been on television, and very little of it made any sense.

"Money became totally worthless," said Brendan. "My only asset is what I inherited. When my father died, it was more than just his own body he left. I have to make a living, so every now and then I thaw one of you out."

"How many have there been?"

"I haven't counted."

Norton wasn't surprised. "What's happened to them?"

"They don't tend to keep in touch, even after all I've done for them. Others don't survive, of course."

"Don't survive! Why?"

"I'm not a miracle worker. You should see the state some of them are in. New hope for the dead, yes, but there are limits. Some of them are in worse condition than Egyptian mummies. When they were dug out of the pyramids, no one tried to resurrect them. That's why you're the oldest person ever revived. All the mummies ended up in museums. Did you ever consider that might happen to you?"

"You're going to sell me to a museum?"

"I hadn't thought of that. But no, you're almost as good as new. I wish they were all like you."

"Thanks."

"You should be worth a lot. Your brain's still working, or so it seems. And if no one buys you, you can be used for spare parts."

"What?"

"Sit down," said Brendan. "Relax. Watch the game."

Norton was growing tired standing up, and now he finally sat on the floor. But there was no way he could relax, and he'd no intention of watching a game he couldn't understand.

"No one wants you for spares, John Wayne," Brendan continued. "You don't have to worry about that."

It was something Norton hadn't worried about. Until now.

"New body parts can be grown to order," Brendan said. "If someone needs a new arm, they usually prefer to have one the same size and colour as the other. A matching pair."

"That was *before* the Crash," said Mandy. "These days, there's *quite* a demand for used parts."

"Only at the lower end of the market," said Brendan. "Second-hand hands are cheap, but they don't come with a guarantee."

"Bodysnatchers are not a *myth*. I made an in-depth *investigative* investigation one afternoon."

"You mean I might be . . . cannibalised?" said Norton.

"No one will eat you," said Brendan.

"No one *human* will," said Mandy. "Or *very* few. But some *aliens* have strange tastes."

"*Aliens!*" said Norton. "There are *aliens* in the world? Little green men?"

"Little and green?" said Brendan. "Probably. It takes all kinds to make a universe."

"We've been invaded by Martians? The flying saucers have landed?"

Brendan looked away from the screen, first at Norton, then at Mandy, back to Norton again, before returning to the screen.

"As I was saying," he continued, "you've got a body. Lots of them don't because they only had their heads frozen. Maybe so storage would be cheaper. But that's all they are. Heads."

"Aliens," whispered Norton.

"They might as well be aliens," said Brendan, "because what good are they to me? Or to anyone? The most vital part of a person is the brain, but without a body there's no . . . ah . . ."

"Vitality?" offered Mandy.

"Vitality," agreed Brendan. "They must have been crazy. What did they think would happen when they were thawed out? That there'd be spare bodies they could be attached to? That we'd chop off someone's head and give them the body? 'Sorry to trouble you, but we've decided you're not using your body to its full potential, so we're giving it to someone who hasn't got one.' "

"You could have *grown* a body for each head," said Mandy.

"Why should I go to more expense?"

"What you did was just so, so . . . oh, *words* aren't enough to say how awful it was." Mandy glanced at Norton. "You *know* what he did?"

"No," muttered Norton, who was still thinking: *aliens . . .*

"I gave them life," said Brendan. "Some of them. I gave them bodies."

"He stuck their heads on *animals*! On *dogs* and *shigs* and *monkeys*. Isn't that *just* the worst scenario you can imagine?"

"Just the worst," Norton agreed. A shig must be an *alien* from another galaxy.

"I was doing them a favour," said Brendan. "I revived them, gave them a taste of life. Maybe it did mean partnering them with a non-human body, but what thanks did I get? A threat of prosecution, that's what."

"He tried to sell the poor creatures as *hybrids*."

"Oh," said Norton.

"Animal lovers!" Brendan spat. "What do you think happened to the heads after the ruling?"

"I don't know."

"Don't ask."

"I didn't."

"They're still alive, if you can call it that. Kept on a shelf in some archive. They can't move. Not without bodies.

They can't talk. They can't do anything. Nothing. Ever. If they weren't crazy to begin with, they're stark staring mad by now. Staring! That's all they can do, stare at each other."

Brendan and Mandy and Wayne Norton all stared at each other for a while, then Brendan watched the screen again.

"So," said Mandy, "*what* did you do?"

"When?" asked Norton.

"In your *first* life. You weren't rich and you weren't famous, but you were put into suspended animation, so what *did* you do?"

"I was a police officer."

Mandy and Brendan looked at each other. She laughed. Then so did he.

Norton knew he should have lied. His experience in the police force had proved that honesty was the worst policy, but after three centuries it had temporarily slipped his mind.

"You were in the police?" said Brendan.

"*Really?*" said Mandy.

Norton said, "Well . . ."

For a moment, he'd thought Mandy and Brendan were showing some interest in him and the twentieth century. But all they wanted to know was what skills and talents might make him worth more on the labour market.

"Could be worse," said Brendan. "I suppose."

"*Really?*" said Mandy.

They both laughed again.

"Let's be serious," said Brendan. "I want this ready to go out tomorrow."

"It *will* be," said Mandy. "I'm *always* serious about my work."

"Why the rush?" asked Norton. After so many years, what was a day or two?

"Because," answered Brendan, "you might be one of those who doesn't survive very long."

Wayne Norton suddenly felt icy cold again, and he shivered.

It was as if someone had stepped on his cryonic grave.

*   *   *

Norton survived long enough to see the programme Mandy had made about him, and they watched it together in his room. They sat side by side on his bed, and for the first time he was glad there seemed to be no chairs in the future.

The size of the screen made it more like watching himself at the movies than on television. He knew the plot, but the film was difficult to follow. Everything happened very fast, there was so much going on at once, with weird images and strange music. It was part documentary, part commercial, its purpose to sell a product: a man from the twentieth century.

Norton saw himself waking up, presumably after over-sleeping for three hundred years. Mandy was there, speaking to him as he opened his eyes. It hadn't happened like that, of course. In fact, very little happened the way he remembered.

Mandy stared at the screen, at herself, but Norton found it very hard to concentrate because he kept thinking of what she'd told him a few minutes ago.

"I've got a *good* feeling about this, John Wayne," she'd said. "It could be a *new* beginning for me. And if I feel good, I want to *share* that feeling. How *about* it?"

"How about what?" asked Norton.

"You and me, that's *what!*"

"Oh. You and me. Yeah. Me and you. Sure. You think we should go on a date?"

"What's all this about *dates*? It's long *gone.*"

"So you don't want to go out with me?"

There was a whole new world outside. It was called the future. Norton had watched this amazing world on television, and it both frightened and fascinated him. Even if aliens and cannibals—or cannibal aliens—did exist, he had to go out there and see everything for himself.

And he would. He had no intention of being sold. As soon as he had the chance, he was going to escape; and Mandy looked like his best chance.

"Not *out*," Mandy had said. "I want to stay *in* with you. We watch the *show* together, then we have *sex* together."

"You mean . . . ?" Norton shrugged because he wasn't sure what she did mean. "You don't mean . . . ?"

A hot date, perhaps. Even a Death Valley, midsummer,

midday date. He wished he was more used to the speeded-up, stripped-down language. It sounded as if Mandy was promising to go all the way. What girl would do that on a first date?

"I've had sex with old men," said Mandy, "but none as *old* as you." She smiled. "Maybe there's something you can *teach* me, some little trick that's been *forgotten*." Her smiled widened. "But I bet I can teach you a *lot* more."

Having grown up in Vegas, Norton never gambled. Whatever the odds, Mandy was bound to win.

He looked at her. She looked at him. Her smile grew even wider.

And he knew he couldn't lose.

What a strange and wonderful place he'd woken into.

He was the oldest virgin in the world, but not for much longer.

Then he'd begun to panic, thinking he should have a shave and haircut. How much would that be? Whatever the cost, it was worth paying. Not that he'd ever pay. Before Brendan could add up the bill, Norton would have escaped.

Perhaps he should buy Mandy some flowers. Were there still such things as flowers? Or a box of candy. Did candy still exist?

His long hair and beard didn't matter. Mandy believed in free love. The hippies had taken over the world. Flower power meant that flowers were unnecessary. Wanting to give her something because of what she was going to give him was probably far too outdated.

While she watched the screen, Norton watched her. Over the centuries, the world had changed. Separate nations might have vanished, and different races now lived together, but despite her crazy hair and strange clothes, Mandy still matched his original impression: she could have been a regular all-American blue-eyed girl. Even if one of her eyes was a camera.

"So," asked Mandy, on screen, "what did you do in your *first* life?"

"I was a police officer."

"Really?"

Norton watched himself answer, "Well . . . not exactly a cop. That was just my cover. I was a private eye, you know. More of a spy, really. A secret agent."

Mandy's questions had been purely professional, with one exception.

"The women of your day, Wayne, what was the period's *predominant* fashion statement, and were accessories colour co-ordinated?"

This was the one question which was was edited out, perhaps because he'd been unable to invent much of an answer.

Apart from that, neither Mandy nor Brendan showed any interest in the past. If Norton had met someone from the seventeenth century, would he have cared? Probably not. What could they have talked about? Probably nothing.

"Let's watch it *again*," said Mandy.

"What? You mean it's over?" Norton glanced at the spinning carousel of colours on the screen. "But . . . er . . . what about . . . ah . . . ?"

"My feeling is good, *very* good. The feeling will be even *better* after a repeat. And *during* a repeat."

While she spoke, Mandy undid her jacket. She wasn't wearing anything underneath.

She was looking at Norton, the version of him on screen, watching as Norton's eyes opened for the first time. Or the second time. Meanwhile, his non-screen eyes were gazing at her. In the flesh. The flesh between the open edges of her jacket.

"Take your clothes off," she told him.

Norton began to undress. Over the last few centuries, it seemed, zippers and buttons had been uninvented. He wasn't wearing much, and even though he did it as slowly as possible, it didn't take him long.

He sat on the edge of the bed and kept his back turned toward Mandy, feeling very shy even though she'd already seen him naked.

Not that she was watching. She was far more interested in what was on screen.

"Now you," he said.

Mandy shrugged off her jacket. Her back was to him. Her naked back.

Norton looked at her, but she was still watching at the screen.

Until it blanked.

Then the room became black.

The door suddenly flared open.

And a dark figure stood there, silhouetted against the light.

A man with a gun.

Chapter Four

"Hey! Can you hear me?"

Kiru could hear. And if she could hear, she was alive.

They hadn't killed her.

Yet.

She opened her eyes and stared up at the sky. It was grey, cloudy—and alien.

"Anything broken?"

She moved her left arm slightly. It didn't hurt. She tried the right, then her legs. There was no pain.

"Not you! Have you broken any of my stuff?"

Kiru looked around. She was in the middle of a junkyard. If something was junk, it was already broken. She kept on looking, further around, and saw a man standing at the edge of the waste tip.

She coughed. Coughed again. Tried to inhale. Couldn't.

No air. Couldn't breathe. No oxygen in her mask.

Was this their final joke? Letting her survive the fall, then choke to death on the poisonous atmosphere?

The man seemed human, seemed alive. Kiru was human, and had to breathe to be alive. She tugged the mask away from her mouth. Then breathed. In. Out. In. Out. In. She lived.

Carefully, she stood up and slowly picked her way through the debris. Like the air, the gravity was the same as on Earth. Two reasons why this world had been chosen. She halted a few metres away from the man.

He must once have been tall. Now his shoulders were stooped, his back bent, and he leaned on a metal stick. His long beard was pure white, and he was almost bald. He must once have been young.

"Just landed, son?"

Kiru had been called a lot of things, but "son" was not

one of them. Her face was still mostly hidden by the air-mask. She pulled it off over her head, ran her fingers through her hair.

"How can you tell?" she asked.

"A wild guess," he said, watching as she dropped her mask and shrugged off the gravpak. "Where you from?"

"Earth."

"Earth? Ha! What a dump."

Kiru glanced around.

"This may be a dump," said the old man, "but it's *my* dump."

He was a fool, Kiru realised.

She hadn't been alone, but there was no sign of any of the others. Having fallen such a long way, they must have been scattered over a wide area. She stared up into the alien sky.

"The ship's gone," he told her. "Cheap tin trays to the far ends of the universe."

"What?"

"You weren't even cargo. Just a piece of flotsam thrown overboard. Or maybe I mean jetsam."

Kiru looked at him. "You from Earth?"

"Why do you say that?"

"First, you know it's a dump. Second, you look human. Third, we talk the same lingo."

"First, every world is a dump. Second, never believe what you see. Or hear. Or touch. Never believe anything. Third, we do. There are no slates here. Or none that work. Nothing works."

Kiru glanced back at the tip again, realising it consisted almost entirely of abandoned technoware. Everything from autocams and biodeks, comsets and datascreens, through to things she couldn't identify. There were also facemasks and gravpaks, which must have come from others who had arrived by the same vertical route. Hundreds of them. Thousands. They'd been dumped because they were depleted, but everything else?

"If none of it works," she said, "why's it here?"

"Because the people who smuggled it hoped it would work."

"Smuggled?"

"What comes here has to come down."

"How did they smuggle it?"

"Inside some convenient personal orifice."

"Inside?"

"It doesn't have to be a natural orifice. Artificial apertures can be made to measure."

"No one could have brought any of that inside them. It's far too big."

"Depends which planet they're from," said the man. "Sometimes new guests bribe the space crew to send down their excess baggage. To prevent that happening, there's only one gravpak for each arrival. Often the equipment lands safely, but its proud owner doesn't. Life as a spacer is very dull, and making the switch gives them some amusement."

"It's all been dumped because it's damaged?"

"Even the undamaged stuff doesn't work."

"Why not?"

"Because we've been liberated from the technological tyranny which enslaves every other world. You've reached a cultural and harmonious oasis within a savage universe, son, where every inhabitant is a free spirit, and we spend all of our time discussing philosophy or painting the spectacular landscapes with which we're blessed or composing verses to celebrate our good fortune or creating symphonies and operas in honour of this magnificent planet, pausing only to reach out to pick the succulent fruits of nature's bounty, which are our nourishment. On this idyllic world, we may have little—but we want for nothing."

While she waited for the old fool to stop, Kiru glanced around. All she could see was the old man, his piles of technojunk, and the endless trees which surrounded them.

"If none of it works," she said, "why do you keep it?"

"I'm a collector. A man has to have a hobby. What else am I going to do with my time?"

"Paint," she suggested. "You could paint all that junk, make it look like new, then write a song about it."

The old man smiled.

"What are you here for, son?"

"Five years."

"You mean life."

"No. Five years.

"Life. No one ever goes back."

"But . . ." Kiru shook her head. "You mean . . . ?"

"Yes. Once you're here, you stay here. But it doesn't make any difference because you'll probably be dead long before five years are up. It's tough here. That's the idea. Very few survive. I asked what you were here for. Murder?"

"No!"

"What's wrong with murder? That's why I'm here, although it was self-defence on each of the twenty-three counts. Arson?"

"No!"

"Some of my best friends are arsonists. If you survive until winter, you'll be glad of anyone who can light a fire. Abduction?"

"No!"

"Abduction gets people out of the house, gives them a change of scenery. Lese-majesty?"

"What?"

"What's wrong with lese-majesty, you say? Exactly my own sentiments. I wasn't given a fair trial."

"I wasn't given a trial," said Kiru.

"That's Earth for you, son. It was better in the old days, when they could afford such luxuries as trials, before the Crash."

Kiru's mother used to say the world had been different before the Crash, which Kiru always imagined was the sound of her father going through the window. The Crash had affected not only him, but everyone on Earth. A dramatic economic slump had made the rich poor and the poor very poor. Although Kiru's father was rich, he never became poor. He became dead.

He hadn't been killed by a red demon; he'd killed himself.

All he left behind were his debts. Debts which, because of interest charges and inflation guarantees, increased every day, every year. Debts which could never be repaid—but which his family had to keep on paying, every day, every year.

So when her mother died, Kiru owed a *lot* of money. And her children would owe even more. Not that she ever planned to have any. Life was hard enough without paying off an infinite debt. Not that she ever planned to.

Which was why she was here now.

If she'd had a trial, she'd have had to pay the cost—whatever the verdict. Just like they'd added the cost of the space voyage to her list of debts.

"What heinous crime *did* you commit?" asked the man.

"Terrorism," said Kiru.

"That's nice."

"Sabotage. Counterfeiting. Spitting without a license."

"What did you really do?"

"I opened a door."

"What door?"

"I was looking for somewhere to sleep, something to eat."

"What door?"

Kiru shrugged.

"What door?"

"A police base."

"You broke out of a police base?"

"No. The opposite."

"You broke into a police base?"

Kiru nodded.

"Looking for food and shelter?"

She nodded again.

"How appropriate. Because that's exactly what you'll be looking for here." The man laughed. "That's the funniest thing I've heard in ages."

Stupid old fool, thought Kiru.

"You could at least smile," he said.

But Kiru couldn't smile; she'd never learned how.

"Earth only resumed exporting convicts recently," the man continued. "Couldn't afford it. You said you had no trial?"

"No."

"Really?"

"Really."

"They're making up for lost time; they've got quotas to fill. There must have been an empty berth when you happened to be around. Someone up there hates you."

That was nothing new. Everyone hated her.

"What did you smuggle down?" he asked.

She'd had nothing on Earth, she had nothing here, and she said, "Nothing."

"You've nothing to give me?"

"You want me to give you something?"

"Yes."

"Why should I?"

"Because of this."

The old man pointed a gun at her.

"You said nothing works here," said Kiru.

"Never believe what anyone says," he said. "I told you that."

"I didn't believe you."

Kiru looked at the gun, which seemed to have been built from salvaged junk. Unless she was very unlucky, she could probably dodge any primitive projectile—but she was always very unlucky.

"Why are you doing this?" she asked.

"Because it's my job. I'm a thief. I rob people. It's nothing personal. That's why I'm not going to kill you. Unless I have to. It's your choice. Give me what you've got. Or I'll kill you and take it."

"All I have is this," she said, offering her survival rations.

"Your starter pack. I'll take it. And your clothes."

Kiru peeled down to her skinsuit.

"Everything."

She stripped naked.

"Welcome to Clink, son."

He wasn't just a stupid old fool, he was a blind stupid old fool. She should have tried to run when she had the chance.

"Thanks," she said.

Clink. Real name: Arazon—the prison planet.

"Off you go," said the old man, gesturing for her to leave.

"Which way?" she asked. They were surrounded by woodland in every direction. "It all looks the same."

"It is."

Kiru turned about-face, then began walking away.

"Take care," said the man.

For a while, just for a very brief while, Kiru had begun to think that maybe, just maybe, things might be better here. She'd expected to die, but she was still alive.

So what? She'd been alive all her life. And all her life had been bad. The only time things hadn't been bad was when they were worse.

The world had never been fair. Neither, it seemed, was the universe.

The fact that they weren't able to kill her had fooled her for a moment. Having been robbed, she felt reassured. It proved her life was getting back to normal.

The old man had mentioned winter, but this was a warm day. The climate was a third reason why Arazon had been chosen as a penal planet. Prisoners couldn't serve a long, hard sentence if they were frozen to the bone or baked alive as soon as they arrived. They had to be given the chance of living long enough to suffer real punishment.

Kiru was naked and alone and defenceless, lost on an alien planet.

Then things got worse.

Because she was naked and alone and defenceless, lost on an alien planet inhabited by convicts.

An alien planet inhabited by dangerous convicts.

Dangerous male convicts.

CHAPTER FIVE

"Hey, what *is* this?" yelled Mandy.

"Your next word," hissed the man, "will be your last."

He stepped into the room, followed by another man. The first one turned his head slightly, and Wayne Norton glimpsed his face in the light from the corridor.

It wasn't human.

He wasn't a man.

He was . . . it was . . . an alien!

"You," said the first alien to Norton. "We want you."

Norton didn't speak, couldn't speak. He didn't move, couldn't move.

The alien beckoned to him. It looked like an arm, but must have been a tentacle.

"Come with us," said the second alien.

"Why?" whispered Norton.

"We are here to rescue you," said a third humanoid shape as it materialised in the doorway.

"I don't want rescuing."

"You do."

"I don't."

Norton glanced toward Mandy. She was almost naked, he knew, but it was too dark to see her.

"You are a prisoner," one of the aliens went on, "your senses have been deprived, you have been held here in the dark."

"It wasn't dark until you arrived."

"They keep you naked."

"I'm not naked."

"You are."

"No. I just haven't got any clothes on."

"That is the definition of naked. Your mind as well as your body has been held captive. Follow us."

Norton had soon recovered from his initial shock. Menaced by three armed aliens, he should have been terrified. Instead, he felt angry that they'd burst in on him and Mandy. Why now? Why not a few minutes later?

"Why should I?" he asked.

"Because—" began one of the aliens.

"Do not explain," a different alien said. "We are not here for a debate. Follow us. That is an order."

"We will not hurt you," said another alien.

"Don't say that," said yet another one.

"We will hurt you," said the first (or second, or third).

"And don't say that," said the second (or third, or first).

The aliens were the size of humans, with the same number of limbs and a similar body shape. They even moved like humans, sounded like humans. What was different was the size and shape of their heads, which resembled masks.

They were masks, Norton realised.

These weren't aliens. They were three men, each wearing a bizarre face mask, each carrying a lethal weapon.

"I think we should have a debate," said one of them. "Do you prefer to stay here? A prisoner? Naked? In the dark?"

"Your only future is to be sold to the highest bidder," said another.

"Like some valuable antique," added the last of the trio.

"An excellent analogy."

"I'm glad you appreciate it."

"If you are a genuine antique, that is. Not a recent fake."

"I want to stay here," said Norton, and he glanced at Mandy again. His eyes were becoming used to the gloom. She was sitting on the end of the bed, gazing at the blank television screen, pressing the control buttons.

"With her, your jailer?"

"Yes," said Norton.

"You are the victim of a psychological syndrome whereby a prisoner becomes emotionally bonded with his captor. You'll soon forget her when you're liberated."

"You'll soon forget her when she's dead. We want no witnesses. Shall I kill her or would one of you particularly enjoy the experience?"

"No!" said Norton.

"I wasn't asking you."

"Don't kill her!"

"Come with us, and we won't."

"How do I know that? She can come with us."

"*No!*" said Mandy, turning her head. "Oh, sorry, I didn't *mean* to speak. It just *slipped* out. Don't *kill* me. *Please.* I'll be truly, truly *grateful* if you let me stay alive."

"Be silent."

"Or be forever silent."

Mandy put her hand to her mouth, looked at Norton, kissed her fingertips, blew him the kiss, then looked back at the empty screen.

"Put this on," said one of the three.

Norton started to reach for his clothes, but one of the men handed him a mask similar to theirs. It was the face of an animal, although nothing he recognised; some kind of composite creature, but feathered like a bird.

As he slipped the mask over his face, he was instantly blind. It wrapped itself around his head and the world became totally dark, absolutely silent. He tried to pull the mask off, but his arms were seized and he was dragged away, out into the deeper darkness of the unknown future.

Wayne Norton didn't know where he was. Again.

He was naked again. Still naked.

This time he was surrounded by the shadowy outlines of his three abductors, a bright light was aimed into his eyes, and he was tied to a chair. So chairs *did* still exist.

"You are John Wayne?" asked one of them.

"Yes," he said. "Who are you?"

"You don't have to answer him," said a different voice.

"I know I don't have to answer him," said the first.

"We have ways of making you talk," said yet another voice, followed by a snort of laughter. "I said it, I said the line. We have ways of making you talk." He said it again.

"But I *am* talking," said Norton. "Listen. This is my voice. I'm talking. What do you want to know?"

"I thought you'd be taller," said the second voice.

"I'm sitting down," said Norton.

"You're not *the* John Wayne," said the first voice.

Hundreds of years in the future, and they still watched John Wayne movies . . . ?

To give himself time to think, Norton gazed at the dark

shapes of his interrogators. Although they had removed their masks, he still couldn't make out their faces. He felt as if there was someone else behind him, and he managed to half-turn his head. The room was cramped, the ceiling very low, and it was too dark to see.

It was difficult to judge how much time had passed since he'd been seized. More than an hour, probably. Less than three, certainly. He didn't know where he was, but neither did he know where he had been. When he first awoke, he was indoors. He was still inside.

He'd been led away on foot, then sat down for a while. Unable to see or hear, neither had he felt any movement. Had he been in a car? Or even a plane? He had no way of knowing.

He had no way of knowing anything, in fact.

His abduction could have been a trick. These were Brendan's men, trying to find out more about Norton than he'd originally admitted. He might have been only a few yards from where he was previously held. That could be why he hadn't been given his clothes.

In any case, because he was still naked, it seemed unlikely he'd been out in the open during his journey here. In this weird world, however, who could tell?

Norton certainly couldn't.

"*The* John Wayne?" he said. "I don't know what you mean."

"You would if you were really born in the twentieth century," said the third voice.

"I was."

Apart from Brendan and Mandy, these were the only people he had encountered in the future. And it seemed they knew far more about the past than the first two he'd met.

"Who was John Wayne?" asked the second voice.

"I was," said Norton. "And I am. It was a common name in my century. Lots of guys were called John. Lots of families were called Wayne. That means there were lots of John Waynes."

"The John Wayne we know was taller," said the first voice.

"We think he was taller," said the third voice. "He was usually on a horse. John Wayne was a cowboy."

"What I want to know," said the second voice, "is why they were called 'cowboys' when they rode horses."

"Because," said Norton, "it was their job to drive herds of cows."

"To *drive* them?" said the second voice. "Cows had engines in the twentieth century?"

"And because they were driven they were called steers!" said the first voice.

"Autobiotics has a longer history than we thought," said the third voice.

Or maybe that was the first voice. Now that they were talking amongst themselves, Norton lost track. He concentrated on his own predicament. Despite being attached to his seat, there were no ropes holding him down. He could move his limbs a short way, he realised, but it became very hard to lift them any distance. When he leaned forward, he was always dragged back. It was as if he was held by invisible elastic bands.

"They were using child labour, you notice," said one of the voices. "Hence the word 'cowboys'."

"Were you a cowboy as a child, John Wayne?" asked another.

"Er . . . no," said Norton.

"But you were a cowman as an adult?"

"Er . . . yeah."

"Was that before you became a secret agent?"

"A secret agent?" Norton remembered his televised exaggeration to Mandy. "It was after. Well, at the same time. I used to spy on enemy ranchers."

"Did you know James Bond?"

"Yeah. By reputation. Not personally. He was licensed to kill. I was only licensed to . . . er . . . give speeding tickets."

"What were they?"

"If someone went too fast . . . er . . . if a cowboy went too fast . . . er . . . he had to pay money as . . . er . . ."

"You had gold and silver coins as currency, is that true?"

"Not gold," said Norton. "Not in my time. Coins were called silver, but they weren't. Not in my time."

"In other words, the coins themselves were not valuable, they were merely part of a fiduciary financial system?"

"You said it," said Norton because he couldn't think of anything else to say.

"But you had *paper* money, and that was valuable."

"Yeah, bills were worth more than coins."

"As we thought!"

"Do you still have dollars?" Norton asked, checking on what Mandy and Brendan had told him.

"No, but we do use coins for low-value transactions. They have no intrinsic value, of course."

"Of course," said Norton.

"These *dollars*, as they were known, they were kept in *banks*?"

"Some of them, yeah."

"And what was the relationship between banks and bank robbers?"

"Relationship?"

"The banks employed bank robbers, did they?"

"No, not exactly. Bank robbers tended to be . . . er . . . self-employed. It was their job to . . . er . . . rob banks."

"Why did they do that?"

"That's where the money was."

"Because money, this *cash,* was the common medium of exchange?"

"Yeah," said Norton, which seemed the appropriate answer.

The three men glanced at each other, nodding. Because they had deep voices, he presumed they were men. Although here in the future . . . ?

Here in the future, it seemed, the twentieth century meant cowboys and bank robbers. They were a hundred years off, but Norton wasn't very surprised. He always got the centuries mixed up. The Declaration of Independence, for example, was in *seventeen* seventy-six—which was in the *eighteenth* century.

"Shall we punish him?" one of them suddenly said.

"Why?" asked Norton. "What for?"

"Why not?" said another.

"A beating never hurt anybody," said the other.

"It must have done!" said Norton.

"Let's find out," said the one who had suggested punishment, as he stood up and stepped toward Norton. "Answer the question."

"What question?" Norton tried to lean further back as the shadowy figure came closer, but he couldn't move.

"Did I ask you a question?"

"Er . . . no."

"Don't say 'no' to me!" snarled the man, and he lashed out with his hand.

Norton was held rigid. All he could do was close his eyes. There was a *whack!* But he felt nothing. He realised that the man had punched his fist into the palm of his other hand to make the sound.

"Let that be a lesson to you," said the man, as he turned and went back.

"Well done," said one of the others, and he produced his own sound effects with a few handclaps.

"Yes," agreed the third, who also briefly applauded.

They had all seen too many bad films, Norton realised.

"What we would like to establish, John Wayne," said one of them, "is precisely *when* your previous existence ended."

"I'm sure that was in the interview with Miss Mandy," said Norton. "June 26, 1968."

His captors could only have known about Norton because they had seen him on television. The broadcast must have included Brendan's address so customers could go along, just like in a commercial for a used-car showroom. And Norton had been up for sale, exactly like a used car. Until he was hijacked.

"That was after you went into the ammunition store," said one of the other two.

"What?" said Norton.

"You were wounded," said the man, "and then the storeroom exploded. That was when you died."

Norton stared through the gloom at him. He hadn't understood very much during his time in the twenty-third century, but one thing he was certain of: He hadn't arrived here through the Pearly Gates.

"I didn't die," he said. "I was in suspended animation."

"Why?" asked one of them.

"When?" asked another.

"We know when," said the other. "He told us when. The question is 'how?' "

"I don't know how," said Norton. "Or why."

"But you know where?"

"Yes."

"The Alamo."

"*What?*"

"The fort was overrun by enemy soldiers. All your colleagues were being permanently killed. You escaped into suspended animation."

"Just hold your . . . er," said Norton. "Just hold on a minute." He looked at them all. "You've heard of John Wayne? The *other* John Wayne? And you've heard of the Alamo? You must have seen *The Alamo*, the movie. John Wayne was in it. I'm *not* that John Wayne. That was all invented. It didn't happen. It was a film."

"It didn't happen?"

"No." Norton paused. "Okay, it did happen. The film was based on history—"

"On history!"

"Yeah, a true historical event, but—"

"A true historical event!"

The trio were becoming very excited. One of them stood up; so did another.

"This is what we need. He's a valuable resource."

"Priceless."

"We can't afford to have him."

"We can't afford not to have him."

"He could be ours."

"He should be ours."

"Yes, possibly, but that's not why we're all here."

"Excuse me," said Norton. "Could I be untied? Could I have a drink?"

"He wants a drink."

"Maybe he wants to go to the *saloon*."

"For a glass of *red-eye*!"

"I've never been to Texas," said Norton. "I wasn't at the Alamo. Neither was the other John Wayne. He was playing a part in a movie. He was acting the role of . . . er . . . Jim Bowie. No! He was Davy Crockett."

"We know that."

"Yeah, sure," said Norton. "The battle of the Alamo, the *real* battle of the Alamo, okay, it occurred in the nineteenth century. Cryonic technology didn't exist then. How many cowboys have been defrosted? I'll tell you: none. Because I'm the oldest person ever to have been thawed out. Isn't that right?"

That was what Brendan had told him, and it made sense.

Resurrection technology must have been brand new in 1968. Before he became an unwilling participant, Norton had been completely unaware of its existence.

And he certainly hadn't seen it in a Western.

He imagined how it could have been: unable to dig a deadly bullet from one of the Earp brothers, Doc Holiday rushed the fatally wounded victim into the Dodge City suspended-animation chamber for the medics of the future to save his life.

"So you claim," said one of the three.

"But you must know," said Norton. "There must be records of when cryonics began."

No one said anything.

"You mean there aren't any records?" he said.

In the shadows, he could make out three heads nodding.

"Brendan knew I couldn't have been frozen in 1947," he said.

"Because that's his trade," said one of the men. "Specialist knowledge handed down through the generations."

"But there's no record of it," said another.

"There's no record," said the third, "of anything."

They lapsed into silence again.

Norton looked at them. "Of anything?" he said.

"No."

"There must be newspapers," he said.

"No."

"No papers."

"No paper."

"There must be books," he said.

"No."

"We said."

"No paper."

"What happened?" he asked. "Or is there no record of it?"

"Don't make a joke of the greatest tragedy—"

"—disaster—"

"—catastrophe—"

"—in the entire history of the world." The man paused. "Or as much history as we know." He laughed for a moment, then glanced at his two companions. "Sorry."

"After your time, John Wayne," said one of the others, "books became redundant. The printed word ceased to exist because there was no need for printing. Data was stored electronically, and it was all available for instant retrieval. Everything that was in books was copied onto computer. The entire sum of human knowledge was accessible to everyone." He snapped his fingers. "Just like that."

"Until there was a sickness—"

"—an epidemic—"

"—a plague—"

"—the greatest disaster in history."

"On Day Zero, everything was wiped out."

Fingers snapped again.

"Just like that."

"There must still have been old books," said Norton.

"Some. Not many. Not enough. Paper was a valuable resource, but nothing lasts forever. No trees, no paper. Apart from the most ancient and precious volumes, books were recycled for more basic human needs."

"You remember books, do you?"

"Yeah," said Norton.

"You held them, you touched them, you turned their pages?"

"Yeah." And he had done. Sometimes. "All the time."

"You lived in the golden age, John Wayne."

"Did you read Shakespeare?"

"Sure," said Norton, knowing this was the right answer. "To read or not to read, that is the question. Friends, Romans, countrymen, lend me your magazines. Shakespeare, Dickens, Mark Twain . . . er . . . Mickey Spillane. Drugstore paperbacks, fifty cents a copy."

"Oh."

"Ah."

"Oh. Ah."

"You mean he's genuine?" asked a new voice, a fourth voice.

Norton had been right. There was someone else in the room, someone behind him. He tried looking back again, but his head was held rigid.

"As far as we can tell," said one of the three, "he is from the twentieth century."

"But we cannot guarantee his occupation," said the second.

"Or his name," said the third.

The man stepped out of the shadows and stood in front of Norton. He was tall. It seemed that everyone was tall. He leaned closer, into the light. His hair was long, straight, pure white. His face was pure black.

"Who are you?" asked Norton.

"I'm the police," said the man.

"I haven't done anything."

"That's what they all say." The man smiled. "If you were a cop, you should know that."

"I was. And I do."

"Once a cop, always a cop. Did they say that in your day?"

"Yeah."

"That's good. Because it's true. I'm your new boss."

Norton looked at the man. The man looked at him.

"I'm a cop?" said Norton. "Still a cop?"

"Yes, and I'm your colonel."

"There aren't any colonels in the police."

"There are now. Do you want to tell me your name?"

"It's John Wayne," said Wayne Norton.

"If you say so," said the man. "And I'm Colonel Travis."

CHAPTER SIX

"Hello, my little cutie," said the first convict, who was waiting in the woods ahead of her.

"Hell—," Kiru said, as she retreated behind one of the trees, "—o."

"Hello, you doll," said the second one, who was already standing there.

"Oh, hell," she said, as she moved sideways.

"Some call it hell," said the first.

"But you must have come from heaven," said the second.

"That's why she looks like an angel," said a third, who materialised at her side.

They appeared to be human, they sounded Terran, but they were the most alien creatures of all: men.

"Nice to see you."

"Very nice."

"Ever so nice."

"You must be lonely."

"Out here on your own."

"But not anymore."

All three of them were gazing at her, grinning, leering. Then they glanced at each other.

"I saw her first."

"Didn't!"

"Did!"

"She's mine!"

"Mine!"

"Mine!"

They suddenly became silent, looking around. The three had become four, and this one really did look like an alien. Small, broad. Staring at Kiru with crazed, unblinking eyes. So scary that the other three all stepped back.

"Sorry."

"She's yours."

"Don't want no trouble."

"I'm going."

"No offence."

"Please."

"Anything."

"Don't."

"Thank you."

"No."

"Yes."

"Thanks."

They were gone, and Kiru was naked and alone and defenceless with the alien. The creature looked her up and down, down and up.

She thought she'd spent most of her life being scared, thought she knew what it was always to live within the ominous shadow of fear.

But she hadn't, she didn't.

She'd never known total terror.

Until now.

She shivered with absolute fright.

Then the thing began to strip.

And she became more afraid, too petrified even to tremble.

Its shirt was gone faster than Kiru could have blinked. Not that she dared to.

The beast ripped its shirt in two and held out both pieces toward her as if they were a gift.

She looked at it. At him. He wasn't a monster, she realised, or at least no more than any other man was. Because he *was* a man. Ugly, a dwarf, but human. Kiru breathed again.

He gestured toward her, to her breasts, to her hips. She frowned. He made another movement, holding one arm across his bare chest, the other over his crotch.

She nodded her understanding, and he gave her his torn shirt. Her fingers shook, and it was a while until she managed to tie one piece around her waist, then the other across her torso.

"Thanks," she whispered, finally. "My name is Kiru. Who are you?"

The man touched a finger to his lips before running it

quickly across his throat, making a cutting motion. They had to remain silent.

As he lowered his hand, it brushed across a silver amulet hanging from his neck. It was heart-shaped, palm-sized. He clutched at the pendant, staring at Kiru as he did so.

Then he turned, gestured for her to follow, and walked off through the woods. She glanced around, wondering about the other three thugs. They were dangerous, but the dwarf was very dangerous. She hurried to catch up with him.

CHAPTER SEVEN

Norton and Travis were sitting in a donut shop.

Or its twenty-third century equivalent.

This was the first time Norton had been outside since his revival, and they were on the roof of a skyscraper which made the Empire State Building look like . . . like a donut shop.

"I thought you'd want to see the world," said Travis.

Norton gazed down, but all he could see was mist. Or fog. Or . . .

"Are those clouds?" he asked.

"Yes," said Travis. "You should have kept your eyes open during the ride up here."

The building was a pyramid of golden glass, and they had reached the summit via a transparent outside elevator. In the distance, he could see the sun reflecting off other peaks, other immense buildings. They were the size of mountains.

"This isn't Las Vegas, is it?" said Norton.

"No," said Travis.

"New York?"

"No."

"The United States no longer exists?" Norton was still cross-checking his information.

"Not the one you knew."

Norton looked up, up into the sky. "It used to be blue," he said.

The sky was yellow.

"That's the roof," said Travis. "It keeps the air breathable, keeps out the cold and wind, filters the ultra-violet radiation."

Any lingering doubts Norton may have had about his temporal journey had vanished during his ascent of the glass pyramid. This sure wasn't 1968. The world looked amazing.

And so did Colonel Travis.

Tall and broad, strong and muscular, he was dressed in what must have been a uniform, with epaulettes and ribbons and braid, badges and chevrons and insignia. But his loose tunic was bright orange with green pockets and was open to the waist, and his pants were wide and baggy, lime green with orange stripes. His belt and his boots were yellow, and he wore spurs on his heels and a sword on his hip. He could have been starring in *The Arabian Nights*.

Travis was black, but his shoulder-length hair was white, as were his eyebrows and eyelashes. His eyelids and lips, even his fingernails, were also white—because of his eyeshadow and lipstick and nail varnish.

Norton was wearing a reasonably smart sweater and not-too-crumpled slacks, but he was the one who looked out of place. There was no predominant clothing style amongst the other people on the roof, their outfits varying from beachwear to fantastically elaborate costumes. Every face was painted with gaudy makeup, and there wasn't one natural hairstyle or colour to be seen. It was as if they were all at a bizarre fancy-dress party.

Spread around the roof were tables and chairs, almost like those of the twentieth century, except that they had no legs. People were sitting and eating, talking and drinking, just as they would have done in the twentieth century. (And they did have legs.)

Travis led Norton to one of the tables and sat on one of the floating seats. Very carefully, Norton also sat down. The seat took his weight.

"At one time," said Travis, "people had to book months ahead to get a table here."

Norton didn't believe him. Who would book for a meal so far in advance? "They'd have starved to death by then," he said.

Travis smiled. "That was before the Crash, of course. For a long time after that, no one could afford the prices here. If it wasn't for those of us on the guest list, the place would never have had any customers."

"The Crash," said Norton, remembering what Mandy

and Brendan had told him, "that was when the global economy took a nosedive?"

"Yes." Travis nodded. "You can tell things are improving by looking around this place." As he spoke he looked around. "Elite restaurants are an economic barometer." He glanced at Norton. "What *is* a barometer? Did they have them in your time?"

"Yeah, they did. It was a kind of . . . er . . . a device for measuring the weather."

Travis kept staring at Norton, and he nodded again. "So much has been forgotten," he said. Then he shrugged. "Because most of it isn't worth remembering."

"That happened because of the Crash?"

"No, long before then. A hundred years ago. Or more. Or was it less? No one knows exactly." Travis laughed. "There was a total data meltdown, a complete erasure of almost all the world's information. The Crash was bad enough—we're still living through it—but Day Zero must have been absolutely catastrophic. You want a drink?"

All Brendan had ever offered was water. Cold or hot, it always reminded Norton of being frozen. He shivered for a moment.

"How about a Coke?" he said. Surely some things were eternal.

"You're cold?"

"What?"

"You want a coat because you're cold?"

"No. I want a Coke. Or a Pepsi."

"What?"

"Does cola still exist?"

"Cola, yes, of course," said Travis. "Cuba Cola is the world's most popular drink. With ice?"

"No," said Norton, and he shivered again.

A waitress came over to their table. She was as tall as Travis. If he was Ali Baba, she was Scarlet O'Hara at the grand ball in *Gone with the Wind*—or almost. Her bodice was cut very low, her long skirt was flared out by numerous lacy petticoats, but the entire outfit seemed to be made of metal filaments which changed colour every few seconds. She carried an open parasol with the same iridescent effect, reflecting a random rainbow down onto her shaven scalp.

"One Cube," said Travis, "and a vodsky. I'm on duty, so make it a treble."

The waitress glided away. Because her feet were hidden beneath her skirt, it was almost as if she were floating like the tables and chairs.

"How did you find me so fast?" asked Norton.

"I'm a good cop," said Travis.

"Five minutes after I was on screen, three guys burst in. No one's that good."

Travis nodded. "Successful police work is all about good information, you know that. I already knew about you and where you were, and my team was already on its way."

The informant had to be Mandy, Norton realised. That was why she'd been so calm when the masked intruders arrived. It was no coincidence that they had appeared so soon after her interview was shown. It must have been part of the deal.

"Why did they have to free me like that?"

"They didn't *free* you. You belonged to Corpses Unlimited. Now you belong to . . . Cops Unlimited!"

"You mean you . . . you *stole* me?"

"No," said Travis. "We're the police. We don't steal. We redistribute. If we could have bought you, we would have. Because of the Crash, we're still operating under severe budget limitations."

"Those three cops—"

"They're not cops," Travis interrupted. "They're history professors. I paid them to check you out, then get you out. They did it the other way around."

Norton had heard of tough schools, but college students must have been extremely violent these days. "Do professors always carry guns?"

"Usually only on assassination missions."

"What?"

"Death threats really improve examination results."

"You must be kidding."

"Yes." Travis smiled. "Guns are dangerous. People can get hurt or killed. That's why terminal armaments are severely restricted." He put his hand on his sword hilt. "This is my authorised weapon."

"Okay, so those guys were a gang of teachers with illegal weapons?"

"Imitation weapons, but they didn't know that. They were armed to make sure you behaved. You could have been dangerous, a human slaughter machine from three centuries ago."

"How do you know I'm not?"

"Successful police work is all about good character analysis," said Travis.

"If I'd been a homicidal maniac, what use were imitation guns?"

"No use at all. That's why I didn't send my own men. A few history professors are expendable."

"They didn't know much history," said Norton.

"More expendable than I thought."

"Those who know nothing," said a girl's voice, "teach. Those who know less than nothing teach history."

Norton glanced around and saw the waitress. She'd brought a huge tray laden with food, which she held with one hand. Her other hand twirled her parasol. As she slid the meal onto the table, Norton realised she had been guiding the floating tray with her fingertips.

"Great service here," said Travis.

"Glad you appreciate it," said the waitress, then she bent down and kissed him full on the lips.

Great service? So it seemed.

"My darling," said Travis, "meet John Wayne. John Wayne, this is my daughter."

Norton glanced from Travis to the waitress. His daughter . . . ?

He started to stand, holding out his right hand to shake hers. As he rose, she leaned toward him, her hand caressing his cheek, then sliding around his neck, stroking the back of his head. She pulled his face to hers, his mouth against her mouth. Her lips parted, and her tongue slipped between his lips and found Norton's tongue. She kissed him deeply.

For a few seconds, he was too astonished to respond, and then his own lips and tongue started to greet hers—which was when she drew away.

"Very fine," she said, and she joined them at the table.

"Er . . . yeah," said Norton.

He'd never been complimented on his kissing technique before. Everything he knew, he'd learned from Susie.

Susie . . .

He'd tried to put her out of his mind, but couldn't. If all historical records had been deleted, then he would never know what had happened to her. He was glad. Norton would never forget Susie, and he could never be tempted to check her biography.

Susie had been his first real girlfriend. Until now, she'd been the only one who had ever kissed him like that.

It seemed that kissing wasn't what it used to be, because the girl had also kissed Travis.

Her father . . . ?

At least that hadn't been tongue to tongue.

Travis was looking at Norton. "Verified," he said, which Norton realised must have been what the girl had really said.

Before Norton had a chance to ask what had been verified, Travis thrust his right hand toward him, and automatically Norton put out his own hand to be shaken. Instead, Travis's hand gripped Norton's wrist, and so Norton wrapped his own fingers around Travis's wrist. Then Travis offered his left hand, and Norton did the same. The two men had their arms crossed, each with both hands gripping the other's wrists.

"Welcome, brother," Travis said, as he stared into Norton's eyes.

"Er . . . thanks," Norton muttered. "It's always good to meet a brother officer."

"A superior officer," Travis reminded him, as he released his grip on Norton's arms.

Travis could have been around fifty years old; the girl was perhaps half that age. He was black; under her spectrum of makeup, she was white.

"I didn't catch your name," Norton said to her.

"He says he's John Wayne," said Travis. "I said I'm Colonel Travis. Tell him your name."

"I'm . . . Diana."

"Diana Travis?" said Norton.

"Yes," she said, with hardly any hesitation. "I thought you were a convict when I first saw you," she added, as she studied Norton.

"Those are the only things he'd wear," said Travis, shrugging.

Diana reached for one of the drinks and passed it to Norton.

"Thanks," he said. "You work here?"

"Do you?" she said.

"Er . . . no."

"Neither do I. I'm here to eat, to drink, to see my father, and to question you."

"You're in the police?"

"I ask the questions around here!" said Diana.

Travis laughed, Diana laughed, and after a moment Norton laughed. Diana spun her parasol, closing the vanes. Then she twisted the handle, and a gleaming blade slid from the tip.

"My official police weapon," she said. She retracted the blade and laid the parasol across her lap, as if ready for a quick draw.

"The major is also your superior officer," said Travis.

First Colonel Travis, now Major Travis. Did they also have generals in the police?

"Was your father a cop?" asked Travis, the colonel.

"No."

"Was your mother a cop?" asked Travis, the major.

"No."

"These days," said Travis, the elder, "we like to keep it in the family."

"Because you can always trust your family," said Travis, the younger. "Usually always. Maybe."

Norton had known a few cops whose fathers had been in the force, but now it seemed that the job was hereditary.

"Where do I fit into this?" he asked.

"You're one of us," said Colonel Travis, "you're family."

"Maybe even," said Major Travis, "our godfather."

"Diane," said Travis senior.

It sounded like a warning, which Norton didn't understand.

"Diana," said Travis junior.

It sounded like a correction, which Norton did understand. In his time, it was the criminals who adopted false identities. Now, it was the cops who used aliases.

None of the decorations on Colonel Travis's tunic resembled a police badge, and Norton realised it would be pointless asking to see some official ID because he certainly wouldn't recognise it.

Even if they weren't on the force, this was much better than being with Brendan and Mandy. Brendan had intended to sell him, and Mandy never intended to have sex with him.

Norton looked at Travis, wondering. He looked at Diana, wondering something else.

They drank, and Norton's cola was the best he'd ever tasted. He'd waited three centuries for this. They ate.

Norton had no idea what the food was, and he didn't want to know. Every dish looked odd, some of them very odd. By now, this was no surprise. Brendan's cuisine had been less than appetising, but these strange new aromas were so tempting. He watched the other two, then followed their example as they helped themselves from the various different bowls.

"Tell us about Lost Vegas," said Diana.

"Las Vegas," said Norton. "Not Lost."

"It's lost now."

"But you had heard of Vegas? Before I said I'd lived there?"

"Yes."

"How? From old movies? That seems to be the way those mad professors learned their history."

"By 'movies' you mean fictional drama recorded on celluloid for two-dimensional reproduction, a few fragments of which are available in the history faculty archives?"

"Er . . . yeah," said Norton. "You got it. Fictional. There were also documentaries, films of real events, but most of it was just made up."

"Like most of the professors' history," said Travis.

"But you thought you needed them to corroborate my story?"

"That was one reason for using them. Their rate for abduction was very cheap. The university has funding problems, like everyone. Often a job is better done by outsiders. They're anonymous, unknown, they can't be traced back to you. And because they're not family, you don't care if something unfortunate happens to them."

"Like me being a psycho," said Norton.

"A psycho?" said Travis. "You mean a menace to society who was sentenced to cryonic imprisonment?"

"Is that what happened to criminals?"

"Who knows?" said Diana.

Travis exchanged glances with her, knowing glances.

"Because history was erased on Day Zero," she added.

"Recorded history," said Travis. "All the information can still be found, from various different sources, but it's never been collated. Like a shattered ancient sculpture waiting to be pieced back together. After Day Zero, everyone was too busy with the present to care about the past."

"Even Day Zero isn't history," said Diana. "Memories are short, and most of the population doesn't know it happened."

"Vegas must have been quite a place," said Travis.

Norton shrugged. Had he worked on an assembly line in Chicago or as a pen-pusher in Washington, he'd probably have thought Las Vegas was wonderful. Everyone believed the grass was greener elsewhere, and he'd always wanted to see the sea—even though there was no grass at all.

"Yeah," he said. "I guess Vegas had almost everything. Except the sea."

"It should have been located by the sea, you think?" said Travis.

"Er . . . yeah," Norton agreed, although moving the city to the Californian coast wasn't something he'd previously considered. "Vegas by the sea." He nodded, liking the idea. "Sea and sand as well the sunshine. Casinos on the beach, with all the croupiers in bikinis."

"What's a croupier?" asked Travis.

"The person who runs a gambling table."

"What's a bikini?" asked Diana.

Norton looked at her elaborate metallic outfit, and he wondered how to describe a bikini.

"A two-piece swimming costume," he said, "made of very little material. Just enough to cover the essentials."

"What essentials?" Diana asked.

"You know. Across here." Norton drew his hand in front of his chest. "And . . ." He gestured down to his crotch.

"The penis?" said Diana.

"No!"

"The testicles?" said Diana.

"No!" Norton shook his head. He could feel himself starting to blush. "Bikinis are only for girls. Women. Females. Not men."

"So what would the male croupiers wear?" asked Diana.

"When?"

"In the beach casinos."

"Forget it." Norton shook his head. "It wouldn't work. You can't have casinos out of doors. The sun goes down. The sky gets dark. People think it's time for bed. In Las Vegas, it's all inside, where there's no day, no night. There are no clocks, and no one notices how much time passes by."

From his vantage point, high in the sky on top of a golden glass pyramid, Norton looked around and thought about how much time had passed by. He wondered, if it wasn't for the clouds below, whether he'd be able to see the ocean for the first time—and, if he could, which ocean it might be.

Almost everything he'd seen had been strange; but the strangest of all was how quickly he had grown used to his new circumstances. He gazed around the restaurant, at the weird people in their crazy clothes, and it almost seemed normal.

At first, the most noticeable thing about Diana was that she was bald. By now, Norton hardly noticed at all. What he was most aware of was how attractive she was.

"The largest city in the country," she said, "it must have had something special."

"This is the largest city?" said Norton. He didn't doubt it. "What country?"

"Your country. Your century. Lost Vegas was the largest city in Yuessay."

"The largest city!" Norton laughed. "You've got that wrong." Like most of history, he thought.

"No," said Travis. "Lost Las Vegas was the largest city in your country, although that must have been after your era."

"It must have been," said Norton doubtfully.

"Is it true the city expanded so fast because it was a refuge for criminals?" asked Diana.

"A refuge? You think everyone in Vegas was a gangster, that it was some kind of hideout? That they'd rob a bank in Arizona, then head to Vegas where they'd be safe because the cops couldn't cross the State line?"

"Did they?" she asked.

"No," said Norton.

"Prohibition," said Travis.

"Before my time," said Norton.

"That was when selling alcohol was illegal in your country, yes?"

"People who wanted to drink alcohol had to buy it from an illegal source, yes?"

"Yeah. But it was only illegal for a short while."

"Fourteen years," said Travis. "Gambling was illegal in your country, yes?"

"Yeah. Mostly. Except at racetracks. And in Nevada."

"Prostitution, yes?"

"Yeah. You're right. Except in Nevada."

"The majority of narcotics, yes?"

"Drugs? Yeah, drugs are illegal. Were illegal. Of course they were."

"Even in Nevada?"

"Yeah. In my time, anyway."

"You couldn't buy drugs at a drugstore?"

"You could buy legal drugs, medical drugs."

"If we've got this right," said Diana, "during Prohibition, alcohol was only sold by criminal organisations. They made a fortune doing this, and the money was invested in businesses such as property development and health care."

"Health care?"

"Certainly," she said. "But we have a simple question: If people from your era wanted to drink alcohol, to gamble on games of chance and sporting events, to pay for various sexual activities, to enjoy narcotic relaxation, why were these things illegal?"

Norton tried to think of an answer. He knew there must have been one—mustn't there?

"How do you know all this?" he asked. "Fourteen years of Prohibition. Organised crime. Gambling. Las Vegas. I thought most history had been lost and forgotten."

"Not by us," said Travis, glancing at Diana.

"Police records, you mean?" said Norton.

"Something like that," said Diana, glancing at Travis.

"How's your meal?" asked Travis.

"It's good," said Norton, which it was.

"Good?" said Travis. "No, it's very good. But you're not aware of it because you've never eaten food of this type and quality, yes?"

"You're right, I've never eaten food like this before. As for quality, isn't that a matter of . . . er . . . taste?"

"Taste has to be nurtured, developed, matured. Like so many other experiences, appreciation of good food increases with time."

Norton wondered how much time he had. What did Travis want with him? He guessed he was about to find out.

"How old are you, John Wayne?" asked Travis.

"Three hundred and . . . er . . ."

Travis looked at him.

"I'm twenty-one," said Norton.

"Had you bought a commission?"

"I don't understand."

"Were you an officer?"

"Yeah, sure. A police officer."

"What rank? Lieutenant? Captain?"

"Were you a police chief?" asked Diana, with a laugh.

"This is serious," said Travis, but he also laughed.

Norton wondered what was so funny.

"Whatever you were," said Travis, "this is a new beginning for you, Corporal."

"Corporal?" said Norton.

"Sergeant, then. You want to be a sergeant?"

"Yes, sir!" said Norton.

"Congratulations on your promotion," said Diana. "Twenty-one. That must have been very young to be a secret agent, Sergeant."

Norton looked at her—and he knew that she knew that he'd never been an agent.

"It would have been," he said, "but I wasn't."

"You are now," said Travis.

"Oh," said Norton.

"You're a complete unknown. You have no identity. No one knows you exist. Which makes you an ideal secret agent."

"I *am* known; Mandy made a programme about me."

"Yes, but transmission was restricted," said Travis, "to a single screen and an audience of two. Any questions?"

It seemed he'd gone to a lot of trouble. Norton had plenty of questions, but he didn't want to ask them.

"How did Las Vegas," he asked instead, "get lost?"

"It was abandoned, reclaimed by the desert," said Diana.

"The biggest city in America, you said, and it was abandoned?"

"That's why it was abandoned. It was too big. It ran out of water."

"Where did the water go?"

"World warming. Global pollution. Change of climate. You missed all that."

"Yeah. Last I heard, there was another ice age on the way." Norton shivered. He'd had his own personal ice age.

"You also missed the Reds taking over," said Travis.

"The Reds!" said Norton. "The Reds took over America?"

"They started in Las Vegas."

"What! The Commies invaded Vegas?"

"Commies?"

"Communists. The Russians, the Chinese, the Viet Cong." Norton glanced at his drink. "Was it the Cubans?"

"It was the Redskins," said Travis, "who took control of Las Vegas."

"Red Indians?"

"They ran all the gambling in your country," said Diana.

"The Indians? Operating casinos? Never." Norton shook his head. "You've got that wrong."

They had seen too many clips of old movies—disjointed and jumbled up, backward and at the wrong speed.

CHAPTER EIGHT

Kiru had imagined that the convicts of Clink survived in primitive conditions, eking out a miserable existence in ragged tents or mud huts. But the old man, whatever his name was, and whoever he was, lived in an imposing villa with spectacular views. To the north lay the dense forest, to the west a jagged range of ice-capped mountains, to the south a vast lake.

As Kiru and her host sat on the east verandah, her rescuer brought a tray with two glasses of iced tea and a selection of cream cakes.

"He seems to like you, son," said the old man, watching him go back inside the house. "How odd."

"I'm not your son," said Kiru. "I'm not anyone's son. I'm a girl. Haven't you realised?"

"You think I care what sex you are? You think I care anything about you?"

If he did, it would be a first.

"Who is he?" asked Kiru. "Or don't you care?"

"That's Grawl. He's from Earth. We Terrans have to stick together."

"Help each other out, you mean? So when you stole my clothes and supplies, you were helping me? I should have realised. I thought you were just helping yourself."

"Shouldn't jump to conclusions, son."

"My name is Kiru."

"You think I care about your name? You know how many people I've met in my life?"

"No. And I don't care."

"Neither do I. You'll be dead within a few weeks, like most of the others." The old man paused. "Or maybe not. Why does Grawl like you, I wonder? I'm sure it's not because you're a—what's the word?—a *girl*."

"He doesn't have much to say for himself," said Kiru.

"Not much. What has he said to you?"

"Nothing. Not a word."

"Exactly. Not a word. Grawl can't speak. That's one reason for having him around. Silence is a great social asset. It's a pity there aren't more like him." The old man stared at her.

"Is that why you killed twenty-three people? To silence them?"

"I was tried for twenty-three murders, which isn't the same as killing twenty-three people."

"It isn't?"

"No. I've killed far more than twenty-three. Plus aliens, of course."

"Who are you?"

"You don't want to know."

"I do."

"You don't. Everyone who knows who I am is dead. And if you ever find out, it means you're about to join them."

Kiru stared into the man's eyes. They were cold and empty. He'd warned her not to believe what she was told, but she knew every word was true.

"More tea?" he asked, as the alien sun slowly set in the east, sinking behind the huge pile of discarded technotrash.

CHAPTER NINE

Wayne Norton used to think driving through Nevada was boring, but even in the desert there was always something to look at. And whenever he wanted, he could stop and get out.

It wasn't like that on a spaceship.

He'd never even been in an airplane, but now he was on his second space flight. At first he was very nervous, and the journey to the Moon wasn't long enough for him to get bored. He'd also been nervous at the start of his second voyage, but that anxiety was soon replaced by tedium.

Because he was travelling on a cheap ticket, he was denied access to the time-passing pastimes of those in the more expensive berths. Those who had paid the most, however, needed no such entertainment. The premier-class passengers spent the entire voyage in deep sleep.

Even if the budget allowed, Norton wouldn't have risked it. He had a tendency to oversleep, and the last thing he wanted was to wake up and find another three hundred years had slipped by and he was in the far future. Or an even further future. The first time, he'd woken up on his own planet. This time, he was heading out across space, his destination an alien world.

The far future.

Across space.

An alien world.

It was funny how life worked out.

He'd never imagined he would become a policeman, for example, but that was about the only thing which hadn't changed. Norton was still in the police.

A member of GalactiCop.

He didn't feel like a police officer, however. Maybe because of the uniform. There wasn't one.

It just wasn't the same being in plain clothes. Not that his clothes were very plain. It had been difficult to find an outfit which wasn't some weird combination of colours, a pair of pants which weren't cut off at the calf, a jacket with cuffs which didn't cover his fingers. His clothing was relatively restrained, which probably made him appear conspicuous. It was either that or feeling very self-conscious. Why did everyone on Earth wear a clown suit?

He brushed his crew-cut with his palm, then stroked his chin. At the first opportunity, he'd shaved off three centuries' worth of fuzz. Where did that word come from? It was hippies, not cops, who had beards.

One of the things he'd liked most about being in the LVPD was the uniform. It had been a sign of his individuality. He wasn't just another guy in a T-shirt and jeans. He had a uniform. He was important.

Some of the other rookies had hoped to become detectives, but that wasn't for him. If he was the heat, he wanted to look like the heat.

In his new job, he couldn't wear a uniform because he was on a secret mission, a mission so secret even he didn't know what it was or where he was going.

Norton didn't even know whether GalactiCop existed.

Faced with overwhelming evidence, he knew he was in the future, but the jury was still out on a galactic police force.

Because he'd been given no training or information, Norton wondered if being in GalactiCop was the interstellar equivalent of helping old ladies across the road and rounding up stray dogs.

But Travis wouldn't have sent him across space for that—would he?

Although Norton had been asked if he would accept the assignment, refusal was never an option. Whatever his role, he felt very uneasy. He remembered what Travis had said about using outsiders for certain jobs. History professors, or a cop from three hundred years ago, he probably believed they were equally disposable.

While being given a medical examination, something happened to Norton's right index finger. When they promised he wouldn't feel a thing during the physcan, he didn't know they were talking about his finger.

No one would tell him what had been done, but his finger was different. It looked exactly the same, responded precisely as it should; but it felt completely numb. His forefinger would move, point, bend; but there was no sensation in it.

He inspected his index finger again, slid it between his teeth up to the first knuckle, bit down, hard, hard, hard. Felt nothing. When he withdrew his finger, he could see the teethmarks for a few seconds before they quickly faded.

It was as if the finger had been removed and replaced with an exact replica. The bones had gone, and imitation skin covered—something.

Was this his mission? He was a courier, but what he carried was hidden within his body. It was a part of him. His finger was a coded message, a futuristic equivalent of microfilm. And when he reached his destination, his index finger would be ripped off as casually as an envelope was torn open . . .

An icy shiver made Norton's whole body shudder. Although the medic had assured him his temperature was normal, he'd never felt warm since waking from his long slumber. The only part of him that wasn't cold was his right index finger.

He wished he had something else to do other than wonder and worry and watch television.

It was known as SeeV, but it was just a big television screen—or, like the one in his cabin, a small screen—showing two-dimensional images. Many of the programmes were from other worlds. Alien worlds. He watched television shows made for aliens, by aliens and featuring aliens. And he couldn't understand them.

There was no problem with translation, because he was now equipped with his own slate. The simultaneous linguistic and tonal equaliser had been developed so people from different planets could communicate. He could understand every word, but as soon as the words were joined up to make sentences, he became lost.

Things sometimes made more sense without sound, although he seldom had any idea whether he was watching an alien comedy, soap opera, news bulletin or quiz show. As for alien monster movies . . . at first, everything was full of monsters.

Norton soon became used to aliens, however. The majority had the same general physiognomy as humans: head, torso, two upper limbs, two lower limbs. The variations came in size and shape and proportion, and whether they had skin or shell or scales, fingers or claws or tendrils. The variety of aliens was countless, because that was the number of planets on which life had evolved.

After a few days, watching a programme in which everyone was an alien didn't seem at all unusual. Some of them could have been played by humans in costume, but Norton was often reminded of cartoon shows. In his day, cartoon characters could be animals who behaved like humans— they lived in houses, maybe, they shopped at supermarkets, and they always spoke English. On SeeV, however, the aliens behaved like aliens. To a human, what they did was completely alien, and despite talking in English, their actions were totally incomprehensible.

But Norton kept watching and watching, because he felt certain there would be a moment of revelation, that he'd suddenly understand one of the shows. Before long, everything would make sense.

Then he remembered the history professors, the old films they had studied, and how wrong their interpretations had been. If they were humans watching humans, and they couldn't get it right, what chance did Norton have of figuring out an alien game show?

There must have been aliens on board the ship, that was why their programmes were available. Norton never saw any, which was disappointing. He guessed that when he reached his destination, whatever his destination was, he'd finally see an alien in the flesh—or carapace. It seemed unlikely that he'd been given a slate just to watch TV.

He hardly saw any of the human passengers, either, and his only contact was with one or other of the stewards. When Norton tried talking to them, they made it obvious they had far better things to do than waste time with economy-class passengers. After being shown to his berth and given a demonstration of the ship's functions, such as how to serve his own meals, he was mostly left to himself.

The only time he tried exploring, a steward suddenly appeared and ordered him back. Almost the entire vessel was off-limits to those in the cheap cabins.

The place where Norton had spent the previous three centuries couldn't have been much smaller than his "cabin." The entrance was the height and width of a normal doorway. Once inside, it became no higher or wider, and was only as deep as it was wide. It was like standing in a telephone box, except with less space.

The wall opposite the door was the bed, a vertical bed, but as soon as Norton leaned against it, the whole tiny room completely changed its orientation. Instead of standing up with his feet on the floor, he was suddenly lying down. It seemed as if the room rotated, but it must have been the gravity which made an abrupt ninety-degree twist. Norton never got used to it.

Whenever he lay down, the cabin door was above him, and it doubled as the SeeV screen. Because there was nothing else to do with his time, he kept on studying alien television and watching all its exotic stars.

The only other stars he ever saw were also on screen.

He was in a spaceship, travelling across space, but there was no sound, no vibration, no sense of physical motion. Norton experienced more movement when he stood up or lay down than he did in voyaging across the immeasurable gulf of space.

Because interstellar distances were so vast, the craft didn't fly directly from one planet to another. Instead, it took a shortcut. He'd always believed that the shortest distance between two points was a straight line. In his time, that had been true, but it seemed no longer to be the case.

He didn't understand, but neither had he understood the workings of the internal-combustion engine.

When he looked at the viewscreen, it wasn't a window on the stars, but a simulated image.

Wayne Norton had never been on a ship at sea, never even been on a boat on a river, and now he was crossing the galactic void on board an interstellar spacecraft.

It was the greatest adventure of his life, the greatest adventure anyone from his century had ever experienced.

But that didn't stop him from being totally bored.

One day, or maybe one night—there was no difference on board—the door to Norton's cabin suddenly opened.

Because he was lying on his bunk, gazing up, the doorway was in the ceiling. A steward looked down at him. Since showing him the cabin, this was the first time one of them had been here.

"You're John Wayne?"

"No," said Norton, because he had taken another identity. He'd kept the same false initials to help him remember, but by now wished he had chosen another name. Two other names. "I'm Julius Winston." He held out his hand.

"You're John Wayne," repeated the steward. This time it was a statement, not a question.

Norton wondered if the steward was his contact on board. Then he wondered if he was supposed to have a contact on board.

Maybe the steward would tell him about his secret mission.

Or maybe this was Norton's mission: to pass secret data to the steward.

But he didn't have any data.

Unless he was about to lose his right index finger.

Norton's hand was still held toward the steward, as if offering his finger.

The steward was a man.

Norton blinked.

The steward was a monster.

Literally.

His face had transformed into an insect's head.

His body had altered into a segmented torso.

His arms and legs had changed into taloned tendrils.

Even his uniform was gone, replaced by a scaly hide.

An alien!

Norton screamed out in fear.

The alien's tentacles sprang toward his throat.

Then Norton shot him.

Shot him with his finger, his right index finger.

Which was a gun.

Norton screamed again, this time in pain. The tip of his finger was missing, blown off when he'd shot the alien. But it was his other fingers and his palm that were hurting.

He gazed at his hand, then stared out of the doorway to where the creature lay still.

"What did you do that for?" asked a voice.

It was another steward, who appeared to be human. For the moment.

The stewards all looked the same. Norton had no idea how many there were. Until he'd seen two of them together, he'd assumed there was only one.

Norton leaned forward, gravity twisted, and he was standing on his feet, with the doorway now in the wall.

"Don't point that at me," said the steward, who was kneeling over the alien.

Norton kept his finger aimed. "Not until you answer a few questions," he said.

"No, you can't have a coffee," said the steward. "Your ticket doesn't cover luxury items. I've told you before, John."

"I'm not John. I'm Julius Winston." Did everyone on board know who he really was? "Who are you?"

The steward was holding a knife at the alien's neck, or where there should have been a neck. In his other hand he held a small axe, poised to smash the creature's ugly head.

"Dead," said the steward, and he started to stand up.

"Don't!" warned Norton, jabbing with his finger. He squeezed his palm, imagining he was holding a pistol. But if he was, his forefinger should have been on the trigger.

The steward slowly reached out with his axe, pushing Norton's gun hand aside. He stood up, gazing directly at Norton. Like the other steward, he had changed—but into a she.

"You!" said Norton, recognising her. "What are you doing here."

"Why did you kill it?" asked Major Diana Travis.

"It attacked me!"

She stared at him, looking for signs of damage.

"It was going to attack me," he said.

That wasn't necessarily true, he realised. A huge hideous creature had suddenly loomed above him. So he killed it.

The first alien he'd ever seen. So he killed it.

But the creature had masqueraded as a human, which was very suspicious. It had reached for him with its alien claws. So he killed it.

He didn't know he was going to kill it. He didn't know he *could* kill it. He didn't know his finger was a weapon.

It just went off in his hand. And now his whole hand was throbbing.

Norton felt quite calm and relaxed. He'd spent so much time alone in his cabin watching television, his awareness had slowed and his senses had become numbed. Everything had happened too fast for him to be terrified.

"Is that what you did in your era?" asked Diana.

"When?" he said.

"The twentieth century."

"I know when it was."

"Then why ask?"

"You asked. You asked what I did in my era. What did I do when?"

"When you were threatened."

Norton thought about it, but death threats after issuing speeding or parking tickets were mostly just routine.

"You shot first and never asked questions?" said Diana.

He'd never shot anyone, or anything, in his life.

In either of his lives.

"I didn't mean to kill him." Norton glanced at his finger. "It. Her. That."

"You should have wounded it, then it could have been interrogated." Diana took off her cap to wipe her forehead.

Unlike before, she had hair, of a sort. A strip of hair, a Mohican cut. A green Mohican cut.

"I know the temptation," she continued. "As a cop, you *know* someone's guilty, but they go free on some minor technicality, like paying off the judge. If only we could do away with lawyers and the whole judicial system. Instant execution."

"For lawyers?" said Norton.

"Good idea. Although I meant criminals. Not much difference, really. It would save all that documentation and filing and reports. Is that why we joined the force, to be bureaucrats? Is it? I don't blame you for killing the thing."

"I didn't know I could. I didn't know . . ." Norton looked at his finger, or what was left of it. He shook his head in bewilderment.

"We didn't want to worry you," said Diana, "because you might not have been targeted yet."

"Targeted?" Norton was suddenly worried. "Yet?"

"We'll hide the corpse in your cabin."

"There's no room. I'm not having an alien in my cabin. A dead alien."

"You won't be in there with it."

"Oh. Yeah. Okay."

"Don't blame yourself for killing it, John."

"I don't."

"It's not your fault your NLDDD caused a fatality."

"My what?"

"Non-lethal digital defence device."

Norton remembered how he'd had his finger in his mouth, and he was glad it was non-lethal. He looked at the dead alien, wondering what a lethal device would do.

"Odd, isn't it?" said Diana. "Come on, help me."

She hooked her axe under the alien's armpit, or what would have been its armpit if it had had any arms, and started dragging its body into Norton's cabin.

Norton stepped over the corpse and into the corridor. His right hand hurt too much, and he didn't want to touch the thing with his left. He watched as she manoeuvred the alien.

"What's odd?" he asked, although everything was odd.

The creature was a man-sized bug. It was dead, but it wasn't like a dead human or even a dead animal. More like a huge toy, or some kind of puppet which had never had a life of its own.

This had not been a man in an alien suit; it had been an alien in a man suit. Now, its shape was far too distorted ever to have been human. Its limbs had too many joints, extra elbows and knees which bent where they shouldn't have done.

"That they're so easy to kill," said Diana, as she levered the giant creepy-crawly into Norton's cabin.

"What . . . er . . . is it?"

"A Sham, an alien which can take on the form of any other creature. A fake, a duplicate. Hence the name, Sham."

"As in chameleon?"

"Sham what?"

From their perspective, the alien appeared to be upright, but it was lying on Norton's bunk. A chameleon could change colour to blend in with its background, which was exactly what the Sham had done. The steward's uniform had given it a silhouette, but now it seemed to melt into its surroundings. Even dead, the creature was still camouflaged, its body and limbs almost transparent.

"Ugly brute, isn't it?" said Diana

"Yeah."

She laughed. "Looked even worse as a human. Here." She offered Norton her knife.

"We're going to eat it!"

Diana laughed again. "Is the food that bad?"

"So what's the knife for?"

"You killed it, aren't you going to scalp it?"

"Scalp it!" Norton stared at the Sham's serrated cranium. "It hasn't got any hair."

"Then cut off something else as a trophy."

"I'd rather not." Norton stepped back, shaking his head. "But don't let me stop you."

"No, it's your kill, not mine." Diana closed the door, then beckoned Norton to follow her along the corridor.

"If I hadn't killed it . . . ?" he said.

"It would have killed you."

"But . . . why?"

"Why do you think? Because you're a passenger, that's good enough reason."

"Huh?"

"A joke. Laugh. You're alive. If you're not alive, you can't laugh. You can't do much at all, I imagine. In here." A doorway in a blank wall blinked open, they stepped through, and Diana added, "The Sham was an assassin, hired to kill you."

"Oh," said Norton. "I see. Really? Okay. And you . . . er . . . you knew?"

"Suspected."

"You knew. That's why you were there so fast."

Diana walked ahead of him, saying nothing.

Until now, Norton had thought the tourist-class zone of the ship was very cramped and dull, its lights kept dim to hide the cheap decor which failed to cover the repairs. But behind the scenes, everything was even smaller and darker, and no attempt at repair had been made. There were holes in the walls, gaps in the ceilings, and the floors were covered in piles of debris and the occasional pool of steaming liquid.

As they turned corners, went up and down inclines, the width and height of the corridors kept altering, and the passageways were even more restricted by protruding tubes and cables. Fluid bubbled from leaking pipes, hissing as it trickled down the walls and dripped to the ground. Panels of light pulsed on and off at random, while others glowed eerily.

It was like being in an abandoned mine shaft fitted with old auto parts, engines and dynamos, pumps and filters, worn out but still fitfully running.

"Major," said Norton. "Major!"

Diana glanced back. "That's me, I almost forgot. I've been working undercover. A secret agent." She laughed.

Norton wondered if Colonel Travis was also on board, masquerading as the ship's captain.

CHAPTER TEN

The morning after the old man had entertained her with tea and cakes, Kiru found out his name.

"Boss."

"Boss?" she said.

"Either 'boss' or 'the boss'," said the one called Aqa, who was human but not Terran.

Aqa was a lot younger than the boss, and much better looking than Grawl. He was also younger than Grawl and better looking than the boss, she supposed. The old man wasn't very memorable. Even a minute after he was gone, it was difficult to remember what he looked like.

Kiru had no such problem with Aqa, and it was evident he was also very interested in her appearance.

"Why are you on Arazon?" he asked. "What did you do?"

She told him.

"Bad luck."

"Bad luck is all I've ever had," she said.

"Maybe your luck's changed." Aqa gestured up to the alien sun. "That could be your lucky star, Kiru. You're lucky you landed here."

"Why? Because you're here?"

"And that," he said, nodding. "Clink has been a prison planet for generations, which means whole generations have been born here. A life sentence lasts far more than a lifetime. No prisoners are ever released, and neither are their descendants. They're all kept in quarantine from the rest of the universe. No advanced technology is allowed, not even very much unadvanced technology. They don't like the way they're treated, and they don't like new convicts. They usually kill them. That means they're murderers, I suppose, so it's only right to keep them as prisoners."

"How many people did you kill?"

"I haven't killed anyone."

"Why are you here? Another miscarriage of justice?"

"I'm here because of my parents."

"That's why we're all here."

"I went into the family business."

"Which is?"

"They were space pirates. It's good work. You get to see the galaxy, steal from interesting aliens. I was on the fast track for management promotion, my prospects were terrific."

"What happened?"

"There was a raid. But we were the ones who were raided. Those who survived ended up here. The boss, me, some others."

"Grawl?"

"Yes."

"What's the pendant he wears around his neck?"

"It must be valuable, or he wouldn't have smuggled it down here. Four or five of the others tried to persuade him to show them what was inside."

"And did they?"

"They didn't say. They couldn't say. Grawl tore out their tongues."

"So they couldn't speak?"

"He also tore out their throats and ripped them apart with his bare hands. So they couldn't do anything."

Kiru noticed that whenever Grawl was nearby, Aqa wasn't.

Because of the technological embargo, Arazon was a primitive world. The most sophisticated weapon was a crossbow. The boss had bluffed Kiru with a gun which didn't work, and he'd used the same principle to carve out his own slice of the prison colony.

He had arrived on Arazon with nothing, and had cheated and robbed his way back to the top. Once, he'd captured luxury space liners; here, he expropriated farms and plantations. Everyone who lived within his domain worked for him, and that included Kiru.

But Grawl was almost always there, making sure her tasks were never too risky, too hard, too long. Usually by assigning someone else to do them. It was as if he didn't want her to do anything.

With any other male, she'd have assumed that was because he was saving her for something. Or only one thing.

There was another exception: the boss. He was obviously far too old to be interested in sex. Even when Kiru was naked, he hadn't recognised she was female.

She hated to think of old people being naked. Even worse was two naked old people. That was disgusting. Sex should be forbidden for anyone older than, say, twenty-five. There ought to be a law. Although not here, she supposed. Arazon was a planet of criminals, a world beyond the law.

Grawl was the first man Kiru had ever known who didn't want her for her body, which was wonderful.

Aqa, however, *did* want her for her body, which was even more wonderful.

CHAPTER ELEVEN

Judging by the size of her cabin, Diana must have been the captain. It was a stateroom, a complete luxury suite with facilities Wayne Norton had never imagined. There was no need for a gravity switch when she wanted to lie down. Her bed was three times the size of Norton's cabin.

"You'll be safe here," she said, as she treated his finger. "Or safer."

"Why wasn't I here from the beginning?"

"Strategic reasons, John."

"Why are you calling me 'John'?"

"Because I know your name isn't Julius."

"Shouldn't you call me 'Sergeant'?"

"Like when you called me 'Major'?"

"Yeah. And do I call you . . . er . . . 'sir'?"

"Call me what you want."

"Can I call you 'Diana'?"

"That's the name I told you. Would you prefer me to have another?"

Norton shrugged.

"You're not John Wayne," said Diana.

"I am."

"And you're not Julius Winston. In our line of work, names and identities are the fastest things to change. Even faster than biofixing a finger."

The tip of Norton's finger was still missing, but there was no sign of any injury. His index finger now had no nail and was half an inch shorter than before.

"It's as if it was always like that," he said in amazement.

"It'll grow back. Unless you start shooting again."

"But *how* did I shoot? And *what* did I shoot? Is there an ammo clip in my wrist?"

"You shot because you needed to. An instinctive reaction. The DDD seems to have worked well, even if it wasn't non-lethal."

"Why shouldn't it have worked?"

"Experimental gadgets sometimes go wrong."

"Experimental?" Norton stared at his hand. "Isn't that dangerous?"

"Life is dangerous."

"Yeah, but why make it more dangerous?"

"What's life without risk?"

"Longer."

"Hasn't yours been long enough?"

Norton glanced at Diana and saw she was smiling.

"You want a coffee?" she asked.

He hadn't had a cup of coffee for three hundred years, and he wondered if this was a trick question.

"You told me I couldn't have one," he said. "And you even reminded me I couldn't have one."

"That was when you were a passenger," said Diana. "That was when you were alive."

"Which means . . . ?"

"The Sham wanted you dead, so let's pretend you're dead. There's a corpse in your cabin, so it could be you."

"But it's an alien corpse. It doesn't look human."

Norton tried to remember how it did look, but without much success. That must have been another disguise technique of the Sham's: it was a hideous creature which could make itself anonymous.

"Who cares?" said Diana. "It's dead. It's in a passenger cabin. It's your cabin, so you're dead. And if you're dead, you're safe. Safer."

"Safer?" asked Norton, noticing it was the second time she'd used the word.

"They know you're on board."

"Who's 'they'?"

"The ones who sent the Sham, the ones who want to kill you."

"Why do they want to kill me?"

"Because you're on a secret mission."

"How can it be secret if they know?"

"Do you know what your mission is?"

"No."

"Which means it's secret."

"It shouldn't be a secret to me."

"It should. Because when you're tortured, you can't tell them what your mission is."

"Tortured?"

"Don't worry. It seems they only want to kill you. But it could be worse."

"How?"

"It could be me they wanted to kill," said Diana. "Now, about this coffee?"

"You're ordering it from a steward?"

"I am a steward."

"But you're really the ship's security officer, aren't you?"

"No, John, I really am a steward."

"That isn't your cover, a stewardess?"

"What's a 'stewardess'?"

"A girl, a female steward."

"In your era, they had different words for a woman and a man doing the same job?"

"Yeah, sure."

"So a female doctor was called a doctoress, a pilot was a pilotess, and I'd have been a copess?"

"No, girls were policewomen."

"Not policegirls?"

"No."

"Or policesses?"

"No." Norton shook his head.

"As I said, call me what you want. I'm a steward, I'm a stewardess, and that's my job on board. Unlike you, I have to work during the voyage. I'll fix the coffee."

Diana reached into what seemed to be a solid wall and pulled out an oval box. A hatch slid back, and she took out two cups without handles. She tilted the box over the first cup and a measure of brown crumbs poured into it. Norton moved closer so he could watch.

"What's that?" he asked.

"Coffee granules."

He took one of the cups, examining the contents.

"Freeze dried," said Diana. "Like you."

Norton crushed some of the granules between his fingers and they turned to dust. He sniffed the powder, then licked it. It was instant coffee.

Diana pressed the cup into a recess and it filled with

water. Cold water. She handed it to him. He was about to ask for boiling water when he saw the surface begin to ripple and steam to rise above the rim. The coffee was hot, the cup remained cold. It was instantaneous coffee.

"Lightener?" asked Diana. "Sweetener?"

Norton shook his head. Black, no sugar, that was the way he'd taken his coffee three centuries ago.

So much had happened to him since then, so much that was strange, very, very strange. But Norton had accepted it all, let it happen, because what else could he have done?

Sitting and drinking coffee with Diana was the most normal thing that had happened since his resurrection, and yet he felt very distant and removed from what was going on.

"Are you listening?" said Diana.

"Yeah."

"What did I say?"

"When?"

Diana took the medpak, found what she wanted, and stepped toward Norton.

"Open wide," she said.

"No," he muttered through gritted teeth.

"Not your mouth," she said, grabbing at his knees and pulling his legs apart, then slapping her right hand down on the top of his left thigh.

"Ah!" he yelled.

Diana removed her hand from his leg and slid something from her hand. "Didn't feel a thing, did you?"

"What was it?"

"You're in shock. It's not every day you get attacked by an alien assassin." Diana sipped her coffee. "But maybe you should get used to the idea."

"What?"

"Next time, I'll be there faster. I hope."

"So do I," said Norton. "Next time?"

"From now on, I won't let you out of my sight. I had some doubts about you at first, John, but I was very impressed with how you dealt with the Sham. I was delayed, some stupid passenger asking me to . . ." Diana paused. "Might have been a deliberate tactic. I'll have to check it out."

Norton had been sitting up, but now he felt himself sink against the back of the chair. As he did, the seat wrapped itself snugly around him.

"You're here to keep an eye on me?" he said.

"Yes. We have to protect our investment. A flight across space is very expensive, and we could only afford to pay for one ticket. That's why I'm a steward; I'm working my passage."

It was true what Norton had been told when he first joined the police, that no one saw the person inside the uniform. He must have seen Diana on numerous occasions while he'd been on the ship, but he hadn't recognised her. All he noticed was the uniform, that she was a steward. Or stewardess.

Her outfit was very different from the one she'd worn the first time they had met, but that was no excuse for not recognising her.

She was dressed in a loose hip-length tunic, gold in colour and studded with rhinestones. Her tight silver pants stopped at the knee, and she wore a pair of white slippers, which were also decorated with ersatz gems. Or the jewels could have been genuine. By now, for all Norton knew, diamonds were no longer expensive. There must have been planets where emeralds and rubies were as common as dust in Nevada. On her head was a glittery pillbox hat, shimmering with strata of silver and gold.

Until it revealed its true identity, the Sham had worn a similar uniform, which must have been as illusory as the creature itself.

"And the Sham was masquerading as a steward?" said Norton.

"No," said Diana. "He, or it, was working as a steward. I thought his name was Heart-of-Peace and he was from Luna. Instead, he was a low-budget assassin. Which means we're minus one steward." She sipped her coffee and looked at Norton. "Or maybe not."

It made sense, he supposed. If the Sham, pretending to be a steward, had really killed Wayne Norton, pretending to be Julius Winston, then the Sham would still be alive, still pretending to be a steward. And so Norton became a steward called Heart-of-Peace.

This meant he had a far better choice of food than the passengers—because he and Diana chose whatever they wanted. Although everything was automated, there were still buttons to press, controls to turn, dials to operate. He didn't know what any of them did, but she made him learn.

"I'm a cop," he said, "why do I need to do this?"

"Because," she told him, "like most creatures in the universe, you need to eat to live. If you don't know how to flasheat food, you'll starve to death."

"You'd let me?"

"Yes."

He believed her.

At first, he was worried his steward's job would entail housework on a galactic scale: cooking, cleaning, dusting, polishing, ironing, washing dishes, doing laundry, making beds. The list of chores was endless. He could never do anything like that. Firstly, it was all women's work, which meant: secondly, he didn't know how.

But a steward was more like a waiter in a restaurant. He dealt with the customers, while everything else happened out of sight. A waiter would bring the menu, take the orders, deliver the meal, but he didn't prepare the food or clear up the mess later.

As he already knew, passengers in his class had to serve their own meals, but the stewards had to make sure all the dispensers were fully stacked. As for doing the dishes, once they were collected and racked, that was also taken care of.

Norton soon came to hate the passengers. They did nothing but moan and complain and ask for the impossible, and even when it was possible he soon learned to be evasive. He could have done his work far more efficiently without passengers interrupting his routine.

At least he was no longer bored.

He was also back in uniform.

"I wish we didn't have to wear such stupid clothes," he said.

"What's wrong with them?" asked Diana.

"They're not so bad on a girl," he told her, which was true. The outfit suited Diana, and he was even getting used to her weird hairstyle. "But a man shouldn't have to wear this kind of thing."

"Why not?"

Norton looked down at his golden tunic, his knee-length silver pants, his jewel-encrusted slippers, and tried to think of an answer Diana would understand.

After going off shift, as now, they would return to her suite. These weren't the usual quarters for a ship's steward, which were no improvement on Norton's cabin. While exploring the ship, Diana had chanced upon a vacant first-class state-room. It was going to waste and so she commandeered it.

"When we first met," Norton said, "you were wearing a long dress." Or what passed as a dress. "A man wouldn't have worn that, would he?"

"Only if it was part of a uniform," said Diana.

"But that wasn't your police uniform, was it? Is there a police uniform?" He paused, then added, "Back on Earth?"

Back on Earth. Such a casual phrase, almost like "down the road" or "on the next block."

"Yes," said Diana. "Of a sort."

"Good. A police officer should have a uniform. People respect a uniform. It gives authority."

"Like being a steward, you mean?" Diana smiled.

So did Norton. "Is there a GalactiCop uniform?"

"I doubt it. How can a galactic force have a uniform? Nothing can be uniform if has to be worn by officers from a thousand different planets. Cops come in different sizes, different shapes, like the planets they're from."

"Planets come in different shapes?"

"You know what I mean. What looks right on one alien race would look ridiculous on another."

"Each planet could have its own uniform."

"On many worlds, John, there's very little respect for law and order. If they're recognised as police officers, they'll be killed. Wearing a uniform would make them an immedi-ate target."

"Is that GalactiCop's function, to bring law and justice to the galaxy?"

"Definitely. Yes. Absolutely. Yes."

He didn't believe her.

"As you mentioned," Diana said, "the day we met I was wearing a dress. You know what it's like."

"To wear a dress? No, I don't."

"Might suit you," said Diana, tilting her head to one side and looking him up and down.

"What?"

"You have to wear all kinds of disguises when you do undercover work."

It seemed that a steward's uniform was nothing compared to the clothing indignities he might have to suffer.

"As I started to say," Diana continued, "you know what it's like, how seeing a cop makes most people uneasy. Not that we care about that, of course, but in many situations it's better if everyone is relaxed and off guard. Which is why I wasn't in uniform that day."

"I thought you were a waitress," said Norton. "And now you are." He smiled.

"I thought you were a convict," said Diana. "So be careful." She also smiled.

It was Norton's relatively normal clothes which had made Diana believe he was from the wrong side of the law, but he asked, "Why would a convict be at an exclusive restaurant with Colonel Travis?"

"For a meal, of course. A last meal."

"Taken to a restaurant before execution?"

"Before transportation," said Diana. "We don't kill convicted criminals. We're far too humane and civilised for that. Those found guilty of serious crimes are deported to Arazon, the penal planet. It's the perfect prison. There's no release, no escape. We don't kill criminals. We let them kill each other."

"You thought Colonel Travis was taking me for a meal before deportation? Is that normal procedure?"

"It could have been a special occasion, like he was saying farewell to an old friend. If there were no criminals, there would be no police. It's inevitable that our professional paths intersect, which often leads to friendship. It must have happened in your era."

"No. Never."

"Really? There was still capital punishment in your era. If you knew someone with a different perspective on criminal matters, instead of letting them dine, you let them die. How primitive and barbaric your world must have been, John."

"No, it wasn't. And you're the one who was talking about instant execution to save on paperwork."

"But you're the one who did it, John. You eliminated the Sham." She pointed her forefinger and closed one eye as if aiming.

"That was self-defence."

"The ultimate self-defence."

Norton examined his right index finger. Half the missing fingertip had already grown back.

He used to imagine himself as a hatchet-man for the mob. It had seemed a very glamorous way of life. A way of life, a way of death. But what kind of person would take up such a career? Maybe it was through living so long that he'd come to realise life was precious. Killing people wasn't very nice. His own life was important, and so was everyone else's. Although not as precious and important as his own, of course.

"I want to talk about this," he said, showing Diana his finger.

"Tomorrow," she said, yawning.

The days had passed by, followed presumably by the nights. Day and night, light and dark, happened back on Earth. On board ship, there were no such things.

Twenty-four hours was the time in which Norton's native planet spun upon its axis. Everything else had become metric (which he was sure he would never get used to), but hours and minutes remained unchanged.

He may have been bored, but as an undercover passenger Wayne Norton had a very easy job. That wasn't the case for Major Diana Travis, undercover crewperson. One passenger, more or less, was of no consequence; but the crew were important to keep the ship operating. With the other shift steward dead, Diana needed assistance.

That was supposing Heart-of-Peace really was dead, which presupposed he'd really existed.

By now, Norton was beginning to wonder if the attempt on his life had ever happened. It had all been so fast, the details such a blur, that perhaps it was nothing but an illusion. There were no such things as Shams. There was no dead alien in his old cabin.

Diana could have arranged the whole event just to scare him, or to rouse him out of his lethargy.

Or because she wanted some help in the kitchen.

"Okay," he said, "tell me something else."

"What?"

"Why am I here?"

"I'm glad you don't want to talk about trivialities, John. After a tough day at work, a metaphysical discussion is exactly what I need. Fix me a vodsky. A mega. Why are you here? Why am I here? What's the purpose of life?"

"Not the purpose of life," said Norton, as he poured the drinks the old-fashioned way: from a bottle into glasses. "Not you. Only me. Why am I here, now, on this ship?"

"Me, me, me. Self, self, self."

"Tell—" He held the drink toward her, slightly out of reach. "—me."

"It's secret."

He knew she'd say that. Even if she had given him an answer, he wondered if he'd have believed her.

"Do you know why, but can't tell me?" he asked.

"Another secret," she told him.

"Where are we heading?"

"Why all these questions? Why now?"

"Because I haven't asked for a while, and I thought I might get some answers this time. Was I wrong?"

"That's another question," said Diana.

The spacecraft didn't have a name. The only reason he thought it should was because ships from his time had names, ships which sailed on the ocean. It seemed that ships which sailed between the stars were more like buses, they had route numbers. And this starbus was on its regular journey.

"Thanks," said Diana, and he realised he'd given her the vodsky.

"We're going to Hideaway," he said.

"You've been talking to the passengers. I keep telling you, they're the enemy. It's treason to communicate with them."

"Are we going to Hideaway?"

"The ship is going to Hideaway."

"So we're going there?"

"The ship is going to Hideaway. First. Then it's going somewhere else."

"Back to Earth."

"Not," said Diana, sipping her drink, "necessarily."

"Will I ever get a straight answer from you?"

"Yes."

"When?"

"You expect two straight answers in a row?"

Norton shook his head. "I guess not." He yawned. "I've sure earned my money today."

"My turn for a question," said Diana. "What money?"

"Don't I get paid as a steward?" asked Norton.

Diana took a mouthful of her drink.

"Okay, then I've got my service pay," Norton said. "Haven't I? I do get paid, don't I?"

"Yes . . . in a way."

"In what way?"

"There are expenses, John. Your ticket has to be paid for."

"By me?" It was as if he'd had to buy the gas for his LVPD patrol car—or maybe even pay for the whole automobile. "What about a refund from when I stopped being a passenger?"

"It's best to keep on pretending you're dead."

"I'm dead, but I still have to pay my fare?"

"Your cabin hasn't been vacated."

"I have to pay to keep a dead alien in there?"

"Julius Winston is dead. If he asked for a refund, don't you think it might seem strange?"

"I guess so." Norton drained his drink.

"The accountants can fix it all, John. With profit-sharing and bonuses, escalators and fixed-price options, you won't lose out."

He had no idea what she was talking about, but that was not unusual.

"Another drink?" she asked.

"Yeah."

"I'll have one, too."

Norton poured two more vodskys.

"How did moles wear their hair?" asked Diana.

"How did who wear their hair?"

"In your era, underground women were known as moles, yes?"

"Underground women?"

"Women, girls, as you call them. Those who associated with the criminal fraternity, the underground."

"Ah!" said Norton. "You mean the underworld, not the underground."

He'd previously figured out that Susie's father must have been involved, deeply involved, with the Las Vegas underworld. And Norton might have ended up underground, six feet deep underground, but instead he'd been deep frozen.

By now, he could remember all that had happened on the final day of his first life. His last memory was hearing a voice say, "Sorry, Wayne." Then Mr. Ash had slugged him.

"The underworld," said Diana, nodding. "Outlaws and bandits, hoods and hitmen, racketeers and bootleggers, gangsters and their moles."

"Moles!" Norton laughed. "They were known as 'molls,' not 'moles.' "

"Molls? Alright." Diana ran her fingers through her green Mohican. "In your era, what kind of hairstyles did the molls have?"

Chapter Twelve

Life was good.

Kiru wished she'd been sent to the prison planet years ago.

She kept thinking it couldn't last. Nothing like this could. Soon, she'd have to pay the price.

Unless she already had. Perhaps the years of misery and deprivation on her home planet had been her admission ticket to the penal paradise of Clink. She now had the best of both worlds. Not Earth and Arazon, but Grawl and Aqa.

Most of her days were spent with Grawl, who protected and watched over her. He couldn't speak, but words were not necessary.

Most of her nights were spent with Aqa. Again, words were not necessary.

One looked alien, but was full of humanity—for her, at least. The other wasn't from Earth, although his most important part—for her, at least—was human enough.

Perhaps, eventually, as she grew older, there might be time for painting and music and poetry. Even, when she was very old, philosophy.

She was right: It couldn't last.

Because then the spaceship arrived.

CHAPTER THIRTEEN

"Come on in, boy. Through here."

Norton halted at the entrance, unwilling to go inside.

"I'm not allowed to enter passenger cabins, I'm afraid," he said. He knew by now that the stewards made up their own regulations, and he wanted an excuse to remain in the corridor.

"Afraid? There's no need to be afraid, boy. I'm not going to eat you. Bring it in."

Norton looked at the passenger, and she smiled at him. She was old, at least fifty, and her hair was silver. Not silver because it had turned grey, but silver like a shiny new coin. Reluctantly, he carried the tray inside, and the door closed.

"If you're not going to eat him, Cass," said another voice, "then I will." The second occupant of the stateroom was another old woman, and her hair was bright gold. "Isn't he the sweetest thing? How did you find him?"

"It's a gift, Peg."

"A gift! For me. You shouldn't have."

"I didn't."

"I'll leave this here for you, madam," said Norton, putting the tray on a table.

"Madam?" said the woman named Cass. "Oh, I like that."

"What's your name?" asked the one called Peg.

"Never mind his name, he's mine, not yours."

"Have you got a friend?"

"Please excuse me," said Norton. "I have to get back to work now, ladies."

"Ladies? Did you hear that, Cass? He thinks we're ladies."

"He's right. I am a lady." Cass laughed. "And I'll prove exactly how much of a lady!"

Norton retreated toward the door.

"You haven't got a friend?" said Peg. "You have now. You've got us."

"You notice how his uniform matches our hair. Silver and gold. He's just made for us."

"It's not his uniform I'm interested in, it's what's underneath!"

They both laughed, and Norton smiled. Although he wished he wasn't here, he wasn't too concerned. He'd seen women like this in Vegas, elderly widows behaving as if they were youngsters, who had come to the city to have a good time and usually ended up getting drunk and making fools of themselves.

Cass and Peg both wore heavy makeup, were dressed in abbreviated outfits which might have suited women less than half their ages, and their faces were tanned and lined by the sun—or *a* sun. If they were wealthy enough to afford a first-class cabin, they might easily have travelled to different solar systems before their voyage to Hideaway.

"Why don't you have a drink with us?" said Cass. "We've got plenty."

Norton knew they had plenty because the tray he'd carried in was laden with various exotic liqueurs. Cass had claimed they couldn't serve themselves because their stateroom's alcohol dispenser was not working. He guessed they must have drained it dry.

"No, thanks, madam."

Norton reached the door. It should have opened, but didn't.

"Have a drink, sweetie," said Peg. "Then we'll let you go. Maybe."

"No, thanks. I don't drink." Because that wasn't true, Norton felt he had to add something, which was, "I don't smoke."

"Why would you smoke?" said Cass.

"Are you a mandroid?" said Peg. "Is there a fault in your circuits? You're not going to burst into flames, I hope."

"I'm not a mandroid," said Norton, although he'd never heard the word. It was something else to put on his list of questions for Diana.

"How do you know?" said Cass. "I'm sure mandroids think they're human."

"I am human," said Norton. "I think."

"He must be human," said Peg. "The price we paid for our tickets, they should only use human stewards."

"If you're human, boy," said Cass, "you drink. Ninety percent of the human body is water."

"Mine isn't," said Peg, as she examined the assortment of bottles. "I never drink water." She laughed.

"Ninety percent of the body is water," repeated Cass, as she looked at Norton. "But it's the other ten percent which matters."

"I have to get back to work," he said.

"This is your work," said Peg. "Pour me a drink, steward."

"What would you like, madam?" Norton turned back into the room.

"You, sweetie."

He halted.

"Take no notice, boy," said Cass. "We're only having a little fun."

"I'd like to have more than a little fun with him," said Peg.

Norton wasn't scared of two old women, and he went to the collection of drinks.

"What's your pleasure, ladies?" he asked, and immediately regretted the phrase.

"Seems we've arrived on Hideaway early," said Peg.

Hideaway, Norton had learned, was an asteroid which had gained a reputation as being the pleasure centre of the galaxy. Tourists from every world headed there to enjoy its extensive variety of exotic diversions, pastimes which were readily available on the satellite but forbidden within their own solar systems.

The spacebus operated a shuttle service between Earth and Hideaway, which meant that Terrans made up the majority of passengers. Norton had seen no aliens on board, except for the one that had tried to kill him.

"What have you got to offer, boy?" asked Cass.

Norton read out the labels from the bottles, which seemed safe enough.

"I'll have that," said Peg, and she indicated one of the

bottles. "It's such a pretty colour. Matches your eyes, sweetie."

"And you, madam?" asked Norton, as he unsealed the cap.

"The same as Cass."

Norton looked at her. He thought she was Cass. It was Cass who'd brought him here, the one with silver hair. The other one was Peg, the one with golden hair, the one who'd already chosen her drink.

The women looked at Norton, waiting for him to pour, then glanced at each other.

"I'm Peg," said the one Norton thought was Peg.

"No, I'm Peg," said the one Norton thought was Cass.

The bottle cap slipped from his hand.

"I'm Pegasus, you're Cassiopeia."

"No, *I'm* Pegasus, *you're* Cassiopeia."

Norton bent down to pick up the cap.

"Names," he heard one of the women say, "are always such a problem."

"They are when you forget your own," said the other.

Norton reached under the table with his right hand.

"Do you have trouble with your name, Heart of John Julian Wiston Wayne Peace?" said the first one.

"It's Julius Winston, not Julian Wiston," said the second one.

Norton froze, not moving.

They knew who he was.

"I can't remember my own false name, why should I remember one of his?"

They knew who he wasn't.

Norton still hadn't moved when a foot came down on his hand, hard, pinning it to the ground. He looked up and saw the two old women staring down at him.

"Dangerous hand you've got there, boy," said the one with silver hair, whose foot was holding him down.

"I don't know what you mean," said Norton.

"Yes, you do," said the one with gold hair.

"It will have to come off," said silver hair.

They were both holding long-bladed knives.

"No!" said Norton. He tried pulling free, but then another foot came down on the back of his neck. "It's the finger," he managed to say, "that's all, just the index finger."

"Oh?" said gold hair, whose foot was on his neck. "You *do* know what we mean?"

"Don't worry, boy. We'll only take off the finger. First."

"Do you want his finger?"

"Yes. Pity it's not attached to the rest of him."

"It is!" said Norton. "It is!"

"Not for long. I'll take the finger. You take the hand. I'll take the forearm. You take the upper arm."

"Then do we go for the left arm?"

"Or one of the legs?"

"Or go straight for the head?"

"Or the heart. He won't be Heart-of-Peace, he'll be Heart-in-Pieces!"

"You're not serious," said Norton.

"We—" said one of them.

"—are," continued the other one, "totally—"

"—serious."

The long black blades were more like swords than knives, and Norton's tormentors took turns swinging them in front of his face, every sweep coming closer and closer. He was frightened, very frightened. When he shut his eyes, he could feel the draft as the swords sliced through the air.

"You're going to kill me?"

"Yes."

"Eventually."

"What have I done? I don't know anything. I've done nothing. I'm innocent."

"What's that got to do with it?"

"Innocent? This isn't a law court, boy."

"It's your death cell."

"I'll tell you whatever you want to know."

"You said you didn't know anything."

"I'll do whatever you want. I'll work for you."

"Pouring drinks?"

"Anything. Everything."

"We don't want anything."

"Nothing you can give us, sweetie."

"Can I say my prayers?"

"You want to pray?"

"If I'm going to die—"

"You are."

"—you should grant me one final request."

"Why?"

"He's right. It's traditional."

"What's your final request? Not to be killed? Refused."

"If he wants to pray, we must let him. He's already on his knees."

"What religion is he? It could take hours."

"We'll give him one minute."

"One minute till we start cutting pieces off, or one minute till we kill him?"

Norton suddenly reared up, trying to break free. It was as if his right hand was nailed to the ground. He raised his head a few inches before it was slammed down again, his face grinding into the floor, and he yelled in pain.

Then he heard an echoing screech, and another, both very close, which blended together and mixed with a chilling yell from the other side of the room.

He caught a glimpse of a shrieking figure hurling itself across the cabin. His captors fell away and he was free.

As Norton rolled aside, he glanced up and saw someone attacking the two old women.

Diana.

She was armed with a short-handled axe. Against two opponents with swords.

All three of them were screaming.

Diana's roar was a battle cry, but the other two were howling in pain, each of them wounded by the knives Diana had already thrown. Silver had a blade embedded in her thigh, Gold had one sticking out of her sword-arm.

Gold dropped her weapon and grabbed the knife handle, yanking it free.

Silver swept her sword at Diana, who ducked aside and brought up her axe, arcing it toward Silver's face, whose blade swung back to parry the blow.

Gold grunted as the blood spurted from her arm, then she sprang toward Diana, the knife aimed at her back.

"Watch out!" shouted Norton.

Diana twisted away, avoiding Gold's knife and Silver's sword, and her opponents collided with each other.

"Are you hurt?" she asked Norton.

"No," he said, as he sat up and crashed his head against the table, knocking it over. "Ah! Look out! Oh!"

Diana side-stepped a sword thrust, slamming her axe

shaft against Silver's blade, then swerved to dodge the knife stabbing toward her neck.

"It's a throwing knife," she said to Gold.

Gold threw the knife, Diana ducked, and then Gold was unarmed.

Diana turned and went for Silver, who defended herself with the black blade. Silver's weapon had a longer reach, but Diana kept dancing out of range. Wounded by the knife buried hilt-deep in her thigh, Silver couldn't follow through fast enough.

Gold reached for the sword she had dropped.

"No!" warned Norton, who was still sprawled on the floor, rubbing his head. He took his hand away, his right hand, and pointed his index finger at the woman.

Gold had seized the sword in her left hand. She was two yards away from Norton.

Two paces, one quick thrust, less than a second, and the sword would be in his chest.

He stared at his finger, willing it to fire.

"I surrender," said Gold, and she dropped her blade and raised her arms.

Keeping his finger aimed, Norton stood up. As he did, his foot became entangled with the fallen table. He tripped and was down on the floor again. Gold made a break and dashed to the door.

"Get—" yelled Diana, as she twisted to avoid being disembowelled—"her!"

Norton jumped to his feet, one of which came down on a liqueur bottle, and he slipped, lost his balance, regained his footing, then started running toward the cabin door.

"Ah-ah-ah!" he yelled, as the pain shot up his leg.

He must have twisted his ankle, and he stumbled, lurching forward, almost fell again, kept upright, but had to limp toward the doorway, where he could only watch as Gold sprinted away along the passage. For an old woman, she was very light on her feet. There was no way Norton could chase after her. He couldn't hop fast enough.

"Stop or I fire!" he shouted, pointing at her.

He knocked into something leaning against the corridor wall, which fell and nearly tripped him, and he stumbled back against the wall. When he looked down he saw a bow, its string stretched taut, and a quiver of arrows on the ground next to it.

"Shoot her!" called Diana.

He picked up the bow, took one of the arrows, notched it, drew back the string.

As he kid, he and his friends used to make their own bows and arrows from bamboo and sticks. Sometimes the sticks had been sharpened, with glued cardboard flights, and they had fired them at targets—and each other. Norton had never hit anything—or anyone.

He sighted the arrow at Gold's vanishing back, then let fly. A moment later, she raced around a corner.

"Darn!" said Norton.

The arrow sped along the corridor. And turned the corner.

There was a distant scream.

"I'll be darned," he muttered.

He glanced into the cabin, where Diana had Silver backed against the wall. Picking up the quiver and slinging it over his shoulder, he took out one of the arrows and notched it into the bowstring, then hobbled along the corridor and around the corner.

Gold lay motionless on the ground. The arrow jutting from below her left shoulder blade must have pierced her heart.

"Get up," he ordered. "Stop pretending. I know you're not dead."

But he knew she was.

He made his way back along the passageway toward the stateroom. Everything was silent. He peered inside the cabin.

Over on the far side lay a motionless figure. In the centre of the room was someone else, someone moving, someone with silver hair . . .

Norton drew back the bowstring, took aim.

"What a mess," said Diana, as she picked up the bottles from the floor and put them back on the table. "I hate this job."

Diana with silver hair.

Norton unnotched the arrow.

"Did you shoot her?" she asked.

"Yeah," he said.

"Didn't I tell you passengers were the enemy?"

"Er . . . yeah . . . but . . ."

"Next time, listen to me. I know what I'm talking about."

"Yeah . . . er . . . yeah . . . and . . . you know . . . er . . ."

"Is that an expression of gratitude?"

"Er . . ."

"I'll assume that's a 'yes.' " She took off her silver hair and showed it to Norton. "Look, a wig! Not even a proper scalp. Was yours the same?"

"Er . . ."

Diana walked out of the stateroom and looked along the passageway.

"Where's the body? Go and get it. Can't leave a dead passenger out in the corridor, we'll only get more complaints."

Chapter Fourteen

It wasn't a big spaceship, just a lander, which did exactly what it was designed for by landing between the lake and the boss's villa.

This was not meant to happen, but it seemed everyone knew it would.

Except Kiru.

"What's going on, Grawl?" she said.

There was no point in asking. Firstly, he couldn't reply. Secondly, she already knew the answer.

It was a break-out.

"Come on, come on, come on!" yelled the boss, waving his metal stick. "All aboard the *Monte Cristo!*"

He stood by the entrance to the lander. With him, encased in camouflaged body armour, was one of the ship's crew.

Kiru watched the group of men and women vanish inside the small craft. These were the core of the boss's regime, the ones who had been captured with him. Space pirates. About to escape, freed by an outlaw ship that had broken through the cosmic chain which kept Arazon in manacles.

"And you, Grawl!" said the boss.

Everyone else had boarded the lander.

Except Kiru.

And except Aqa, who had been away since yesterday.

Grawl gestured toward the ship. Kiru shook her head. He grabbed her wrist. It was the first time they had ever touched. She tried to hold back, but he was far too strong, and he pulled her toward the hatch.

She didn't know whether to go with Grawl or stay with Aqa. Whatever she decided, it would be the wrong choice. That was the story of her life.

"Not her," said the boss. "There's no room."

The crewman levelled his gun at Kiru. It looked real. It was real. The most powerful weapon on the whole planet.

Grawl released Kiru, then pretended he was counting down on his fingers, until only his right thumb remained. He peered all about, then shrugged a silent question.

"Yes," said the boss, "one more, but where is he? Where's Aqa?"

Which was what Kiru had wondered last night.

"One minute," said the crewman, through his visor.

"Aqa!" shouted the old man, staring around.

There was no sign of movement.

"Aqa!!"

"Forty-five seconds."

"Aqa!!!"

No one else was in sight.

Except Kiru.

Grawl jerked his thumb toward her.

"Want a ride?" asked the boss.

She looked at him, looked at Grawl, looked at the ship.

"Thirty seconds."

"An empty berth when you happen to be around," said the boss. "Someone up there likes you."

It wasn't someone up there. It was someone down here.

"Twenty seconds."

The boss threw away his stick and stepped into the lander.

Grawl followed, then turned to look at Kiru. It was her decision.

"Ten seconds," said the guard, as he also went on board.

Grawl winked at her. It was the first change of expression she'd seen him make. Like Kiru, he never smiled. The universe wasn't funny. It was a serious place. Deadly serious.

He'd killed Aqa. Killed him so Kiru could take his place. He must have liked her, really liked her, to do that. Too bad about Aqa. He was okay, more than okay, but their relationship had only been physical. There were plenty more like him. Plenty more in the universe. But Grawl? Grawl was different. They had a real rapport. He was a true soulmate, and she felt they could see into each other's hearts.

She boarded the ship and it blasted free of the prison planet, out into orbit.

CHAPTER FIFTEEN

"Who were they?" asked Wayne Norton.

"Passengers," said Diana. "Good passengers."

"*Good?*"

"Yes. The only good passengers are dead ones."

"You said I shouldn't have killed the Sham, so it could have been interrogated. Couldn't you have questioned those two? You didn't have to kill them."

"I only killed one of them, John. You killed the other."

"No, it was the arrow."

"Arrows don't kill people, people kill people. You shot the arrow, didn't you?"

"You told me to."

"You were only obeying orders, you mean?"

"Yeah. No. I shot the arrow, but then it whizzed round the corner like a guided missile."

They were in her stateroom, and he'd knocked back several nerve-calming alcoholic beverages. She had drunk one glass, probably because she had no nerves to calm. Norton put down another empty glass and held out his right hand. By now, it was no longer shaking.

He didn't feel as if he'd killed Gold, although logically he knew he had. Maybe if he'd seen her fall because of his bowshot, it would have been different. Or if she'd died in hand-to-hand combat, the way that Diana had killed Silver, he could accept he was the direct cause of her death.

In a similar way, when he'd killed the Sham, Norton had felt nothing. But that was self-defence, wiping out an ugly alien critter that had tried to murder him.

Now he'd shot an old lady in the back, and it was no different from squashing a bug underfoot.

"Were they space pirates?" he asked.

Diana stared at him. "What do you know about space pirates?"

"Only what I've seen on SeeV."

"While you've been on board?"

"Yeah."

"They show dataplays about space pirates to spaceship passengers?" Diana shook her head in bewilderment. "Good. I hope it scares them."

"They were on the alien stations."

"What's an alien station?"

"Television for aliens. Broadcasts I picked up while flicking through the channels."

"What?" Diana frowned. "Oh, yes, I know what you mean. This ship used to be on the interstellar run to different worlds, which must be why there's so much alien programming available." She sipped at her drink. "Some of us have been too busy to watch SeeV."

Norton wasn't sure what was worse, watching television all the time or being a steward. One difference was that when he watched TV, he saw people being killed; now that he was a steward, he had to do the killing.

"Tell me about space pirates," said Diana.

"I've seen them on screen, how they take over spaceships. They start by killing the crew."

"That's why you thought those two geriatrics were galactic buccaneers? To hijack a spaceship, first wipe out the stewards. I always knew we had the most important job on board."

"They kill all the crew, steal the ship, hold the passengers for ransom. Is that what happens?"

"Happens? Happened, you mean. Maybe. It's all ancient history. Although not as ancient as you."

"Space pirates don't exist?"

"What you've seen is very exaggerated. It's entertainment, nothing to do with the real universe."

"Spaceships don't get stolen?"

"They do, but not very dramatically. It's all done through fraudulent documentation."

"Oh."

"You seem disappointed," said Diana.

"No," said Norton, and he shook his head in disappointment.

He'd watched pirate-busters on SeeV and wondered if that was one of GalactiCop's roles. From what Diana said, that was entirely possible: It sounded dull and boring and routine and monotonous enough.

Norton studied his hand. His finger was its original length again, and the nail had grown back.

"Why couldn't I fire my non-lethal finger?" he asked.

"Because it's a defensive weapon. When you're under threat, the reflex kicks in and blasts out a stun shot."

He remembered how Gold had raised her hands to surrender as soon as he pointed his finger at her.

"What use is that?" he said.

"Very little. You should be able to fire at will, not let your weapon decide. I'm glad I haven't got one."

"It's not standard issue?"

"I told you, it's experimental."

"Am I the experiment?"

"Yes, you're a guinea pig." Diana paused. "What was a guinea pig?"

"A small furry animal, I think it was a rodent, used in medical experiments."

"Did the experiments kill them?"

"Why?"

"Because that would explain why they're extinct."

"Will I become extinct?"

"No. Or not because of the NLDDD. Unless it completely fails, of course."

Norton tapped his right forefinger against his empty glass. A gun was a cop's right hand. In his case, his right hand was a gun.

"I'm not a steward," said Diana. "If you want a drink, pour one yourself."

"Why me?" asked Norton, examining his finger—which was also the barrel, "and not you?"

"I'm a major, you're a sergeant."

Norton poured himself a drink.

"I'll have the same," said Diana. "Sergeant."

"Yes, sir!"

Norton gave an exaggerated salute. The tip of his right index finger hit his forehead, and he wondered how close he was to frying his brains.

"So a stun shot is non-lethal?" he said.

"Except to a Sham."

"What is a stun shot?"

"A painful and immobilising pulse of energy," she said. "I don't know the technical details."

"Who does?"

"The manufacturers. You were fitted out under a sponsorship deal. They want to see how their new defence device performs under operational conditions. In return, they paid for your ticket to Hideaway. And in return for that, you're supposed to write an efficiency report."

"Am I? Anything else I should know?"

"Don't bother with the report. What can they do?"

"What else have they done?" Norton asked. "My finger's become a gun. Is there any other part of me with a new improved active ingredient?"

Diana shook her head.

"Not even an electric battery in my wrist?"

"The energy comes from your own bioganic system."

"My what?"

"Take a drink."

Norton did.

"To take a drink," said Diana, "you lifted your hand. To lift your hand, you used your muscles. To use your muscles, you need strength and stamina."

"Finger-bone connected to the wrist-bone, wrist-bone connected to the arm-bone," sang Norton.

"You're drunk," said Diana, and she sipped at her glass. "It would be interesting to correlate your degree of inebriation with the accuracy and amplitude of the NLDDD."

"And write an efficiency report?"

"It must be like running. After a hard sprint, you have to stop and catch your breath. After a volley of stun shots, you're exhausted, and your body needs time to reload."

"So I'd need a rest, a drink, maybe a meal, perhaps a snooze, before I could fire again? Great weapon. How can I get rid of it?"

"It's an implant, grafted into your nervous system, fused with your bones. You can't get rid of it."

"I can't, but you can. I've swallowed enough anaesthetic. Chop it off, please."

"You've numbed your brain, not just your finger. I'm not cutting it off."

"Okay, I'll do it. Give me your axe."

"No," said Diana. "I won't let you cut off your finger. And it's not an axe, it's a tomahawk."

"Tomahawk? I thought it was a cleaver from the kitchen. Not the kitchen. What's it called? From the galley."

"And you thought these were galley knives?" Diana held up one of the blades she'd thrown at Silver and Gold.

"Yeah."

"Could be interesting. Fighting with kitchen utensils. One hundred and one ways to kill with a spoon."

"A tomahawk and knives are your police weapons, you mean?"

"Yes."

"That's all you have?"

"It's not such a good idea to deploy maximum firepower on board a spaceship. In most circumstances, blowing a massive hole in your enemy is the best way to make them see your point of view, but not when it also means blasting a hole through the ship's hull. Space travel and heavy munitions don't mix. But this is perfect." She put the axe down between them. "Don't chop off your finger. You'll have to clean up the mess."

"What about cleaning the cabin?"

"What's wrong with it?" Diana glanced around. "Are you saying I'm untidy?"

"Not here. Where we left the bodies."

"Forget it, John. We're off duty."

"But we can't just leave the corpses there."

That was what they had done with the Sham, but that was different. The Sham wasn't human. Locking up its body in Norton's old cabin was bug disposal.

"We're off duty," Diana repeated. "Permanently. We've almost reached our destination. That's why you're getting so drunk. We're celebrating the end of the voyage."

"So it's a party!" Norton raised his drink. "Cheers!" He drained the glass and reached for the bottle. "You're not drinking much." He poured himself another.

"Ship duties are over, but I'm still on police duty." She examined her glass, took a sip. "I might have to rescue you again."

"What?" Norton suddenly felt very sober. "Who from?" He picked up the axe.

"If I knew that," said Diana, "I'd be dealing with them."

The first tomahawks were made of stone, then of metal, their heads mounted on wooden shafts. This was neither stone nor metal, head and handle forged into one potent piece of armament.

"But there might not be anyone else," Diana continued. "Those two could have been the last. They probably waited until the end of the journey because it gave them a better chance of escape. And if they'd killed you earlier, they'd have been without a steward."

Norton gripped the axe in his right hand, and it felt as if it belonged there. It was already a part of him, far more than the NLDDD. He made a practice stroke, swinging the weapon through the air, then another.

"Top of the range weaponry for starship combat," said Diana, as she watched him. "Strange, isn't it? Knives, hatchet, bow and arrows, all our ancestral weapons."

"Ancestral?" Norton remembered something he'd kept meaning to ask. "Is Colonel Travis really your father?"

"Biologically?"

"Yeah. Is he really your father?"

"Yes. Why?"

"Because he's . . . er . . . coloured, but you're not."

"Coloured? What colour?"

"Black. He's black. His skin is black. Yours is white."

"So's yours."

"Yeah. I'm white, you're white, but Travis is coloured."

"White isn't a colour, is that what you're saying, because it reflects all light?"

"I don't know what you mean."

"And I don't know what you mean."

"Your father," said Norton, "what is he? What race is he?"

"Race?" Diana frowned. "Ah! I know what you mean. In your era, you'd have said, let's see . . . an aboriginal. Yes, an aboriginal."

"So he's Australian?" That made sense, although it still didn't explain why Diana was white.

"No. That's another continent. It is now, and I'm sure it was in your era."

"Yeah, it was halfway around the world." Norton shrugged. "That used to be a long way."

" 'Aboriginal' means native to a particular region. What about 'Native American'; was that the term in your era?"

Norton glanced at the tomahawk he was still holding. "Are you talking about Red Indians?"

"Yes. You said that before, back on Earth. Red Indigenes. Names change."

"So I've found out."

"Native Americans. Tribal Nations. Aboriginals. Autochthons. Amerindians. Red Indigenes. That's what we are, Reds."

"You mean—" Norton looked at Diana, at her Mohican haircut—"you're the last of . . . you mean . . . you and your father . . . you're both Red Indians?"

"And you," said Diana.

Norton laughed. He took a swig from the bottle. Then he laughed again.

"You are," Diana told him.

"You're crazy."

"That's an opinion. But you're a Red Indigene. That's a fact. I verified it."

"Verified?"

"You remember."

Norton touched his lips. How could he forget?

"You're not one hundred percent," Diana continued, "but no one is. There have been no pure-blood braves for a long, long time."

"Are you telling me," said Norton, as he gripped the tomahawk tightly in his hand, "that one of my . . . my ancestors was a Red Indian?"

"Certainly. Where does your thick black hair come from?" Diana glanced at his head. "The hair you had when we first met."

It was possible, he supposed. Although it was unlikely any of them had arrived on the *Mayflower*; both sides of his family had lived in the United States for several generations. Family legend said that some had been pioneers, heading out West on wagon trains; others had sailed around Cape Horn and reached California during the gold rush; some had fought for the Union, others for the Confederacy; some had herded cattle, others had built railroads.

All of American history ran through his veins, so who was to say there wasn't some Red Indian blood in there?

"That big nose," said Diana, "where did that come from?"

"I haven't got a big nose."

"Alright, it's a strong nose. And the way you shot that arrow. It was instinctive; you were born to it. Like me."

She walked across the cabin and picked up her bow, pulling back on the string, aiming at an imaginary target.

"Diana the huntress," she said. "Goddess of the Moon. That's me. Roman mythology."

"What . . . but . . . what . . . ?"

Norton shook his head, trying to dislodge the rest of his question. He had much to ask, but he felt in no condition to understand any answers. He was very tired, completely exhausted.

"What about Day Zero?" suggested Diana. "We remember the past through oral history. We remember Lost Vegas. We remember everything. We're the only ones who do. The word 'Redskin' was pejorative, but we adopted it and became proud to call ourselves Reds. We were cheated out of our land, but then we took it all back."

Norton reached for his glass. There seemed to be three of them in front of him. His hand missed them all.

"Time for bed," said Diana.

"Very," said Norton.

"Very what?"

"Very . . . fication. Do you want to . . . very . . . fy me again?"

"Not much. And I don't think you could. Come on, it's time to get horizontal."

"Very . . . good."

"On your feet, John."

"I want to . . . to . . . here . . . stay here."

"You must stand up before you can lie down."

"Can lie . . . lie down . . . here."

"Stand up. That's an order."

"Can't . . . bad . . . bad leg."

Diana hauled him to his feet and dragged him over to the bed. This was where he'd slept ever since leaving his own cabin. It was also where Diana had slept. But it was a big bed. He had one side, and she had the other.

Every night he waited and watched and wished. He'd never even seen her undress.

Norton felt totally weary, totally drunk. Maybe tonight

was his chance. Diana would think he was so far gone that she'd peel off her clothes while she was in the same room. Maybe she would even help him remove his outfit.

She did neither.

He lay on the bed where she'd let him fall, trying hard to stay awake. When Diana finally climbed into the far side, he stretched out his hand toward her, but it was heavy, so heavy, and she was so far, far away. Before he could reach her, sleep overwhelmed him.

Wayne Norton had been the oldest virgin on Earth. Now, it seemed, he was the oldest virgin in the universe.

CHAPTER SIXTEEN

"Where are we heading?" Kiru asked the boss.

It was best to speak to him because he was the one Grawl was least likely to be jealous of. And least likely to kill.

Grawl hadn't killed Aqa for himself, she supposed. If that were the reason, he'd have wiped him out months ago. Grawl had eliminated Aqa for Kiru's sake, which proved what a good friend he was. His concern was more than that, however, different from that. It was almost like—

Kiru tried to break her line of thought. Her father had betrayed her by committing suicide. He'd only killed himself. For himself. Whereas Grawl had killed someone else. For her.

"Would you like some refreshment, Kiru?" said the boss.

It was the first time he had used her name, she realised. He actually knew who she was.

"I'd prefer an answer."

"Have both. You're the only one who doesn't know where we're going, so I'll tell you. Make yourself comfortable."

They were in the boss's cabin on board the outlaw ship. She gazed at the wall behind him, where a huge black screen sparkled with the lights from countless stars. It was an amazing sight, capturing her gaze and seeming to draw her deep within.

"Once you've travelled the galaxy, Kiru, no one planet can hold you. Not even Arazon. We're back, and the whole universe is ours to pillage and plunder!"

"What about me? Am I a space pirate, too?"

"You've got a wonderful reference: you were on Clink. But you might not be suitable as a professional pirate. It's a vocation, a calling. Many are called, few are chosen. It takes years to become fully qualified. There's a very high failure rate. You'll have to study, go on field trips, study again, do research projects, more study, pass all the exams."

Kiru managed to look away from the screen. "What?"

"Have you heard of Hideaway?"

She shook her head.

"The most famous leisure planet in the entire universe? The greatest pleasure asteroid in the whole galaxy?"

She shook her head again. There had been very little leisure or pleasure in her life—until she became a convict.

"That's the way it should be," said the boss. "No one should know. Hideaway was hidden away. It was our secret headquarters. A fantastic place, unbelievable, indescribable. You'll see what I mean when we get there."

As she looked at the boss, Kiru wondered why she'd once thought of him as being old. Compared to herself, he was, but so were most people. He was also older than Aqa. Or older than Aqa had been. The boss was in his middle years, his hair thick and dark, his cheeks and jaw unlined. He was quite an attractive man, in fact. Why hadn't she noticed until now?

"We're going to Hideaway?" she said.

"Yes. It will be ours again. This time it will stay ours. And stay a secret. We have to concentrate on our core business. The miscalculation last time was to move into subsidiary activities. The start-up costs were far too great. We sacrificed most of our primary cash flow, invested too deeply in capital projects which depreciated much more rapidly than forecast. I know what you're thinking."

"You do?"

"That all this could be claimed as tax losses, yes? But not when all we had was a deficit. Hideaway is one of the prime real-estate sites in the galaxy. We had it. We lost it. We lost everything."

Kiru nodded, as if understanding. "That's why you were on Arazon?" she said.

"Indirectly. It was the end result of a series of badly judged business decisions by the previous chief executive."

She nodded again.

"I admit," admitted the boss, "that after our relocation to new premises, he made tremendous progress in restructuring the company for its niche market. We were poised for expansion throughout the galaxy, negotiating to franchise our reputation as brand leader. Then almost exactly the same thing happened. We lost our new headquarters as well. Would you believe it?"

Kiru shook her head.

"The company was suddenly caught up in a ruthless trade war. My predecessor became the victim of corporate raiders and suffered the ultimate cancellation of his contract. We were totally downsized, and almost the entire personnel were made redundant. Those of us efficient enough to stay out of the red were given an involuntary transfer to Arazon. Thank you, Grawl. I was telling Kiru about the hostile take-over which liquidated the organisation's entire capital assets."

Grawl had brought in two elaborate cocktails and a choice of savoury snacks. He paused for a moment, glancing at the boss before setting down the tray.

"When the Algolan war fleet attacked our last hideout," the boss explained.

Kiru wished he'd said that in the first place.

"Thanks," she said as Grawl handed her a drink.

Although everyone on the ship probably believed she and Grawl shared more than just their cabin, they were all wrong.

At first, Kiru couldn't understand why the boss had said there was no room on board for her. It had been cramped inside the lander, but the escapees soon transferred to the parent ship when the *Monte Cristo* spliced into the *Monte Carlo*.

As the renegade craft set course across the universe, Grawl chose their quarters. There were two extra berths in the cabin, but no one claimed them.

It was only later that Kiru realised no one dared.

CHAPTER SEVENTEEN

Wayne Norton gazed in awe around Hideaway.

The entrance hall was vast, the size of an entire Vegas casino, so big that the floor curved down toward the near horizon.

And it was full of *aliens* . . .

Most of those he saw were humanoid bipeds, but the range and variety of colours and shapes and sizes seemed limitless.

Despite their differences, these weird beings had one thing in common: They were all tourists, and they'd come to Hideaway to have a good time, to spend their money gambling and whoring and drinking—and indulging in whatever other "pleasures" existed on the artificial asteroid.

But Wayne Norton was here because he was working. He was a cop, just like in Las Vegas.

"Welcome to Hideaway, sir."

He looked like a man, his appearance both human and male. He sounded Terran, using fluent fastspeak.

Norton wished there was an alien in the reception booth because he could have tried his slate. But that wasn't how the Hideaway check-in system operated, where everyone was met by a member of their own race. Or apparently of their own race.

Diana had briefed him on board ship, and what Norton was faced with was an illusion. He wasn't human. He didn't exist. He was a computerised simulation, his familiar appearance designed to reassure visitors.

Norton felt uneasy. The only other non-human in disguise that he'd encountered had been an alien assassin. And he was the intended target.

"Everyone's a winner on Hideaway," continued the

man—the computerised simulation of a man—"and I hope you'll be very lucky."

"Thanks."

"Will you be here long, sir?"

"Probably a couple of days."

"Just for the weekend?"

Norton nodded. He didn't know whether it was true or not, but Diana had told him to say his visit would be very brief. All this way, countless trillions of miles, travelling for endless weeks. Just for the weekend.

He guessed GalactiCop hadn't found anyone to sponsor his stay and could only afford the room rates for two days.

Anyone who could pay their fare to Hideaway was allowed on to the planetoid, which meant that spaceship crews were prohibited. It wasn't just a question of money, Diana had said, but of security. Space crews were notorious for causing trouble wherever they went. In return for keeping their crews on board, high-ranking officers were given access to the pleasure planet.

"Are you carrying a weapon?" asked the sim.

Like all plain-clothes officers, Norton had a concealed weapon. Concealed in his hand. Inside his hand, in fact. Which meant he wasn't carrying a gun. Not really.

"No," he replied, "I'm not."

"Will you follow me, please, sir? This will only take a minute."

"What will?"

"A technical formality. Nothing to be concerned about."

Norton had heard the phrase before, had used it himself, and his earlier unease now became concern.

The simulation walked toward a wall, then through it. There was no doorway; he stepped through the wall itself. It was the kind of thing an illusion could do. Norton reached out, and his hand vanished into the wall. Maybe it was the wall which was an illusion. He walked through and found himself in a small room, empty and featureless.

The man sat down. Norton hadn't noticed the chair.

"Please be seated."

Nor the other one. He sat down.

"What name are you using?"

There was no pretence. They expected him to give a false name. For a moment, Norton was tempted to give his real name. But only for a moment. He could be anyone he wanted to be. Identity documents no longer existed. There were no passports or driving licenses anymore, and neither were there any modern equivalents. They were so easy to forge that they were useless.

Wayne Norton could be anyone he wanted to be.

He remembered his exploits with the bow and arrow, and he said, "Robin Hood."

"And you're from Earth?"

"Yeah."

"Travelling through falspace can affect the memory, Mr. Hood. There's something you seem to have overlooked. Any idea what it might be?"

"No."

"You cannot enter Hideaway with a weapon."

They knew he had a gun, so there was no point denying it.

"You will have to leave," added the simulated man.

"I can't leave. I've come for . . ." Norton still didn't know why he was here, but he added, "pleasure."

"This is certainly the place to find pleasure, Mr. Hood, but first you must remove your weapon."

Norton looked at his right hand. "Yeah, I'd love to, but . . ."

"We will remove it for you. It also means removing your right hand, of course."

"Removing! My hand!"

"You'll still have the left one. You can have your other hand back when you leave."

"No! I'm leaving now."

"If that's what you want." The computerised man stood up, and Norton did the same. "Thank you for coming." He offered his hand, and they shook. For an illusion, he had a very firm grip. "Now you can go on through."

"Go on through to Hideaway?"

"Certainly, Mr. Hood. Your room is on level 8364, co-ordinates XJ-17/VF-306."

"What about my hand?"

"You can keep it. It was a joke, Mr. Hood. Hideaway is a fun place. We weren't going to cut off your whole hand. The index finger is all we need."

Norton glanced at his right hand. Thumb, three fingers.

Three . . . !

His forefinger was gone. The sim had stolen it when they'd shaken hands. He hadn't felt a thing, couldn't feel a thing. There was no blood, no pain. It was as if the missing finger had never been there at all.

He glanced at the simulation's hands, which were both empty. There was no sign of his amputated finger.

"As I told you, Mr. Hood, you can have it back when you leave."

Norton sat down again, and the chair he hadn't noticed was there again.

"Anything else I can help you with?" asked the sim. "I can point you in the right direction. Even if you can't."

"If I can't what?"

"Can't point. That's another joke. You've got to think of this detachedly."

"Another joke?"

"You *do* have a sense of fun! You'll find plenty of that on Hideaway, Mr. Hood. Isn't that why you're here?"

"Er . . . yeah."

"In that case, do you need something for the weekend?"

"What?"

"The absolute totally ultimate bugstrap. At a bargain price. Plus twenty-five percent sales tax, naturally."

"What's a bugstrap?"

The sim laughed, stopped, stared at Norton. "You don't know, do you?"

"That's why I asked."

"It's like a bugbelt. But of a more intimate and personal nature. You understand?"

"I don't. What's a bugbelt?"

"You're not wearing one?"

"I don't think so."

"A bugbelt is essential to every space traveller. You can't afford to be without one, Mr. Hood. Because it's classified as a necessity, there's only ten percent tax."

"But . . . what is it?"

The sim explained that because humans had evolved on one world, they were biologically suited to live only on that world. Anywhere else but Earth, they needed a spacesuit for protection against everything from microbes to raindrops because every type of alien "bug" could be lethal.

The early personal-defence suits were very cumbersome and restrictive, and had been superseded by bugbelts which performed the same function. These could also protect the wearer from extremes of climate and dangerous radiations, as well as compensating for differences in gravity.

And Norton didn't have one.

"Do I need a bugbelt?" he asked. "You mean it isn't safe here?"

"Hideaway is the safest place in the universe, Mr. Hood. The whole environment is sanitised for your protection. Hideaway can comfortably accommodate beings from every inhabited world. Different levels have different gravities or temperatures or atmospheres to make every client feel at home. Or almost at home. Whenever I go on vacation, it's the little differences I appreciate. I'm sure it's the same with you. But some differences are too extreme." The sim shrugged a human shrug.

"Do I need a bugbelt?" Norton repeated

"It's not a question of need, is it, Mr. Hood? It's a matter of comfort and convenience. A man of your status shouldn't have to endure any unnecessary stress and effort. I would also advise a bugcollar."

"A bugcollar? What's that for?"

"For the safe ingestion and digestion of non-human food."

"You mean . . . *alien* food?"

"Alien to you, yes."

"I have to eat alien food?"

"You don't have to. This is Hideaway. You can do whatever you want. Or whatever you can afford. I assume that a man of your obvious sophistication and refinement would wish to visit one of the many non-human levels to sample some of their cuisine."

"I don't think so." Norton shook his head.

"You can't imagine what you're missing."

"Yeah, I can." Norton shuddered as he remembered some of the meals he'd seen during his career as a steward—and all of those had been for the human palate.

The sim slowly nodded its simulated head. "For most people in your situation I can offer a really excellent deal. Bugbelt, bugcollar, bugstrap. A package of three. But if you only want the bugstrap, why not have the absolute pinnacle of the range? Combining total safety with ultimate satisfaction. And the price? It's so low I'm almost ashamed to tell you in case you I think I'm working for a charity."

"I still don't know what a bugstrap is."

"Everyone's a winner on Hideaway, Mr. Hood, but what if you want to play a different game? When you hit the jackpot, a bugstrap is absolutely vital. You understand?"

Norton said nothing. Because he didn't.

"Congress," said the sim.

"Washington DC," said Norton.

"What do you mean?" asked the sim.

"What do you mean?" asked Norton, then he said, "Oh." Because suddenly he understood.

"Do you need medical assistance?"

"No."

"Are you sure? Your face has turned an odd colour."

It had turned red, Norton knew. And not because he was an Indian. He was blushing with embarrassment.

A bugbelt allowed humans to visit alien worlds without harm. A bugcollar let them safely eat alien food. And a bugstrap . . .

Norton tried not to think about it.

"There must be something you've always wanted," said the sim, "something you can't find anywhere else in the entire galaxy. If you can imagine it, I promise you can find it on Hideaway. You can get anything your heart desires."

"Anything?"

"Anything and everything."

"How about some decent clothes?" said Norton.

CHAPTER EIGHTEEN

Hideaway was fantastic, or so the boss had said, unbelievable and indescribable. Kiru could only take his word for it because she'd seen nothing of the exterior and not much more of the interior.

According to legend, the asteroid was built aeons ago, in another galaxy, by a race of mysterious aliens. Long extinct, all that remained of them was the enigmatic world they had created.

It was a small planet with its own even smaller sun, a star that blazed at its very core, a perpetual source of solar energy and propulsion. Hideaway was a world without limits. Sliding into falspace as if it was a spaceship, it could reappear at the far edge of the galaxy.

Once, it had been the hidden headquarters of the pirate fleet. They had turned it into a pleasure planet, the ultimate hedonistic experience. Now, it was owned by an even more secretive and sinister organisation: the Galactic Tax Authority.

The space pirates had boarded the asteroid via a long-forgotten staff entrance. All Kiru saw were dark, narrow tunnels and the dark, narrow room into which Grawl led her. Having covertly breached Hideaway, the invaders split up, each to his or her or its own appointed task, ready to launch their assault at the same precise time.

Grawl put a finger to his lips, and opened the door.

"Don't leave me alone," said Kiru.

He closed the door, leaving her alone.

It was locked, of course, but she didn't want to go anywhere. Grawl was protecting her again, keeping her safe while he and the others went about their work. All she could do was wait. She kept listening for the sounds of violence. The pirates were heavily armed, and she guessed it would not be a peaceful take-over.

Time passed.

She heard nothing until the door opened again. Grawl came back in and gestured at her. The gesture was obvious. She was to undress.

Was this it, repayment time?

Kiru watched as Grawl removed the silver pendant from around his neck. This was the first time; he even slept with it on. He gestured at her again, impatiently. There was nothing she could do except obey.

As she took off her clothes, the alien entered the room.

She had seen aliens before. There were alien convicts on Arazon, there were aliens among the pirates, and there were even aliens on Earth. Since the Crash, it had become a cheap place for a holiday, a cheap place to buy land, a cheap place to buy anything. Including humans.

Was that it? Grawl had sold her to the alien?

She thought the thing was wearing body armour, but realised that was its skin. The creature was big and bulky, covered in a hard shell; its four eyes were on stalks; its six limbs were clawed. It was a monstrous, scaly insect.

Kiru stood naked and trembling and terrified.

Grawl's heart-shaped amulet was passed from fleshy hand to chitinous claw.

"Trust me," said the alien. "I'm a doctor."

"What are you going to do?" whispered Kiru.

Then it told her.

She had been wrong. Wrong from the very start.

Because Grawl *did* want her for her body.

All of it.

CHAPTER NINETEEN

"Show us your genitals," said the topless blue alien, via the simultaneous linguistic and tonal equaliser.

"Er . . . ," said Wayne Norton. "Is that really necessary? I only want a suit."

The alien stepped toward him.

"Or just a jacket," said Norton, as he backed away. "Forget about the pants. In fact, forget about all of it. I'll go. Sorry to have troubled you."

He retreated toward the doorway, but it didn't seem to be where it was when he'd come in.

"You can't leave empty-handed," said the alien.

"Yeah," said Norton. "Yeah, of course, I understand, yeah." He glanced around the room. This was meant to be a clothes shop, but there were no clothes on display. "A necktie. I'll buy a necktie, okay? Any tie. Just give me a tie, then I'll go."

"A necktie is some type of restraining garment?"

"It goes around the neck." Norton mimed putting on a tie, making the knot, pulling it tight.

"For strangling your enemies, we understand. But we are a couturier. We make clothes to personal order, not weapons. You've come to the wrong boutique."

"I'll go. Let me out. Please."

He kept looking for the exit, but couldn't see it. He couldn't even make out the size or shape of the room because it was almost completely hung with diaphanous fabrics, all of which seemed to float in the air from invisible washing lines. The multi-hued material was also scattered all over the floor, making it very soft and spongy. The atmosphere was thick with perfume, a mixture of heady fragrances so strong Norton could taste them as well as smell them.

"You're from Earth, we believe," said the alien.

"How do you know?"

"Because you look like an Earth person. We like Earth persons."

"Oh, good."

"Some Earth persons."

"Oh."

"Our name is Xenbashka Bashka Ka. We are from Algol, and our traditional greeting is 'Show us your genitals,' but we believe this is yours." The alien held out its right hand. "How do you do?"

This is an alien, thought Norton.

I'm with an alien.

"Howdy," he said.

Talking to an alien.

The only other alien he'd met was the Sham, which had tried to kill him.

The Algolan was tall and blue, with cropped white hair, pointed ears, and huge, sloping eyes. And bare breasts. Blue but bare. With hard nipples. Hard but blue.

He tried not to stare.

Breasts. Nipples. He'd never seen any before. Not for real. Not in any colour. Not human breasts. Not female human.

Was the alien female? It didn't matter, except to another alien of the same species.

Female, male, or whatever other alien sexual variety there was, it was of no interest to Wayne Norton, Earthman. None at all. Absolutely none.

He started to offer his own hand, his right hand, then hesitated, remembering his missing finger.

"Is something wrong?" said Xenbashka Bashka Ka. "You refuse to greet us because we are an alien?"

Norton wondered why the alien kept saying "us" and "we." The words were a direct translation, so that must have been how Algolans referred to themselves.

"No," he answered, shaking his head. "It's this." He held up his hand, showing his fingers.

The alien did the same, for comparison. Its hand was like Norton's, with three fingers and one thumb, although each was tipped with sharp claws.

Norton held up his left hand, with its full set of fingers.

Then the alien held up its left hand. Three fingers, one thumb.

"Ah, you're deformed!" said Xenbashka Bashka Ka.

"I'm not deformed," said Norton.

"You're an alien, of course you are."

Xenbashka Bashka Ka suddenly growled, showing its teeth. They were long and sharp, like fangs, and Norton quickly stepped back.

"We know what it's like to be hideously ugly," said the alien. "But it doesn't matter, not here. If you're from another planet, even the most beautiful alien can look like an ugly monster. Or vice versa."

Xenbashka Bashka Ka growled again, and Norton realised it wasn't a threatening noise. To him it sounded like a growl, but to the Algolan its meaning was different. A laugh . . . ?

"Do you want a pair of gloves to hide your deformity?" asked the alien.

"This really is a clothes shop?" said Norton, as he peered around. The silky drapes which engulfed them both must have been fabric samples.

"No."

"Oh."

"There's nothing you can see which you can buy."

"Oh. Yeah. Then I'll go." He kept looking around. "If I can."

"But we can make whatever garment you want. What would you like?"

"Er . . ."

"Something like you're wearing?"

"No." Norton was still in his steward's uniform. He could have changed before leaving the ship, but it was the only outfit which was half suitable.

"Something like we're wearing?" asked the alien.

"No!"

"What's wrong with it?"

"Nothing. On you, it's fine."

Norton didn't know the word for what the alien was wearing, although presumably there was one in the Algolan language. The garment was a pair of pants that began half-way up the chest and ended below the knees, and it appeared to be made from hundreds of small green bricks cemented together with mortar, each layer of which was a different colour. The alien's elbows were similarly covered. It also wore a pair of transparent clogs, and Norton could see that each foot had four clawed toes.

"Show me what you want," said Xenbashka Bashka Ka, and blue fingers touched what looked like a watch strapped to a blue wrist.

The air between them shimmered for a moment, then a figure materialised in the room.

Norton moved away as the shape suddenly appeared. It was a naked biped, still and lifeless. A tailor's dummy. A full-sized duplicate of himself, in fact. Even its right index finger was missing. As were the genitals. Norton looked down. So did Xenbashka Bashka Ka. The alien's head rocked from side to side. An Algolan shrug . . . ?

"Pants," said Norton. "Long, loose pants."

Alien fingers danced across what wasn't a wristwatch, and a pair of trousers appeared on the mannequin.

"Down to the ankles," said Norton, and the pants grew longer. "Waist lower. Around the waist."

He'd thought he was coming to choose some clothes, not design a complete costume for himself. His favourite outfit, the one he felt most comfortable in, had been his Las Vegas Police Department uniform. Because he was an undercover cop, it probably wasn't a good idea to wear something like that, even though no one would recognise it, not here, not now.

Norton had another idea. The more he thought about it, the more he liked it. Why not the kind of snazzy suit James Cagney or Humphrey Bogart wore when they were gang bosses?

Yeah, why not?

The Algolan was an expert at interpreting Norton's hesitant approximations, and very quickly the image became clothed.

Double-breasted jacket, wide lapels, razor-sharp creases on the pants. Belt—no, make that suspenders. Starched shirt. Vest with fancy buttons. Polished spats. Necktie.

"We don't do weapons," said Xenbashka Bashka Ka.

"A necktie isn't a weapon. It's a piece of material that goes under the shirt collar, then hangs down over the buttons."

The alien soon designed a necktie which met Norton's specifications.

"That looks great," said Norton, studying what had been created.

"What colours do you want?"

"None." Gangster films had all been in black and white, and so Norton's suit had to be in monochrome. "White shirt, everything else black."

Xenbashka Bashka Ka operated the wrist control, and the jacket and vest and tie and pants and suspenders and shoes all became black.

"The customer is always right," said the Algolan, "but that isn't."

Norton nodded his agreement. The outfit looked far too formal. The jacket seemed like a tuxedo. More than anything, the dummy resembled a head waiter.

"What do you suggest?" he asked.

"How about stripes?"

"Stripes?" Norton immediately thought of sergeant's stripes, but chevrons on the sleeves would spoil the effect. "Like this."

The Algolan added pinstripes to the jacket and pants, and wider diagonal stripes to the tie, which diluted the severity of the black. That was how black and white movies looked, Norton realised. They were different shades of grey.

"Yeah," he agreed, "like that. Now I need a hat. What were they called? A fedora? Like a stetson, but not as big."

Under his direction, Xenbashka Bashka Ka created a hat that looked almost perfect. But there was something wrong, something missing.

"A band," said Norton. "It needs a band."

"You want music coming out of your hat?"

"No, a band of fabric, above the brim, going around the crown. Yeah. Like that. Not so wide. Yeah. Yeah. That's it. That's it!"

The perfect gangster suit, straight out of the late thirties, early forties—*nineteen* thirties, forties, naturally. It was a classic, there had been nothing like it for centuries. Norton gazed at the design in admiration.

"How many would you like?" asked the alien. "Two sets of everything?"

"Two, yeah, why not?" Then he realised why not. "Er, what about payment?"

"If you couldn't pay, you wouldn't be on Hideaway."

"Exactly." Norton nodded. "Exactly."

"And if you can't pay, you'll wish you weren't on Hideaway."

"Oh."

The alien growled, but Norton stood his ground. A growl meant laughter. Maybe.

A clawed finger tapped the circular gadget, and the no-longer-naked mannequin vanished.

"How long before it's all made?" Norton asked.

"A few minutes. If you want, we can dispose of what you're wearing and you can put on your new ensemble."

"Yeah."

"Would you like a bag to carry your other new clothes? We can make one in any style you wish."

Norton thought about it. "I want one shaped like a violin case."

He'd never seen a violin case, except in the movies—and neither had he ever seen a violin—but he demonstrated what he meant.

"Like this?" said the Algolan, and another manifestation appeared between them.

"More like," said Norton, gesturing with his hands, "yeah, that, only not as much, yeah, there, that way, with a kind of . . . yeah."

The alien's creation looked close enough.

"We need your name," said Xenbashka Bashka Ka.

"Wayne," he said. And immediately wished he hadn't. "Why do you need my name?"

"So that we will be paid."

Norton had checked in as Robin Hood, but it was too late to give the Algolan another name—although not too late to give his complete one.

"I'm Duke Wayne," he said.

"You're a duke?"

"Yeah."

"We are royalty."

"That's nice."

"You must already know who we are."

"No."

"But you must."

"No. Why?"

"Because you're here to assassinate us."

"What?"

"Our real name is Janesmith of Algol."

"Pleased to meet you."

"Princess Janesmith of Algol."

"Very pleased to meet you." Norton wondered if he was expected to bow.

"You must have discovered our identity."

"I haven't discovered your identity. You told me who you are."

"We are Princess Janesmith, heir to the imperial throne of Algol."

"I didn't know."

"Xenbashka Bashka Ka is our assumed name, but everyone on Hideaway knows who we really are."

"I told you, I didn't know."

"We are a direct descendant of the First Empress, six hundred and fourteen generations ago. Why should we hide under a false identity? We are Princess Janesmith, next in line to the imperial crown."

Janesmith wasn't a very alien name, although that was the fault of the slate. It *was* a female name, however, and princess was a female title. If that's what the alien really was.

"Why's a princess running a clothes shop?" asked Norton.

"If you know who we are, you already know the answer."

"All I know is what you've told me. You say you're Princess Janesmith."

"We are, and therefore we're a threat to our sister, Marysmith, Empress of Algol. Only an aristocrat, even an alien aristocrat such as yourself, is permitted to eliminate that threat by assassinating us. Are you here to execute us, Duke Wayne?"

"I don't think so."

"You're not sure?"

"Yeah, er, I'm sure. Sure I'm sure."

But Norton wasn't sure. He wasn't sure about anything. It was a reasonable assumption that his secret mission was not to kill Princess Janesmith, alias Xenbashka Bashka Ka.

He wouldn't have been brought halfway across the galaxy for that—would he?

"If you're not going to kill us," said Princess Janesmith, "shall we have sex together?"

"Sex?"

"Yes."

"Together?"

"Yes."

"No!"

"Why?" asked Janesmith. "Is it because we're ugly? We think you're very ugly, but we'll close our eyes and imagine someone else."

"You're not ugly," said Norton, and he realised he meant it.

Despite her blue skin and her strange appearance, the Algolan was better looking than a lot of human women. If she was a woman.

"If we weren't a princess," said Janesmith, "we'd have been drowned at birth."

"You are, er, female, aren't you?"

"We are, but we don't look very feminine because we're deformed."

She looked feminine enough to Wayne Norton, and what he could see definitely wasn't deformed.

"But my genitals are not deformed," the princess continued, "and they're compatible with yours."

"Er . . . how do you know?"

"Because of my research on male Earth persons. You're certain you are male?"

"Yeah. Totally. All male."

"And because you are an aristocrat, you can have sex with us."

"Can't we, er, wait?"

Norton kept backing away, hoping to reach the wall, then feel his way around to the exit. He moved slowly, hoping that Janesmith wouldn't follow. But she did.

"Why wait?" she asked.

"Er . . . shouldn't we get to know each other better?"

"What for?"

"Because, er, it's nice to talk first."

"Is it like foreplay for you if we talk?"

"No, I mean, er, yeah. So, er, what's a princess like you doing on a planetoid like this?"

"We're trying to have sex."

"Have you been on Hideaway very long?"

"Far too long."

"Nice place you've got here."

"It's not nice, and it's not ours. You think we want to be here, making impossible clothes for temperamental aliens? We're here because we're trapped, paying off our debts."

"Through gambling? You lost your shirt?"

"We never wear a shirt. If we wanted a shirt, we could make one. As a young princess, we learned embroidery. It's one of our three skills. It's also our qualification for this demeaning job we were forced into after being abandoned on Hideaway. And who abandoned us here?"

"Who?"

"An Earth person. A male Earth person."

"Oh," said Norton. "But you said you liked Earth persons, Earth people."

"Some Earth persons. One male Earth person in particular."

"Me?"

"Not you. He was so handsome, so strong, so wonderful, so perfect." Princess Janesmith gazed up, remembering. "Definitely not you."

While her eyes weren't on him, Norton retreated two steps. There was still no trace of the wall, let alone a doorway, just more and more drifting lines of soft material. One by one, they were as light as gossamer, whatever gossamer was; together, they were almost impenetrable. He kept his arms behind him, yanking the layers of flimsy fabric aside, trying to force his way back.

Janesmith seemed to have no problem with the stuff, simply brushing it aside as she remorselessly pursued him.

"But he abandoned you," said Norton.

"He wasn't to blame. It was another Earth person who left us here. When we find him, we'll make full use of our second skill."

"What's that?" Norton didn't want to know the answer, but he wanted to keep Janesmith talking.

"Death," hissed the Algolan, baring her fangs. "We

killed three of our sisters. They called us the ugly sister. Now they're the ugly ones. Ugly corpses!"

If Janesmith was considered ugly, then her other sisters must have been absolutely beautiful. When they were alive.

"We should have executed Marysmith when we had the chance," added Janesmith. "We wouldn't be here now, slaving like a peasant. We would be Empress. Empress of Algol!"

Janesmith flexed her claws, and her whole body seemed to ripple. There was something almost feline about her exotic features, her lithe shape, her supple movement.

"From what you say, Algol isn't a constitutional democracy?"

"What?"

"Crowns and thrones, princesses and empresses. You don't operate the one-vote system?"

"We have a one-vote system," said Janesmith. "The Empress is the one with the vote."

"What about 'one man, one vote?' "

"On Algol, men are nothing. Their only purpose is for pleasure and for siring children."

"Oh."

"We've talked enough. You must be aroused by now."

"Er . . . no."

"You soon will be. Our third skill, the other royal talent we spent so long perfecting, is the art of sensual enjoyment."

Norton could no longer move. He was Janesmith's helpless prisoner, entangled in a spider's web of gauzy fabric, drugged by the exotic aromas that filled the air, trapped by her hypnotic alien eyes.

"Now we will have sex, Duke Wayne," she said. "That is an imperial command."

Princess Janesmith stepped toward him, her arms going around his shoulders, and she pulled him close. Their lips met.

He didn't want to, but he couldn't resist. No longer in control of himself, Norton's mouth opened. They kissed.

And kissed. And kissed.

He'd never been kissed like this. Her tongue sinuously twined around his, explored his mouth, his palate, his throat. He felt her warm breasts against his chest, while her fingers clawed up and down his spine. His passion rose, his ardour grew.

She finally released him, licking her lips with her tongue. Her forked tongue.

Wayne Norton watched as the Algolan princess discarded her clothes. Her strange garment began to unravel, falling apart brick by brick, revealing more and more of her blue flesh.

He'd never seen a naked girl before, either human or alien.

Until now, the closest he'd come had been gazing at photographs in *Playboy*.

Tits and ass, that was all a centrefold would reveal. The secret heart of the female anatomy was a complete blank.

Janesmith stood nude in front of him.

He should have bought a bugstrap.

Norton's heart was racing, his mouth was dry. He had waited so long for this moment. Slowly he looked down, down her perfect blue body, until his eyes finally focused on her crotch.

Where he saw—

He blinked.

Where he saw what looked like—

It couldn't be!

Could it?

Teeth!

Two sets of tiny curved fangs waiting to devour their prey.

Their male prey.

He suddenly felt very dizzy. His head was spinning and he started to f

a

l

l

.

.

.

He'd waited forever for this moment, for Susie to strip off her T-shirt and reveal what she'd let him touch but never see. Her breasts were wonderful, everything he'd dreamed of.

So shapely. So firm. So blue.

So blue?

Then she unzipped her jeans. The colour matched her boobs. As her denims dropped, she tucked her thumbs into the elastic of her briefs and started to slide them down.

This would be the ultimate revelation, the forbidden zone he had neither seen nor even been allowed to touch.

She was naked and soft, he was naked and hard.

Susie smiled, leaning forward to kiss him. He always loved the way her tongue snaked into his mouth. That was because her tongue was forked. He'd never noticed before. And her teeth were so very sharp. Why had he never realised?

Because this wasn't Susie . . .

She was someone else, someone different, someone *alien*!

That was when he woke up.

With a scream.

He opened his eyes wide, discovered he was naked, and closed his eyes again.

Not wanting to, not wanting not to, he slid his right hand down his body. He'd already lost a finger on Hideaway. Had he lost something else, something infinitely more vital?

It was still there and he sighed with relief as he grasped it in his palm.

Then the door blinked open and a naked girl stepped into the room.

"Susie?" he said.

"Shut up," the girl said.

She was naked but not defenceless, and she pointed her gun at him.

"Who are you?"

She wasn't Susie, but at least she wasn't blue.

"Don't stare at me when you're playing with yourself!"

He hadn't woken up. This was still his dream. He'd stare at her if he wanted to. Which he did.

She was good looking, of course. How could a fantasy girl be otherwise? Tall and slender, but with all the necessary curves. Her hair was red, curly, and short, in two places.

"You're human?" she asked, moving closer to him. "From Earth?"

He wondered how he had got back to his room. But if he was still asleep, he might not be in his room. Where were his clothes? His new ones, his old ones, any clothes. He wouldn't have been naked by choice because it made him feel even colder. Neither would he have chosen a null-bed, lying suspended in mid-air.

As the girl came nearer, he covered his groin with both hands. She tapped his hands with the gun. He let go.

"Just checking," she said. She glanced back at the invisible doorway. "You're my alibi. I've been here for an hour. Two hours. Understand?"

She climbed onto the nullbed, straddling him, and he didn't notice any teeth.

"Stop staring at me!" she ordered.

"I can't help it."

"Then close your eyes."

If his eyes were open, then he couldn't have been asleep. Unless he was dreaming he was awake.

"Is this real?" he asked the naked girl above him. "It's not a dream?"

"I'm not a dream, I'm a nightmare. One mistake, and I'll blow your brains out." She touched the barrel of the gun to his groin.

"If you're in trouble," Norton said, slowly, carefully, "I can help."

"How?"

"I'm a police officer."

"Ha!"

"I am."

She looked at him, really looked at him, for the first time.

"That's all I need," she muttered. "One wrong word, and you're dead. Or one wrong move. Uhhh!"

"What?"

"Ohhh! Keep still."

He was desperately trying not to move. But there was a part of him which he'd never really been able to control, a part which had never been so close to its female equivalent, a part which now he couldn't control at all.

"Don't!" she warned.

He was scared of the gun, but his other part knew no fear. When she pressed the weapon harder against him, it pressed harder against her.

"Uhhh," she sighed.

"Ahhh," he agreed.

Her eyes gazed down into his, and it was as if she could see deep within him, down into his very soul, knew everything about him, was aware of every thought, could read every secret.

She leaned forward, and her lips brushed lightly against his. Then she sat up again, the gun sliding away from his body as she slid even closer.

"If we're both going to, ohhh, die, we might as well make the most of what we've got left."

"Die?" He was already entering paradise.

"Shhh," she told him. "Lie back ahhhnd think of the uhhhniverse."

Reality or not, this was the best dream of Wayne Norton's long life.

CHAPTER TWENTY

"The alien's claws were surgical instruments," said Kiru. "It was going to cut me open, put Grawl's pendant inside me, turn me into an android, make me a zombie!"

"How did you get away?" he asked.

"I dived to one side, toward the door. The alien spun around and one of its claws hit Grawl, knocking him out. Instead of stopping me, the thing went to Grawl. Because it was a doctor, I guess. So I grabbed Grawl's gun and ran."

"Wow."

They held each other close and they kissed.

"Don't let them get me," she said.

"Never," he said.

They kissed again.

By now they had introduced themselves. His name was James Bogart.

"You're really from Earth?" asked Kiru.

"The twentieth century," said James.

"Where's that?"

"It's in the past. You know, history and all that stuff. I was born over three hundred years ago."

"No," said Kiru. He was lying. He was a man. Of course he was lying. "Humans don't live that long."

"I was born in 1947," he said. "I've spent most of my life, if you can call it that, in suspended animation. I was revived just a few months ago."

Kiru looked at him, but he was looking at himself.

"This is the first time I've felt warm in three centuries." James turned his attention to her. "You've finally thawed me out, Kiru."

"You look good for an old man. Everything still seems to work well."

"Seems to, yeah."

"What's so funny?"

"Nothing. Why?"

"You keep smiling."

"I'll stop," he said. "If I can keep doing this."

They kissed. Again. Then they did something else again.

Kiru was very impressed with the nullbed, it was so flexible and versatile. Hideaway certainly provided the best in guest facilities. And it had also provided her with the perfect guest.

"How did you know his name?" asked James, after a while.

"Whose name?" she asked.

"Grawl."

"Did I say his name?"

"You did. But he didn't. You said he couldn't speak."

"He couldn't. He didn't. The alien did. That's how I knew what they were going to do to me."

"The alien told you Grawl's name?"

"Yes."

"And did it introduce itself?"

"Why all these questions? Don't you believe me?"

"Now you're the one asking questions."

"I was in terrible danger. They were going to erase my mind, take over my body."

"Terrible," said James, but he was still smiling.

He obviously didn't believe her, he seemed to think she was here simply for his amusement.

"I'm still in danger, James. We both are. They could find us here."

"Like you found me here?"

"I told you, when I got away I made for the human levels."

"And you chose me."

"No. Yours was the first door I came to."

"But they chose you."

"Who did?"

"Grawl and Doctor Lobster. Why you?"

Kiru shrugged.

"Probably because you're perfect, Kiru. Young, attractive, sexy. I couldn't imagine a better victim."

"You say the sweetest things."

"You were visiting Hideaway, relaxing on vacation, and Grawl just came along and abducted you?"

That was what she'd told James, and she wished she was better at telling lies.

"I'm sure that must be illegal," continued James. "Even here. Shouldn't we report it to the authorities?"

"No!"

"Why not? You escaped. He'll try it again, and the next girl might not be as lucky."

"He's dangerous. He kills people."

"How do you know?"

Kiru tried to think up an answer which fitted in with the rest of her story.

Did it matter whether James believed her? He didn't seem to care whether Kiru believed him, and his own story was far less credible than hers. Three centuries in suspended animation?

"Because I do," said Kiru, which sounded very feeble even to her. "Because he killed Aqa," she added.

"Who?"

"Aqa. My previous lover."

"Previous?"

"I'm sorry, James, but you aren't the first man in my life. I've had sex before. Which is why I'm so good at it. I've practised. Unlike you."

"What do you mean?" James was no longer smiling.

Kiru said nothing, because there was no need to explain. They both knew exactly what she meant.

Because she'd never done it with a first-timer, it had taken a while to realise. James was clumsy and inept, although that was nothing new. Despite his enthusiasm, he was also a little shy, a bit hesitant, a fraction uncertain. By themselves, none of these meant much. Added together, they meant only one thing.

James Bogart was a virgin.

Or had been until an hour ago.

"I've had sex before," he said.

"Doing it with yourself doesn't count."

"But I have."

"I'm sure you have."

"No, I mean for real. I've had sex before. Plenty of times."

"It isn't an accusation. We all have to start with some-one, James, and I'm honoured to be your first. You're a good pupil and a very fast learner."

"This guy, Aqa," said James, "Grawl killed him when he abducted you?"

"Don't change the subject."

"I'm not."

"You are. I want to know why a good-looking man like you never had sex till now."

"Er . . . you think I'm good looking?"

"Compared to Grawl, you are."

James looked down from the nullbed on which they were entwined to where Kiru had dropped the gun.

"Where did you get that?"

"From Grawl, I told you. Why are you asking?"

"Because I'm a cop. That's my job. I ask questions."

A cop? Kiru wasn't sure whether that was a lie or not. She glanced at the massive weapon. "Grawl probably stole it. Are you going to arrest him?"

"For stealing the gun?"

"If that's more important than trying to steal my brain."

"This is out of my jurisdiction." James paused. "I think. In any case, I haven't got a gun."

"Take mine."

"I haven't got any pants."

"Neither have I."

"I had a gun when I arrived."

"I had pants."

"But I was disarmed." James lifted his right hand.

"No, just disfingered. I noticed." Kiru held his hand, kiss-ing it where the finger had been removed. "Because that's important to a girl."

"Important? What do you mean?"

"This important," she said, taking his left index finger, licking it, then demonstrating.

"Oh," he said.

"Oh, oh, oh," she said.

One thing led to another, and then another, as Kiru turned James's mental gymnastics into ones of a more phys-ical nature. It was only when the nullbed drifted against the wall that Kiru noticed how small the room really was.

Hideaway itself was completely spherical, and there

wasn't a straight line anywhere in the asteroid. The illusion of space in the room was created by the curvature of the walls, the floor, the ceiling, all of which merged into each other at angles that deceived the eye.

"How did Grawl get the gun onto Hideaway?" James asked, eventually. "If I'd tried bringing in a weapon that size, I'd have been disarmed up to the elbow."

"He smuggled it in. He smuggled himself in. He's a pirate."

"A pirate? You mean a space pirate?"

"Is there any other kind?"

"But they don't exist."

"They do," said Kiru. She shouldn't have said this, admitted that she knew what Grawl was. Now that she'd started, she might as well continue. "A gang of them is attacking Hideaway."

"When?"

"Now."

"Shouldn't we tell somebody?"

"No. They'll know. It's too late. They'll find out."

For the second time, James had stopped smiling. He was also studying her the way a cop would.

"Who are you hiding from?" he asked.

"Grawl."

"Who else?"

"The alien doctor."

"Who else?"

If James really was in the police force, she couldn't tell him the complete truth. But if he was, he could provide the perfect alibi.

She had arrived on Hideaway with the pirates. If their assault on the planetoid failed, she didn't want to be arrested as being one of their number.

But if the pirates succeeded, then she had to escape from Grawl. Either that or destroy his body before he could destroy her mind.

"Everyone," said Kiru. "Except you."

Zeep-zeep-zeep.

"What's that?" said James.

"It's the door," said Kiru, as she quickly reached for the gun. "Did you have doors three hundred years ago? There's someone outside."

"Why don't they come in?"

"You didn't have doors? This is your room, James. That's your door. People can't come in unless you let them."

"You came in."

"I'm different."

"How different?"

Zeep-zeep-zeep.

"I open doors," Kiru said, as she aimed the weapon at the optically stretched blank wall.

"With a gun?"

"No."

Kiru could open doors. Any door. Every door. Doors that were totally secure. Except to her. Opening doors was her talent. A talent which had landed her in a lot of trouble over the years, but which had sometimes helped her get out of danger. That was how she'd escaped from Grawl, and that was how she'd got into James's room.

The comscreen showed no one outside, but there was a small box lying on the ground. Kiru stood guard as the door blinked open, and James reached for the box. It was black, metallic, studded with spikes and fastened with a chain.

He brought it back into the room. The chain was tied in a bow, almost as if the box had been gift-wrapped.

"Could be a bomb," said Kiru.

"Is it a bomb?"

"How should I know?"

"Do we open it?"

"How should I know?"

James unfastened the box and carefully opened the lid. They both peered inside. It was full of slimy blue worms, squirming and writhing. He slammed it shut, but not before something dropped out. The size of a playing card, it was furry on one side, like animal hide, and there was writing on the other side.

"What's it say?" asked Kiru.

"I can't read alien."

"You don't have to." She rubbed a finger across the fur.

"A small token of my affection," spoke the card. *"In gratitude for your first royal performance. From an anonymous admirer."*

"Who's it from, James?" asked Kiru.

"I don't know," he said. This was the most obvious lie of all.

"You're blushing."

"I'm not!"

A wriggling blue shape slithered from the box and dropped out, then squirmed across the floor. James yelled and jumped away. Kiru squashed the bug with the gun barrel.

"Must learn how to fire this," she said, as she bent down to examine the dead worm. "Looks delicious. Want a taste?"

"No!" James quickly tied the box shut and put it down in the furthest corner—which wasn't very far.

"Why not? It's a box of chocolates."

"It's not."

"It is if you're an alien. Who's sending you chocolates, James? Is there someone else in your life?"

"No, no one."

"No one sent you a gift-box of worms?"

"Er . . . someone . . . er, just someone I met earlier."

"This someone was an *alien*?"

"Yeah, but—"

"And was this alien a *she*?"

"Yeah!"

"Because you can't always tell with aliens."

"Of course she was female. Anyway, I didn't do anything. How could I have done? With an alien!"

James was standing in one corner of the room, as far from the metal box as possible. Kiru sat on the nullbed, which floated between him and the black box.

"She was a princess," he said.

"Did she change from an alien when you kissed her?"

"She's a princess because she's the daughter of an empress."

"She told you that?"

"Yeah."

"And you believed her?" Kiru shook her head. "What was she like?"

"I don't want to think about her."

"Maybe not, but she's been thinking about you. Was she pretty?"

"No. She was *ugly*. With claws and sharp teeth and . . . and more sharp teeth."

"She must have been gentle with you. No sign of any cuts or bruises. But if that's what you want, James, if that's what you like, I can bite and scratch." Kiru beckoned him toward the nullbed. "Come on over here."

He obeyed. She sank her teeth into him, dug in her nails. Not too too hard, but not too softly. They began again.

Then the bed suddenly dropped to the ground. For a moment, Kiru thought they had exceeded its capabilities.

"Under arrest," whispered a voice, an inhuman voice, an alien voice.

They were surrounded by a group of ghostly figures.

But at least they weren't pirates—or so Kiru hoped.

"Where other you?" added the voice. It had no one source, each syllable seeming to come from a different direction.

Kiru and James disentangled themselves and drew apart, gazing up at their uninvited visitors.

"Two you?" sighed the voices. "Four limbs, no eight?"

"Yeah," said James. "Two of us. Humans. Two arms, two legs. Each."

The newcomers were no more than vague shapes, without depth or outline. There was nothing to focus on, and at first Kiru couldn't even work out how many of them there were.

Four guns were aimed at her and James, from four different sides. So there might have been four of the wraiths.

"Half space pirate you," breathed the quartet.

"Half?" said Kiru.

"They mean one of us," said James.

"Not me," said Kiru.

"And not me," said James.

"Two criminal. One criminal. All criminal. All capture. Hideaway safe. Hurrah!"

"Who are they?" asked Kiru.

"A security squad, I think," said James. "Those pirates, they must all have been caught."

"Good," said Kiru, narrowing her eyes as she tried to focus on one of the intruders.

They were almost transparent, but they made the room seem even smaller.

"You space pirate half," came the soft accusations. "You space pirate all."

"I want to make a statement," said James.

"Number," said the phantoms. "Twelve to one."

"What?"

This was Hideaway. A world of risk, of gambling, of random chance, and so Kiru said, "Seven."

"Lose."

"I want to protest," protested James.

"Number."

Kiru said, "Nine."

"Lose."

"I demand to see my lawyer," demanded James.

"Number."

"Six," said James, a moment before Kiru could speak.

"Win. Who lawyer you?"

"Er . . ."

"Who lawyer you? No? Lose. Prisoners you. All leave. Now."

Kiru and James looked at each other.

"We're under arrest," he said.

"Seems like it," she said.

"They think I'm a pirate. But I'm not."

"Tell them, not me."

"It's all a misunderstanding," he told them. "I'm a police officer, I'm in GalactiCop."

"All cop. All criminal. All go."

"Can I have my clothes?" asked James.

"Yes."

"Can I have my gun?" asked Kiru.

"Yes. No. No gun. No clothes. No thing. Yes. One thing."

The black metal box floated up toward James, lifted by an invisible hand or tendril or mandible.

"No leave Hideaway no thing," sighed their ghostly captors. "Everyone winner Hideaway."

CHAPTER TWENTY-ONE

"You aren't smiling now," said Kiru.

"What's there to smile about?" asked Norton.

"They haven't killed us."

That was something he hadn't thought about.

"Yeah," he said, and he gave a smile.

"Yet," added Kiru.

Norton surrendered his smile.

He had grown used to rooms without doors, without windows, but this one didn't even have walls. It was spherical, so small they had to curl up to fit within its contours. They lay side by side, facing one another, hip to hip, knee to shoulder.

It seemed hours since their ghostly captors had brought them here. The room was as bare as they were. There was only one other object within the sphere: the spiked box that Princess Janesmith had sent.

Every now and then, the casket would rock and sway. The worms inside must have been trying to ooze free.

Norton glanced away from the metallic box, toward Kiru, then studied their circular cell, which didn't take long, before looking at the girl again.

"This is for real, isn't it?" he said.

"I don't understand."

"Neither do I." Norton shrugged. "Is this an illusion?"

Kiru looked at him, touched his chest, slid her fingers against the curve of the wall, then said, "How should I know?"

"I mean everything. Not just an imaginary cell. Are you a simulation?"

"Sometimes I wish I was. Are you?"

"Who knows?" Norton examined his right hand, with its three fingers. "But I think I'm real, and so are you. I think."

"I'm glad to know it."

"So this is actually happening, here, right now, to us. You agree?"

"I never doubted it."

Wayne Norton had come to Hideaway to work. Even if he didn't know what that work was. But then Kiru had arrived and it seemed he was being forced to enjoy himself, whether he liked it or not.

Which he did. Very much. Very, very much.

Because she was his dream girl, specifically designed for him.

Back in Las Vegas, if the casinos wanted to smooth over a problem with a high-roller, he would be given a free room—and a girl to go with it. Hideaway must have run a similar system, and Norton qualified as a VIP. He couldn't remember exactly what had happened when he'd been with Janesmith. Not that anything could have happened. Of course it hadn't.

But maybe because Janesmith hadn't treated him the way she should have done, the management had provided compensation in the form of a naked redhead.

Or perhaps they had discovered he was in GalactiCop. It was always good policy to keep in with the police, which could also be why they gave him a fantasy girl who pretended she was in danger and had come to him for help.

When Norton realised Kiru was a computerised simulation, he'd felt cheated. For a moment. By then it was too late to bother, and so he'd continued enjoying what was offered. Which was why he had been smiling. Until he'd been arrested as a space pirate.

"Do you ever doubt the evidence of your own senses?" Norton asked.

"If I can see it," said Kiru, looking at him, "that's good enough for me. And if I can touch it, that's even better." She leaned harder against him.

Norton used to believe that, but not anymore. There was no such thing as objective information. It all became twisted to fit the false perspective. Everything was subjective.

He had no way of telling what was going on.

Perhaps he was the victim of a drug-induced hallucination. Spiked by Janesmith's spiked teeth.

Perhaps he was dreaming, still deep in his three-century sleep.

Perhaps he was unconscious, stunned by Mr. Ash's treacherous blow.

Or perhaps he was in a spherical cell.

If he could choose, this was his choice: He hoped he was in a cell with a beautiful nude redhead because that meant all they had done together had been real.

As a fantasy, it had been great.

But as reality, it was Wayne Norton who had been great.

"You're smiling again, James."

Out of habit, he'd given a false name. James Bogart sounded a lot better than Humphrey Cagney.

"Am I?" he asked, as he kept smiling.

"What have you got to be so happy about? Anyone would think you liked being here."

"I like being with you, Kiru, although I'd prefer to be somewhere else with you. This is obviously a mistake, and once I've been questioned they'll let me out, and then I'll be able to help you."

"You mean that?"

"Yeah," he said, and he did.

"It's a pity no one's going to question you," said Kiru. "For both our sakes."

"Of course I'll be questioned. That's standard procedure everywhere."

The authorities had every right to be suspicious of him. Norton had attempted to enter Hideaway with a hidden weapon, which didn't look so good, and they had discovered him with Kiru, which must have appeared even worse.

But he was confident that everything would be cleared up. Only the guilty had anything to fear, and Wayne Norton was completely innocent.

Yeah, he was.

"This isn't everywhere. This isn't anywhere." Kiru glanced around, which only took a split second. "I didn't mean to get you into this mess, James. All I wanted was to get out of one."

She was a criminal, a space pirate. He couldn't believe a word she said, shouldn't trust a thing she did. It was because of her that he was trapped. She was trapped with him, of course, and she was also naked and gorgeous and . . .

Norton tried to ignore her, which was almost impossible. The room was so tiny, his body was always touching her nude, soft, warm, supple flesh. He focused his attention on the black box.

"Why," he asked, "did the pirates come to Hideaway?"

"Maybe they were looking for treasure. How should I know?"

"Because you're one of them."

"I'm not! Would Grawl have tried to robotomise me if I was?"

"The spook squad who arrested us thought you were a pirate."

"And they thought you were one!"

"Only because I was associating with you."

"Associating? Is that what they called it in your day?"

"Yeah. Mixing with a known criminal. You."

"I came to Hideaway with the pirates, but I wasn't one of them."

"You admit you were with them?"

"On the same ship. But you know what it's like, you can't choose who you sit next to on a long flight. I didn't want to be mixed up with space pirates, so I had to pretend I was on Hideaway before they arrived."

"With me as your alibi?"

"Yes."

"So I could have been anyone? You chose a room at random, broke in, and threatened the occupant, who happened to be me."

"Lucky you. It's true what they say: Everyone's a winner on Hideaway."

"For every winner, there's a loser."

"What have you lost, James?"

"My clothes, my freedom." Norton held up his right hand to start counting, then realised that wasn't a good way of demonstrating.

"Your finger. Can't blame me for that. Or your clothes. What else have you lost? Your virginity. Okay, I apologise."

"And what have you lost? Nothing. Not even your clothes. You didn't have any."

"I've lost nothing, but I've found you. You're my treasure. My buried treasure! I'm so glad they dug you up."

"Why should I believe you? You're using me."

"I wouldn't use just anyone. What do you think I am?"

"A space pirate."

"How can I convince you?" It was Kiru's turn to raise her hand, as if swearing an oath. "I am not now, neither have I ever been, a space pirate."

Norton wanted to believe her. He met her gaze. Her eyes were so open, so honest, so limpid, so perfect.

"Believe me," she said, "I'm not a pirate."

He believed her. His instincts would never have allowed him to associate with a criminal. He leaned forward to kiss her.

"I'm an escaped convict," she said.

"What?"

She silenced him with a kiss.

"No!" He moved back as far as he could, which wasn't very far.

"I'm still the same girl, James. Don't pretend you're not interested. I can see the evidence with my own eyes."

"Evidence? I bet you know all about evidence!"

"I'm going to tell you a story. My story. If you don't want to listen, then leave."

She told him. He listened. Because he couldn't leave.

". . . and then the worst thing in my whole sad, rotten, miserable life happened," Kiru concluded, "I met you."

Norton had to admit that Kiru's autobiography was sad, rotten, miserable. If it was true.

"Look at it this way," he said, "things can only get better."

"Or, if I look at it this way—" she twisted her body until she was upside down, her feet braced on the curved ceiling—"you certainly look better."

It was Norton's job to be suspicious, and he knew he should never trust a dame, but Kiru's story had mesmerised his mind. Now she was hypnotising his body with her superb physique.

It was Kiru who had finally warmed him up after his frozen voyage through time. Having slept so long, he'd never fully awoken. Until now. It was as if he'd been sleepwalking, letting others run his life.

Not anymore.

After all that had happened since arriving on Hideaway, Norton should have been exhausted. He felt tired, but his mind was totally alert for the first time in centuries. From now on, he resolved, no outsider would control him.

"Oh," said Norton, losing his resolution as he looked at her, "no."

"Oh," said Kiru, as she looked at part of him, "yes."

"We can't."

"We can."

"How? There's not enough space."

"I'll show you," said Kiru, and she did.

"Shhhh," said Kiru, putting a finger to her lips.

"Why, am I boring you?" said Norton, who was narrating his biography.

"Shhhh," repeated Kiru, and this time she put a finger to *his* lips. "You hear anything?"

Norton shook his head.

"Sounds like an alarm," said Kiru. "Like an emergency siren on a spaceship."

"Hideaway is a spaceship. Of a sort."

"Not this sort. We're probably on a convict ship."

Wayne Norton looked around, but all he could see was the inside of the small sphere where he and Kiru were trapped. The surface was white, and it gave off a dull glow. If it was made of glass, it would have been like the inside a goldfish bowl, without the water. Which was just as well because he couldn't swim.

"We can't be," he said.

"We can be. I've been on one before. Not like this, inside a cell like this, but it feels the same, feels like a convict ship."

"How did we get here?"

"Transferred inside this piece of baggage." Kiru tapped the side of the sphere. "We're cargo. They must have captured all the pirates who attacked Hideaway, and we're on our way to Clink with them."

Norton had first heard about the penal planet from Diana. Arazon, also known as Clink. Then he remembered something, something very important. "My finger! They were going to give it back when I left Hideaway!"

"They let you keep all the rest. After what you did, some planets would have chopped off everything."

"What did I do? Nothing."

"On most worlds, captured pirates are executed immediately."

"I'm not a pirate."

"They think you are. And that's enough. Now be quiet!" Kiru put her ear to the side of their cell. "There's trouble outside."

She reached over to the small metal box. Before Norton could stop her, she untied the chain.

The lid sprang back and a blue worm oozed out. It was so fat it almost filled the box, so fat there was no room for any others. There were no others. It had eaten them all. Tiny fangs snapping as it searched for something else to swallow, the worm slid slowly across the cell, leaving a sticky trail of blue slime.

"And there's trouble inside," said Norton, pressing himself hard up against the curved wall. "Why did you do that?"

"I felt sorry for them. For it. Do you want to be locked up in here?"

"No."

"And that poor little thing doesn't want to be locked up in there. Time to go, James. It's our turn to get out."

She opened the door.

Norton was watching the worm, so he didn't see what Kiru did, but a round hole appeared almost directly above them.

"How did you do that?"

"I told you. It's my trick. I open doors."

"You could have done this earlier?"

"Yes."

"Why didn't you?"

"It wasn't important then. It is now. Listen."

Yow-yaw-yee-yaw-yow-yaw-yee-yaw.

Norton could hear the howl of a siren. He straightened up for the first time in ages, slowly sticking his head through the exit. It was so dark that he could see nothing, so cold that his breath condensed in a white cloud. He ducked back down again.

"What's going on?" he asked.

"I don't know, but we'd better get out of here quick. They can see the door's open."

"Who can see?"

"We're in a cell, James. Prisoners are usually kept under observation."

"You mean there's a camera?"

"Of course."

"We've been watched? All the time? Even when we were, er, associating?"

"When we were *what*? Ah, yes." Kiru nodded. "Of course we were being watched."

"Oh. No. Oh."

"They're aliens. They don't care. They're not interested. We're a different race. It's like watching animals. What kind of animals did they have in your time? Dinosaurs? Would you be into that? Watching dinosaurs *associate*?"

"I wasn't a caveman. I'm not that old."

"Let's get out of here, James." Kiru stood up. "If we stay here, this is a death cell."

She climbed out into the unknown, and Norton followed. He was glad she didn't reach back to help the blue worm escape. They found themselves in a high, narrow passage, and the alarm sounded even louder than before. It was cold, very cold.

Yow-Yaw-Yee-Yaw-Yow-Yaw-Yee-Yaw.

Norton looked to the left, but it was too black to see anything, looked to the right, with the same result. He stared, unblinking, from side to side, trying to adjust his eyes to the darkness. The only illumination came from a few tiny orange lights which blinked on and off, on and off, at ground level.

"We've got to get away before we freeze to death," Kiru said. She put her hand on his arm, and her fingers already felt colder.

Norton shivered. He'd been frozen before. Frozen alive.

"Stop," ordered a hollow voice behind them. "Escape no."

"Escape yes," said Kiru, and she ran.

"Under arrest," said the same voice from ahead of them.

One voice, two shapeless shapes drifting along the corridor toward them, trapping them in the middle. Two serious weapons held by spectral limbs.

The creatures were the same as the phantoms which had arrested them earlier.

As Norton walked to where Kiru had halted, he looked up, down, all around. There was nowhere to go.

"James!" said Kiru.

What would Cagney have done? Or Bogart? Or John Wayne?

Norton clenched his fists.

When the first alien came close enough, he lashed out, slugging it on the jaw, or where it should have had a jaw. His right fist sank deep into the thing's face. It was cold, like plunging his hand into freezing water.

The alien rocked back on its footless feet, then fell over. Norton spun around to confront the other one.

"You hurt you?" The second hazy creature had stopped and appeared to be gazing down at its companion.

"Hurt *you*!" shouted Norton.

He punched the thing in its middle, and his fist seemed to go straight through. When he tried to pull his arm out, it was trapped. His hand became even colder, growing numb.

"Me hurt me," said the alien. It doubled up, then collapsed.

Norton's arm came free.

What was left of it. It was severed at the elbow.

That was why it was numb, because it wasn't there.

His whole body became instantly ice cold.

First, his index finger. Now, half his arm.

He'd also lost his voice, couldn't scream out his horror and fear and pain. No, not pain. There was none. No feeling because there was nothing left to feel.

"James, that was, that was so . . . so prehistoric!" Kiru was gazing at him in total admiration.

"M-my arm-m," he stammered, shivering, showing her his stump.

"My caveman!" She reached out for what wasn't there, touching where his fingers should have been. "It's cold."

As he watched, his arm slowly reappeared. It was transparent, but still there! Each bone of his skeleton was clearly visible, gradually becoming covered with sinew and muscle. Every vein and artery could be seen through his by-now-translucent flesh. Finally, the skin reappeared, and he was whole again. Except for the missing finger.

Norton rubbed his left hand over his forearm. It was still too cold, still numb, but warmth and feeling were returning.

The two guards remained down, but not all the way down. They rolled from side to side, suspended a few inches above the ground, which was visible through their hollow bodies.

Perhaps that was because the security spooks were still on Hideaway. By now, Norton had accepted that Kiru was right. He and she were no longer on the pleasure satellite.

When the shadowy shapes had first appeared in his room, Norton felt he was in a daze, halfway between dreaming and waking. But it was an imagined dream because Kiru had been real.

He wasn't sure of the guards' reality. It was as if they were only half there, a projection from another dimension.

When they spoke, he'd understood them even without a slate. They hadn't used words, he now realised, but thoughts. His mind had picked up their meaning.

Kiru reached down for one of the ghostly guns.

"No!" warned Norton.

But he was too late. As soon as she touched the barrel, her fingers sank into the weapon, and she screamed with pain.

"It's cold!" She jumped back, shaking her hand, then stopped and stared. "My hand! It's gone! It's gone!"

"It hasn't," said Norton. "It's a trick. I can see it." He reached for her hand. "I can feel it." He put his other arm around her shoulders, holding her close.

"Where? Where?" said Kiru.

"Here. Here." Norton rubbed her icy wrist and palm and fingers.

"I see it," Kiru whispered, holding her hand in front of her face. "It's coming back."

The gun was as out of place as the ethereal guards. From what Diana had said, such a powerful weapon couldn't be used on board a spaceship because it would puncture the hull.

But maybe that was what had already happened, why there was an emergency, why the siren was screaming louder and louder.

YEE-Yaw-YOW-Yaw-YEE-Yaw-YOW-Yaw.

"Look," said Kiru.

Norton glanced around in time to see the two amorphous aliens float upward and touch, then overlap, their shapes merging as they absorbed one another. Two became one, still no more substantial than before, but now each upper limb held a weapon of its own. One barrel was aimed at Norton, one at Kiru.

Then the double alien's single head turned slowly away. A second later, its body twisted around more quickly. Another second, and the pair of guns also changed direction. The guard sped away, quickly fading into the darkness, its feet never touching the ground.

"Now we should go," said Kiru.

"We're on a spaceship," said Norton. "There's nowhere to go."

"Are you coming?"

"Where?"

"With me."

"Yeah."

Hand in hand, they hurried along the passageway.

"It must be great being a cop," said Kiru. "You've got to teach me how to hit people."

"I don't believe in violence," Norton said. "That's why I became a law-enforcement officer, to help prevent senseless violence."

"Sensible violence, James, that's what the universe needs."

Yow-YAW-Yee-YAW-Yow-YAW-Yee-YAW-Yow.

They dashed along corridors, down steps, down ramps, always down, and it seemed to be getting colder, colder, the air thinner, always pluming into white clouds as they exhaled, but the clouds growing paler as the ship ran out of air.

"What's going on, Kiru?"

"The ship's in danger. I don't know why. We don't have time to find out. But blow-ups happen. We're getting out of here."

"How?"

"By lifeboat."

She led the way, never hesitating.

"How do you know where to go?" he asked.

"Didn't you learn emergency procedure on your voyage to Hideaway?"

"No."

"Maybe there were only lifeboats for the crew. Like here. You can bet there aren't any capsules for prisoners."

"On my ship it must have been women and children first."

"First class, you mean? No lifeboats for anyone else?"

"No, I mean women and children first into the lifeboats."

"How quaint. Women and children first. That's me twice over."

"You're not a child."

"I am compared to you, old man. But neither of us will get any older if we keep talking. Save your breath, James, and follow the lights."

Norton had been aware of the pulsating orange lights which lined their route, but it was only now that he realised the lights actually marked the escape route.

YOW-Yaw-YEE-Yaw-YOW-Yaw-YEE-Yaw-YOW.

Apart from the siren and the soft sound of their feet slapping against the floor, there was no noise. There was no one else around, no one else running for the lifeboats.

"Why's there no panic?" said Norton. "Where is everyone?"

"If this is a convict ship," said Kiru, "they're still locked in their cells. That's where the panic is."

Norton halted. "We've got to get them out."

Kiru also stopped, ran back to Norton, grabbed his hand, and pulled. "No, we haven't. Come on! It's too late."

Norton didn't move.

"You can't get them out," said Kiru. "You can't open the locks."

"But you can."

"What? Grawl could be on board. You expect me to free him, give him another chance to wipe my mind?" Kiru stared at Norton. "And what do you think they'll do to you, James? They won't thank you, they'll kill you."

"Because I'm in GalactiCop?"

"That's a bonus. They'll kill you because you're not a pirate. Compared to what Grawl will do to me, you'll be the lucky one."

Kiru let go of Norton's hand and stepped away. In the gloom, he saw her shrug her shoulders.

"But I could be wrong," she said.

"They wouldn't hurt us, you mean?"

"No, I mean we could be the only ones on board. We weren't captured with the pirates, so we might not be with them now."

Yow-YAW! Yee-YAW! Yow-YAW! Yee-YAW! Yow-YAW!

"And the ship might not be about to go supernova," added Kiru. "This could be a false alarm." She turned away. "Goodbye, James, it was nice knowing you."

"Wait."

He caught up with her, their fingers interlocked, their icy lips briefly brushed together, and they continued their descent through the doomed ship.

"Almost there," said Kiru, as they rushed down to another level.

Norton wondered how she could tell, but didn't have the energy to ask.

They turned another dark corner and Kiru stopped.

Ahead of them, in the dim light, a handful of bulbous hatches sprouted from the bulkhead.

"They all seem to be there," said Kiru. "I thought we might have been too late, that the crew would have taken them all."

Norton's theory was that this was a ghost ship, without even a skeleton crew.

"Escape capsules," Kiru continued. "Spacers call them 'coffins.'"

"I've already spent three hundred years in a coffin."

"You came out of it alive, James. And I want to get off this ship alive. You're my good-luck charm."

"How do we get inside?" asked Norton.

Kiru reached up, and a moment later one of the hatches swung open.

"Told you," she said.

"Women and children first," said Norton, and he cupped his hands for her to step into. "I hope you know how to drive one of these things."

"So do I," she said, and she kissed his lips.

As Kiru rose up to the capsule, he kissed her shoulder, her breast, her hip, her knee, her ankle.

YEE-YAW-YOW-YAW-YEE-YAW-YOW.

"Now you." Kiru reached down for him.

Norton raised his arms, and their wrists and hands locked

together. Then a hint of movement in the gloom caught his eye and he looked around.

One of the shadow guards glided through the icy darkness, straight at him. It carried no weapon, but its arms were poised to haul him away from safety. If Norton fell, he'd also drag Kiru out of the capsule.

"Let go!" Norton yelled.

"No!" cried Kiru.

He tore himself free, saw Kiru fall back into the lifeboat. As he began to drop, the spectre collided with him.

But instead of a violent impact, instead of thudding against Norton's body, the alien passed *through* him . . .

Every atom of Norton's body was drained of heat. His entire being was plunged into the abyss of absolute zero. His blood froze in his veins. His heart ceased to beat. His whole existence ended.

He was dead. Totally dead. Not at rest, as he had been during suspended animation, but completely without a trace of vitality.

The only thing Norton had left was his brain, his final thoughts, which were of Kiru.

She was only a few yards from him, but the distance was a galaxy away. Since they met, this was the first time they had ever been apart.

How long had he known her? Two or three hours? Five or six? Eight or nine? There was no way of telling. However long it had been, it wasn't long enough. He wanted to be with her, stay with her, continue their association.

He'd never felt this way. Not for three centuries. Not even then. Not like this.

Wayne Norton was in love. But now it was too late.

All was dark, all was over, all was silent.

YOW! YAW! YEE! YAW! YOW! YAW! YEE! YAW! YOW!

Except for the sound of the alarm—

BAMABAMABAMABAMA!

—the noise of the ship being ripped apart—

"James! James! James!"

—and Kiru calling his name, or what she thought was his name.

He could hear.

Which meant he was alive.

He could feel the vibrations of the ship being destroyed.
Wayne Norton had been reborn.

!!!!! POWPOWABAMAPOWBAMMMMMM !!!!!

But the spaceship was going through its death agonies.

He was lying prone on the deck.

His life had begun anew, but his future would be very
brief.

He had been in darkness, but now there was light.

The light from the stars. Visible through the rips in the
hull.

Pulling himself to his feet, he took a final gasping breath
as the last of the ship's air was sucked out into the vacuum
of space.

The hatch to the lifeboat was still open. A fraction.

Norton stretched up, but couldn't reach. He jumped, slid
one hand in through the gap, then the other.

He was floating. Gravity was gone. Only his grip on the
hatch prevented him from being sucked out into the infinite darkness.

The hatch moved. Slightly. Then slightly more. Then
more. More. And he slipped through, tumbling down. The
hatch snapped shut.

He closed his eyes in relief, and opened his mouth to
greedily drink in the air.

"Honey," he breathed, "I'm home."

He opened his eyes.

Saw someone.

Not Kiru.

He was in the wrong escape capsule.

With Grawl.

CHAPTER TWENTY-TWO

"James!" yelled Kiru. "James!"

Then the hatch slammed shut, and she knew it wasn't such a good idea to try to open it, not if she wanted to live.

She sank down on to the floor and wondered if she wanted to.

All was silent. The emergency siren could no longer be heard. The escape capsule must either have been ejected from the main ship, or the ship no longer existed—or perhaps both.

It was warm inside the lifeboat, warm and light, but she'd willingly have spent the rest of her life in the cold and dark if she could have been with James.

He had sacrificed himself for her, and now she was alone.

Alone again, as she had been for almost all of her life.

"And who are you?" enquired a voice.

Kiru looked up quickly. There was a human standing at the far end of the capsule, or a figure that appeared to be human. If so, he seemed to be male; but because he was dressed, she couldn't be certain. Within the confines of the capsule, he seemed even taller, broader, than he really was. His face was black, his hair was white, and he was wearing a dark outfit of loose trousers and long jacket.

"Who are you?" said Kiru, as she stood up.

The man smiled, looking her up and down, and said, "I asked first."

Kiru put her hands on her hips and tried to out-stare him. Without success. He kept studying her naked body.

"I'm delighted you're here," he said.

"What do you mean?"

"To be joined by a lovely young thing such as yourself, that's what I mean. What a pleasure."

"You're not getting any pleasure from me!" said Kiru.

The man held up both hands in a placatory gesture. "You misunderstand, my darling. When one gets to my age, one doesn't bother about that kind of thing anymore. Which doesn't mean one can't appreciate the physical perfection of a nubile young beauty such as yourself."

As he spoke, he slowly moved toward her. Kiru glanced around for some kind of weapon, but there seemed to be nothing she could thump him with.

The man followed her gaze, and he also studied the lifeboat. It was small, compact. All that could be seen of the interior was a short corridor, about three metres high, one metre wide. The floor and sides were matte, metallic, and Kiru knew that below and behind them was all the survival gear and rations. The capsule was fully equipped for several people, but would be ideal as a single cabin.

If she had been here alone, she wouldn't have wanted anyone else suddenly coming in. Apart from James.

"It ain't much," said the man, "but it's going to be our home. I think we should get going."

"Going? Where?"

"This is an escape pod, my sweetheart. So we escape."

"I'm not your sweetheart."

"Whatever you say, my love."

The man turned, making his way back to the end of the capsule. He raised one hand, rotated his wrist, pointed, and a screen appeared on the wall. Then he started waving his hands in front of it.

Kiru hadn't moved from the hatch. Although the capsule was larger than the spherical cell, that wasn't saying much, and she wanted to keep as much distance between herself and the man as possible.

"What are you doing?" she asked.

"Don't worry your pretty little head over that. This is man's work."

Kiru felt a movement. The lifeboat was in motion. Slipping away from the convict ship. Away from James.

But the ship no longer existed. Neither did James.

She had to forget about him. It would be easy. He was just a man. She'd hardly known him. He was nobody to her. And now, he was nobody at all.

Kiru didn't believe anything James had told her, or not much of it. He might have been a policeman, but what kind

of person became a cop? The kind of person who couldn't
be trusted. James couldn't help telling lies. Three hundred
years old? He probably wasn't from Earth. He probably
wasn't even human. She was much better off without him.

"Yeah," she said.

"I'm glad you agree," said the man.

Kiru realised she'd spoken aloud, trying to convince herself by vocalising her thoughts.

"Women, bless them," the man continued speaking, as
he continued gesticulating in front of the screen, "just don't
have the reflexes and co-ordination to pilot a starship. As
long as you know your place, my dear, we'll get on fine."

"What is my place?"

"In the galley."

"You mean I've got to row the lifeboat? Chained to an
oar?"

"The galley is the kitchen."

"Ah! I cook and clean for you?"

"If only. It's all compact food, flasheated in five seconds."

"Good."

"It's not good. If we can cook and eat in ten minutes,
how do we pass the rest of the time? This is going to be a
long voyage, my precious."

"I'm not your precious. I'm not anyone's precious. I'm
not a love, not a dear, not a darling. My name is Kiru."

"Delighted to make your acquaintance, Kiru. Is that it?
Just one name?"

"We were too poor to afford more than one."

The man laughed.

"What's funny?" demanded Kiru. "It's true." It probably
wasn't true because she must once have had a family
name—because once she had a family. "I'm from a poor
planet. It's called Earth."

"I know."

"How do you know?"

"I couldn't help noticing, Kiru, that you're not wearing
a slate. But you understand me, which means we're from
the same planet."

He had been gesturing at the control screen all the time.
There was no longer any sense of movement, but Kiru
knew the capsule was now speeding through space. Away

from the debris of the convict craft. Away from James. Heading for . . . ?

She'd been about to ask their destination, but this was a more important question.

"You're from Earth?"

The screen vanished and the man walked back from the far end of the lifeboat, which was only several long strides away. He stood in front of her, looking down, and nodded.

Earth was just one of thousands and thousands of inhabited worlds, an average little planet with no distinguishing features—or even distinguished features. Since leaving her native planet, almost everyone Kiru had met claimed to be from Earth. The boss, Grawl, James, and now this man. But they were all men. They could all have been lying.

Kiru had been very nervous at first, but now that the man was so close that she could look up his nose and see his nasal hairs needed a trim, he wasn't so intimidating, and she was no longer scared. Even his nose hairs were white, as were his eyebrows and lashes.

"Do you have a name?" she asked.

"Plenty of them," he said. "Unlike you."

"Do you have a name I can call you?" she asked.

"Eliot Ness," he said.

There was something familiar about the man. Kiru had never seen him before, or at least not the way he looked now. But appearances could be changed, and no one was ever who they seemed to be.

In retrospect, she knew how much the boss had altered during the voyage from Clink to Hideaway, although she was now unable to picture him in any of his guises. That must have been part of his masquerade, to block the memory of anyone who saw him. He might not have changed at all, but he had controlled Kiru's perception of his appearance: He had never been an old man, but he had made her believe that he was.

Despite his ability to transform himself, she felt sure Eliot Ness wasn't the pirate boss.

Neither was he Grawl. Because if he was, Kiru would have lost her mind by now. Literally. And Grawl would have claimed her body.

She also knew that he wasn't James. Because he would

also have claimed her body, although in a much more pleasant and far less fatal way.

James was outside the lifeboat when the hatch had closed, by which time Eliot Ness was already inside. James was gone, dead and gone, dead and gone and forgotten.

"You should put something on," said Eliot Ness.

"I haven't got any clothes," Kiru told him. "I haven't got anything. I was a prisoner on a convict ship. That was a convict ship we left, wasn't it?"

"Depends on your perspective."

"From where I was, there wasn't much of a perspective. Were you locked up?"

"Depends on your definition of 'locked up.'"

"If you weren't a prisoner, you must have been working on the ship."

"Working? Me! You think I do manual labour?"

"How should I know? Are you going to tell me what you were doing on board?"

"You wouldn't believe me."

She wondered how he knew.

"As I told you, Kiru, we're in this together. We've got to be friends."

She looked around again for a weapon.

"Or at least not enemies," Eliot Ness added. He stepped back, reached up to the bulkhead, and part of the wall slid away. Leaning inside, he took something out, threw it to her. "Not very flattering, but they'll fit almost every known race in the galaxy."

Kiru unfolded what he'd given her. It felt warm to the touch but looked like a huge plastal bag.

"Aren't you going to put it on?" he asked.

"Not with you watching."

"But you're already naked."

"So?"

Eliot Ness shrugged, then turned his back.

Kiru couldn't work out where to begin. There didn't seem to be any sleeves or legs or neck. The garment clung to her as she examined it. When she tried to pull away, it moulded itself to her skin. She twisted to free herself but instead became more entangled. The thing slid up, around, over, and suddenly she was no longer naked.

It was looser than a bodysuit, but even more comfortable, supporting her where she felt weak, warming her where she was cool. She was completely covered from toe to head, with only her face and hands exposed.

"Um," she said. "Um, um, um, um, ummmmmm."

"It's called a symsuit," said Eliot Ness, as he took out another and unbuttoned his jacket.

"You're already dressed. Why do you need one?"

"Because I prefer survival to annihilation. The suits will slow our metabolism and allow us to live longer."

Kiru didn't want to turn her back on him, but neither did she want to watch him undress. As he took off his clothes, she looked away.

"What are they made of?" she asked, running her fingers across the strange material. It had felt cold and hard at first; now it was warm and soft.

"That's like asking what are we made of."

"You mean they're . . . *alive*?"

"It's better than wearing something dead. People used to do that, did you know? They wore dead animals. Leather and fur."

"This is some kind of *animal*? Some kind of *alien* animal? Is it dangerous? Could it eat me?"

"More like a plant than an animal. It won't eat you, but you could eat it. They're dormant until they come into contact with a living creature, then they start to interact, working symbiotically with your body."

Kiru glanced around. Eliot Ness was dressed in his own colourless symsuit. Only his face remained visible, his long white hair covered by the fabric. His hair wasn't that colour because of his age. He was old, of course. Everyone was old to Kiru. But he wasn't *old* old, really old, not the way the boss had pretended to be.

"Shall we celebrate our survival by having something to eat?" he said. "With only two of us on board, we don't have to ration ourselves. For a while."

"Now my chores begin, you mean?" said Kiru.

"I'll do it," said Eliot Ness.

In a very brief time, his whole manner toward her had changed. He must have been as surprised as Kiru was to find that there were two of them in the escape capsule, and the way he'd first spoken to her showed he had been as wary of her as she was of him.

He found the food, flasheated two meals, made two seats and a table appear out of the walls, and they ate.

"Don't think of this as food," he said. "It's fuel to ensure our survival."

"Tastes fine to me." The meal was far better than most of what she'd eaten during her life. "How do you know where everything is? How come you can pilot this ship? Where are we going?"

"The eternal questions. Where are we going? Where do we come from? What's the purpose of life?"

"I'll settle for the first two. Where did we come from? No, where did you come from? Why were you on that ship? Were you being taken to Clink?"

"Clink is for common criminals. I am neither."

Kiru was about to tell him that she'd been on Clink, but decided it was best not to say anything about herself yet.

"Where are we going?" she asked.

"Escape pods are designed to head for the nearest inhabited world. That isn't necessarily where I want to go, so I reprogrammed the controls."

"What if I want to go there?"

"Hideaway? That's nearest. You want to go back?"

"No, not there."

"Where *do* you want to go?"

It made no difference, and Kiru shrugged. "Where are we going?" she asked.

"You won't have heard of it."

"Where?"

He told her, and she hadn't heard of it. Not that it made any difference because she didn't believe him. They were probably heading somewhere else, to some other planet she'd also never heard of.

"If you weren't being taken to Clink," Kiru asked, "what were you doing on that ship?"

"What makes you think it was heading for Clink?"

"That's where we came from."

"We?"

"Ah . . . ," said Kiru.

"You mean the convicts who broke free from Arazon and then attacked Hideaway?"

Kiru nodded. "I was with the space pirates, but not *with* them. If you know what I mean."

"You thought you were on an excursion trip for jail-birds? A relaxing holiday on Hideaway, then back to the prison planet?"

"Okay, I was guessing." Kiru shrugged. "I was captured, locked up, I'd no idea where I was or where I was going. But you seem to know."

Eliot Ness nodded. "I thought I knew. Then I discovered what was really happening." He paused, shaking his head in disbelief. "So I made my excuses and left. How did you work out what was going on?"

Kiru hadn't worked out what was going on. And she still didn't know. She shrugged again because it could mean anything.

"You're a clever girl, Kiru."

No one had ever called her that before. In fact, very few people had called her anything. She'd spent most of her life being ignored. When she was a kid no one took any notice of her, and as she'd grown up, no one ever listened to what she had to say. Eliot Ness, however, had no alternative. As well as not talking about herself, she should say as little as possible about anything, or else he'd soon discover she wasn't as clever as he thought.

"Lucky for us the ship had escape pods. Even luckier, this one is still functional." Eliot Ness glanced around. "So far."

"Don't all ships have lifeboats?"

"No. And probably not ships with a suicide circuit."

Kiru stared at him. "It was no accident? The ship was deliberately destroyed?"

"Yes. We were on board a time bomb."

Despite her symsuit, Kiru shivered, and her voice was a whisper as she said, "We were meant to die?"

"Most people are meant to die," said Eliot Ness. "But I have other plans."

Kiru was born more than three hundred years after Wayne Norton.

In those three hundred years, Earth had revolved around the sun three hundred times.

In galactic terms, that was less than the blink of an eye.

When their distant ancestors were still struggling for survival in the fertile slime of Earth's primeval ocean, a globule of molten magma erupted from the white-hot core of a star in a remote solar system.

For hundreds and hundreds of millions of years, this lump of alien ore had drifted across the galaxy, its course varying every few aeons as it came under the gravitational influence of the nearest star. Every sun it approached, every speck of interstellar dust it encountered, every single atom of hydrogen created on its course, helped guide the meteoroid toward its destiny.

CHAPTER TWENTY-THREE

Wayne Norton stared.

Of all the sentient beings in the universe, of all the mindless creatures in the galaxy, how had he ended up trapped inside a lifeboat with Grawl?

It had to be him. Norton had heard all about Grawl from Kiru, and there was nobody else who could possibly match such a description.

He was short and seemed almost as wide as he was high. His shapeless overall couldn't disguise the strength and power of his body. Even his bald head looked muscular.

Grawl was like a bullet.

A bullet might miss its target, a bullet might only wound.

Grawl was more deadly than a bullet.

He kept looking at Norton.

Norton took a step back, tried to take another, but he was up against the bulkhead. He had to get out.

If he left the escape capsule, he'd die.

Definitely.

If he stayed, he'd also die.

Probably. Possibly. Maybe.

"I'm so sorry to intrude, sir. I wonder if I might share this lifeboat. Your lifeboat. I won't be any trouble, sir. You won't even notice I'm here."

Grawl gazed impassively at Norton's naked body. His hand went to the heart-shaped pendant around his neck, stroking it.

And Norton realised that although he might not die, his mind could be erased and replaced.

Which was just as bad.

Or worse.

He stood more chance of surviving the frozen vacuum of merciless space than he did with Grawl.

"Okay. Yeah. Sure. Sorry to have bothered you. I'll leave. Now. Immediately. At once. Even sooner."

Norton turned. The hatch was shut, and he couldn't work out how to open it. He wished Kiru was here.

No, that would be far worse. Kiru trapped with Grawl.

For a moment he'd thought that might be the case. Kiru had climbed into the capsule, found Grawl already there, and she'd been forced to hide.

But the lifeboat was so small, with every cubic inch assigned its own vital function, there was nowhere to hide. If Kiru was here, Grawl would have known.

She must have been in another escape capsule. When the ghostly guard attacked, Norton had rolled beneath a different lifeboat and lost his bearings.

He ran his hands over the hatch, searching for a lever or button or handle. As he did so, he felt a vibration. The lifeboat was moving, dropping free from the doomed spaceship.

Norton glanced around at Grawl, who was no longer holding the amulet. He didn't want to annihilate Norton's brain and take over his body. The body he wanted was Kiru's, and who could blame him for that?

He nodded, once, slowly, almost imperceptibly.

"I can stay?" said Norton.

Grawl did nothing. He didn't move, didn't nod, didn't react. Most importantly, he didn't shake his head.

"Thank you, sir, that's very kind of you, sir. My name is Wayne Norton. I'm very pleased to meet you."

Norton stepped forward, holding out his right hand.

Grawl looked at the hand, and kept looking. Norton realised he must have been counting his fingers, and he let his hand fall back, clasping it with his other one to modestly cover his groin.

"Had to leave in a hurry," he laughed. "No time to get dressed."

He knew Grawl couldn't speak, but if he let Grawl know that he knew he couldn't speak, then Grawl would know that Norton knew who he was. A little knowledge was a dangerous thing.

As was Grawl.

"I, er, didn't catch your name, Mr. . . . ?"

Grawl still didn't move or react.

"Ah, well, maybe we speak a different language. Maybe we're from different worlds. Although you look human. And you can tell that I am. Ha, ha, ha!"

Grawl blinked.

"Where are you from, sir? I'm from Earth, myself. Nice little place."

Grawl was also from Earth, of course, but Norton had to pretend he didn't know.

He wondered how he could ever become friendly with Grawl. It was inevitable they'd become more than casual acquaintances. In an escape capsule like this, there was no alternative.

Well, no, there were several alternatives—the most likely being that Grawl would kill him.

The guy had probably never had a friend in his life, and Norton would never be on more than nodding terms with him—because that was all Grawl could do, nod or shake his head.

Norton was still standing by the hatch. He leaned against the bulkhead and folded his arms, trying to look casual. But uncovering his private parts probably wasn't such a wise move under the circumstances—under most circumstances, in fact.

He shifted position, resting his left hip and shoulder against the wall, which meant he was side-on to Grawl, and he let his right hand drop down across his thigh, shielding his most vulnerable area.

"So," said Norton, and he nodded.

Grawl did nothing except look at him.

"Here we are."

Grawl still did nothing.

"Yeah."

Grawl continued to do nothing.

Norton supposed that was all there was to do, although he wished Grawl would look elsewhere while doing it.

There was far more room in the lifeboat than in the cell, and at least he could stand upright; but Norton felt much more cramped, far more of a prisoner.

It was going to be a long voyage.

"Are we going anywhere, do you know? Are we just drifting?"

A long, silent voyage.

They stood looking at each other for a long while. In silence.

To pass the time, Norton thought of a whole series of questions which Grawl could answer with a single nod or shake of the head. Asking them would also have passed the time. But even if Grawl replied, it wouldn't have been much of a conversation, and Norton decided to save them for later. In case Grawl ever became more communicative.

Suddenly, Grawl moved. He raised both hands, and Norton quickly stepped back as far as he could, which was all of eighteen inches. Grawl held his left hand up, sideways to Norton, and rested his right hand horizontally across the fingertips.

His hands were in the shape of a single letter.

" 'T'?" said Norton.

Grawl nodded.

While he waited for Grawl's second letter, it was Norton's turn to do nothing. But then Grawl turned away and opened a cupboard in the hull of the lifeboat. It was full of jars, pots, and containers, and he set to work. He made himself a drink. It must have been tea, Norton realised, something he hadn't heard of for hundreds of years.

"Tea!" he said. "Oh, I see. You meant 'tea' the drink, not 'T' the letter. Sorry. I didn't understand. I thought you were spelling out something, and I was waiting for the next letter, and I thought, 'This is going to be a long conversation if he has to signal every letter.' Yeah. Please. I will have a cup of tea. Thanks. Kind of you to offer. It's not my favourite drink. I'm more of a coffee type of guy. But at the moment I'll drink anything. No. Not anything, of course. Tea will be great. Really great. Really. I can't think of anything better. Thank you very much. Yeah. Please. Yeah. Thanks."

Grawl turned around again, raised his right hand, lifted his index finger. For a moment, Norton thought he was mocking him, doing something Norton no longer could. Then Grawl put his finger to his lips.

If anyone else had made such a gesture, it would have been a simple request. When Grawl did it, it was a menacing threat.

Norton became silent. But didn't get a cup of tea.

He watched as Grawl pulled a handle on the wall, and

part of the bulkhead was transformed into a seat. Grawl
sat down and drank his tea.

There was a similar handle near Norton. He pulled it,
and a shelf slid open, hitting him in the groin.

"Ahhhhh! Ohhhhh! Uhhhhh!"

When Grawl glanced at him, Norton immediately became silent again, clutching at himself in agony.

Grawl had killed Kiru's previous boyfriend. If he even
suspected that Norton knew Kiru, ever found out what they
had done together, Grawl would rip him apart.

What had happened to Kiru? Had her capsule survived
the detonation and escaped safely? Even if it had, he'd
never see her again. The galaxy was a big place.

Despite that, Norton planned to spend the rest of his life
looking for Kiru.

If he had a life.

Which all depended on Grawl.

Space is cold, silent and infinite.

The chance of two different objects from different eras
and different parts of the galaxy being on convergent tra-
jectories is incalculably small. The probability is higher than
zero, however, and even a one in a trillion trillion chance
is likely to occur once every trillion trillion times.

So it was with the escape pod and the chunk of ancient
galactic debris.

The two objects, one natural, one synthetic, were travelling in different directions, at different speeds. Although
the former was much smaller than the latter, had there
been a less tangential collision it was the lifeboat which
would have emerged as the smaller. Much smaller, in fact.
Transformed into thousands of very small particles.

They passed one another in less than a millisecond, only
a few cubic centimetres of matter attempting to co-exist in
the same three-dimensional area of space during that time.

The effect on the meteoroid was minor. It lost a tiny
fraction of its mass and an even lesser percentage of its
velocity, although its path across the galaxy now differed
by almost a complete degree of arc. On it went, on and on,
out into the universe, forever and ever.

The spacecraft suffered damage to its tail, losing a heating fin and part of a propulsion unit, and it was also showered with countless dust particles.

A lifeship could survive without a heating fin, without a propulsion unit; but those within the ship could not survive without the air which began slowly leaking out through all the microscopic holes in its hull.

CHAPTER TWENTY-FOUR

"What's that?" asked Kiru, as the lifeboat suddenly shook and she heard a loud bang.

The vibration only lasted for a moment, then everything was still and silent again.

And Kiru realised the sound had been outside.

"I don't know," said Eliot Ness. "It's as if we hit something. Or something hit us."

They looked at each other. The only thing outside was space. Empty space.

"If anything was wrong," said Kiru, "wouldn't there be an alarm?"

"The warning system was switched off when I disabled the distress signal."

"There's no distress signal?"

"No. We don't want anyone tracing us."

"We don't?"

"We didn't. But—" Eliot Ness stood up and went to check the control screen—"we do now."

"What's happened?"

"You were right, Kiru. We've been hit. We're always getting hit by interstellar dust, and the hull is constantly sealing itself. The particles pass straight through the ship, straight through us."

"Through us?" Kiru glanced down at herself. There were no marks in her symbiotic suit. She pulled it open, examining her torso for holes.

"In and out," said Eliot Ness. "Too fast and too small to cause much damage. Our bodies are like the hull. Self-repairing." He sat down again. "This time, there was more than dust. One of the propulse lines has been wrecked, which will slow us down, and one of the thermofins is missing, which will cool us down."

"We're going to freeze?"

"Yes, but don't worry about it."

"Why not?"

"Because we'll already be dead by then. Pressure inside. Vacuum outside. Too many holes in between. All the air's going to leak out."

Kiru took a deep breath. While she could. "How long have we got?"

"Forty-two hours, eighteen minutes and thirty-six seconds. Plus or minus three hours, twenty-two minutes and nine seconds. Approximately." Eliot Ness paused. "That's for both of us."

"With the symsuits on?"

"That is with the suits."

"What about an escape capsule?"

"This is an escape capsule. Lifeboats don't have lifeboats."

"Just checking," said Kiru. "Looks like we should have headed for the nearest inhabited world."

"We wouldn't have arrived there yet."

"But we'd have gone in a different direction, so we wouldn't have been hit. At the beginning, we were only a few hours away from Hideaway."

"A few hours, a few minutes. It means nothing. Or it means the same. In falspace, everything is relative."

Space travel was not *across* space, Kiru was aware, but *through* it. Because interstellar distances were so vast and voyages lasted so long, very few solar systems could ever be reached within a lifetime—either human or alien. The quickest route between two planets was non-linear, skipping across true space and time, dancing through false time and space.

Falspace was a dangerous realm, where ships still vanished: wrecked by the storms of time, torn apart upon the reefs of space, trapped in the endless depths of eternal flux. The one way out was via an escape pod, buoyed up to the surface after the vessel had sunk: Lifeboats could only travel in real space, in truspace.

Which was why they took such a long time to get anywhere.

And why few survivors lived long enough to make planetfall.

"In any case," said Eliot Ness, "the pod wouldn't have recognised Hideaway as a destination. It doesn't have fixed co-ordinates."

"That's not what you said at the time."

"Neither of us wanted to go there."

"That was then. This is now. I'll go anywhere."

"There's nowhere near enough. Not even in ninety-one hours, twenty-one minutes and thirty seconds. Twenty-nine, twenty-eight, twenty-seven . . ."

"Maximum air supply for one of us?"

"Yes."

"What do we do?" asked Kiru. "Wait to die?"

"That's not my preferred option."

"How about the distress signal? Can't you switch it back on? Or is being rescued too far down on your priority list?"

"It depends who rescues us."

"Beggars can't be choosers."

"I've no experience of the choices available to beggars."

"If someone answers the distress signal, they have to be on your list of approved rescuers? Otherwise you'll say, 'Thanks, but I don't like the colour of your ship, I'll wait for the next one'?"

"No one, Kiru, is going to rescue us."

"No one will hear the signal, you mean?"

"Even if they hear it."

"By the time they reach us it'll be too late?"

"No one is even going to try to reach us. Why should they? What's in it for them? You and me, what are we worth? I'm the most precious person in the universe. But only, it seems, to myself. Space rescue isn't a charity run by humanitarians. Or even alientarians. There just aren't enough philanthropic selfless altruists in the galaxy."

"People like you?"

"That's right. Launching a rescue is very expensive, even making a detour takes time and money. And it can be dangerous. Sending false distress signals is a pirate tactic to lure ships to their doom. As I'm sure you know."

Kiru ignored the last remark. "What can we do?"

"We can rescue ourselves."

"How?"

"By becoming a very attractive salvage opportunity. We need a fast rescue from the nearest planet, or we have to

snare a ship out of falspace with a lucrative rescue pro-
posal."

"How?"

"Like this," said Eliot Ness, as he returned to the control screen.

Kiru watched him. There was something different about
him. Different but familiar. This was the first chance for a
long time that she'd had to study Eliot Ness while his attention was concentrated elsewhere.

She wasn't sure exactly how much time had passed, but
they had been on the lifeboat at least three weeks. Or perhaps it was nearer to three months.

There was nothing within the pod to mark the passage
of time. (Or nothing that Kiru knew about.) The symsuits
slowed all their biological functions, making it even harder
to judge how long they had been together.

On board, there was nothing to do except sleep, eat and
talk, sleep, talk and eat, sleep. There was something else they
could have done, something men and women had done together since the dawn of time, but Eliot Ness always behaved like a perfect gentleman. He never made any
advances, but kept his distance and allowed Kiru her own,
small space.

She often wondered how he would react if she made the
first move. It was only an idle thought, but she had plenty
of time for idle thoughts. He wouldn't refuse her, she knew.
He was a man, so how could he? He was old, but not that
old. And the longer they were on board, the smaller the
relative difference in their ages would become. In another
ten years, say, he might be twenty or twenty-five percent
older; but Kiru would be fifty percent older.

It was a depressing thought, almost as bad knowing she
had less than a hundred hours to live.

Kiru had soon become used to the size of the capsule
and learned where everything was. (Or everything Eliot
Ness wanted her to know about.) What she didn't learn
was anything about Eliot Ness, who successfully evaded all
of Kiru's questions about his life. Despite this, he always
had plenty to tell her. She'd never had much education,
but thanks to her personal tutor she was on her way to
becoming a galactic graduate.

Eliot Ness seemed to have been everywhere, to know

everything. If not, he must have had a datadek grafted onto his brain. Or else he was lying.

Kiru had told him her own life story, which wasn't worth lying about, although she stopped when she reached Grawl's attempt to obliterate her brain and steal her body. She didn't want to remember what had happened after, her few fantastic hours with . . .

. . . whoever he was, whatever he'd been called.

"Who are you?" Kiru asked, as Eliot Ness turned away from the screen.

He smiled and shook his head.

"Aren't you ever going to tell me?" Kiru said.

"No, but I'll tell you who you are."

"Who?"

"You are Princess Janesmith."

"Who?"

"She's the elder sister of Marysmith, Empress of Algol," said Eliot Ness. "I met her on Hideaway when I was having some clothes made."

This was the first time he'd ever referred to being on Hideaway. Kiru had wondered if perhaps he hadn't been on the pleasure asteroid. He could have been on the ship when it arrived and stayed on board when it departed.

"You went to Hideaway to buy clothes?" said Kiru.

"I was there. I needed some clothes. Princess Janesmith made me some."

"A princess made you some clothes?"

"Forget the clothes, Kiru." Eliot Ness paused, smiling briefly. "If I remember, that's what you'd done when I first met you. The important thing is: from now on, you will be Princess Janesmith of Algol."

Everyone else had a false identity, now it was her turn.

"Why?" she said. "Give me one good reason."

"So I can survive," Eliot Ness told her. "Or you might prefer another reason: so you can survive."

Kiru nodded, but she was thinking of something else, of someone else. James. Before meeting her, he'd been with an Algolan princess. She was the one who sent him the box of blue worms. She had to be Janesmith, had to be the same person.

"Your younger sister, Empress Marysmith, inherited the Algolan throne," said Eliot Ness, "and she—"

"My younger sister?" Kiru interrupted. "I mean, Janesmith's younger sister?"

"On Algol, it's the youngest, not the eldest, who inherits everything. The youngest daughter, that is. Sons don't matter. The Algolans have got everything back to front. The females are in complete control, the males are totally subservient."

"That's insane."

Eliot Ness nodded his agreement.

"They must be absolutely crazy," Kiru continued. "Imagine a solar system run by women. Gossiping all the time. Comparing their hair, their makeup. Talking about babies. Going shopping. How long could an empire like that last?" She shrugged. "Longer than Earth's recorded history, isn't it?"

"Yes, yes," said Eliot Ness. "Never mind that. As I was saying, Marysmith, Empress of Algol, wants you, Janesmith, her elder sister, dead."

"Why? Because she, I mean me, because I keep borrowing her clothes?"

"It's because you're next in line to the crown. While you're alive, you're a constant threat to your sister. That's why Empress Marysmith has issued an imperial death warrant. She wants you dead, and so her whole planet wants you dead."

This, at least, made sense to Kiru. Everyone had always wanted her dead.

"If a whole planet wants this princess dead," she said, "isn't it dangerous to pretend to be her?"

"Only if you're on that planet."

"It isn't the one you want to go to?"

"No."

For some reason, she believed him.

But for some other reason, she still wasn't very reassured that this was a good idea.

Then she remembered where she'd first heard of the Algolans. They were the ones who had attacked the pirates, wiping out their secret base, causing so many of them to wind up on Clink.

"Don't the Algolans have a war fleet?" said Kiru.

Eliot Ness looked at her, obviously wondering how she knew, then nodded.

"Wherever Janesmith is, a battle squadron can suddenly blitz in and destroy the entire world she's on?"

"Well, yes, in theory. But in practice, a royal death warrant is just a formality, nothing but ancient protocol. The real Janesmith is on Hideaway. If I know that, the Algolans know that."

"I don't want to be her."

"You'd prefer the certainty of dying here, very soon, rather than risk the remote possibility of execution by an alien bounty hunter?"

"Do I have any choice?"

"Trust me," he said, "I'm not a doctor."

CHAPTER TWENTY-FIVE

Wayne Norton had been right about his lifeboat voyage with Grawl.

It was long.

Long and quiet.

As quiet as could be, in fact.

He soon learned to say nothing, to ask nothing, not wanting to discover what measures Grawl would use to enforce his "no talking" edict.

Norton could understand why spacers called the lifeboats "coffins": This felt like living death.

The only thing which broke the monotony were the cups of tea and the meals which Grawl gave him. Preparation took all of a minute, and Norton really envied the few minutes of distraction which Grawl found every day.

Days became weeks. Counting was Norton's only pastime, but every addition was even more depressing. There seemed to be enough supplies on board the lifeboat for a lifetime. Both their lifetimes.

Had he lived so long for this? To be cast adrift on the endless ocean of space for the rest of his life?

The long voyage grew even longer.

CHAPTER TWENTY-SIX

"Welcome to my humble spacecraft, your majesty," the first fat alien said to her. "Your wondrous presence lights up the whole ship."

"Your divine being illuminates the entire galaxy," the second fat alien said to her.

"Shut your toxic aperture!" said the first fat alien to the second fat alien. "I am captain, and I am talking to the transcendent princess. Please forgive this obscene intrusion, your terrific excellency."

"You fetid excrement!" said the second fat alien to the first fat alien. "I am the one who is on duty. Not that it is a duty to greet your imperial magnificence, but rather the greatest privilege of my entire life."

The two aliens were both identical, both almost spherical. Round scaly heads balanced on top of round scaly bodies. Grey on grey, with huge grey eyes. Small and squat, reptilian and repulsive.

Who were they? What were they doing here?

Also, where was *here*?

And what was *she* doing here?

She said nothing, did nothing, and tried to remember.

One of the round aliens said, "My whole existence has been a prelude to this moment. Having reached this pinnacle of achievement, from hereafter my career is on the decline."

The other round alien said, "You must ignore my insubstantial crew, your great greatness. I will have it expelled into space like the putrid garbage it is. Say the word, and I shall also step out into the void so the entire ship can be yours and you are not contaminated by my wretched self."

"Please, your acclaimed wonderfulness, ignore this anorexic peasant. If such is your wish, of course. Whatever your glorious self commands or desires, it is yours. While you are on board, this ship is your ship and I am your captain," said the other spherical alien.

"No," continued the previous one, "*I* am your esteemed luminescence's captain. It was I who came to the rescue of your unique superlativeness. I seek no compensation for all my exertions and expenses, although if your prestigious self were to offer a reward for your salvation I would not be so rude and ignorant as to refuse any such tokens of gratitude."

She was on board their spaceship. They had rescued her.

But what had they rescued her from?

She felt exhausted, unable to stand, hardly even able to move. Although there were only two of the grotesque aliens, she was surrounded. The creatures kept rolling from side to side, wobbling all around her, and she couldn't tell which was which. As they were exactly the same, it made no real difference.

She had found herself in a huge spherical room which was so bright she had to narrow her eyes, and yet it was a negative light which seemed to defy the laws of physics. The vast room was so bright that it was almost dark. The aliens were grey, and so was she, but they all cast brilliant shadows against the curved floor, the distant walls, the high ceiling.

The shape of the room seemed very familiar, reminding her of somewhere else, somewhere much smaller.

She tried to remember where it was.

And *who* she was.

"Does your majestic majesty understand me?" said one of the round creatures.

"Yes," she replied.

"Paradise!" said the alien which had last spoken. "Did you hear that, you emaciated dirtbrain? Our honoured guest addressed me. Me! Not you."

"Can you hear me?" said the other grey alien, as it bobbed up and down and around. "Can you hear me? Can you? Can you?"

"Yes," she repeated, "I can hear you."

"Heaven, absolute heaven!" said the same alien. "This revered high personage can also hear me, you malnourished bacteria."

Their heads were gnarled and wrinkled with creases and cracks which could have been eyes and ears and noses, but there was nothing which moved like a mouth while they spoke. The sounds the aliens made seemed to come from deep within them, echoing and gurgling upward through layers of bubbling fat.

They were only half her height, although probably four times her weight, and she wondered if she should have been scared of them. She was too confused even to be nervous.

"Have you found the correct reference yet, you virulent wart?" said the other alien, or perhaps the one who had just spoken.

"Here it is, you starving excuse for a life."

For the first time, the two round creatures became still, gazing up at an array of multicoloured lights which hovered in the air a few metres above their round heads.

"This odd being does not look like an Algolan," said one of them.

"Maybe it is a bad picture, germ-features," said the other. "Try a different reference work."

The lights blinked out, to be replaced a moment later by another rainbow of luminescence. The aliens remained motionless, staring at the glow.

While they looked up, she looked for an escape route. She wasn't in danger, not yet, but that might not last. Even if she could recognise a way out, that might be even more risky.

Her body was slumped, her shoulders stooped, and her knees bent. She tried shifting her legs to become more comfortable. They would hardly move. It was as if her feet were stuck to the floor, which made the idea of escape even more theoretical. She peered up at the phosphorescent swirl, but she could see no pattern.

It seemed the aliens, however, could.

"Almost the same illustration, you disgusting skeleton."

"This being is not an Algolan, you insignificant amoeba. I have been fooled."

"That is not difficult, you moronic excrescence."

"You were also deceived, you gullible cyst."

"Not at all. I have always had doubts, you supporting scab. If it was a princess, why did it have no jewels or treasures or offing works of offing art?"

"None that you recognised, you cultural savage. Algolan or not, this is an alien. Everything on board the lifesaver was alien. I do not yet know what is worthless and what is priceless. That is why I loaded the complete craft on board."

"That was my initiative, you mendacious particle."

She was wearing a slate. That was how she understood what was being said; but that was all she did understand.

The aliens appeared to know far more about her than she did, but she was aware it wouldn't be the best policy to ask who she was.

"Your distress signal claimed you were an Algolan princess," said one of the aliens.

"I am Princess Janesmith of Algol," she said, and she wondered why she'd only now remembered the name.

"Janesmith," she said, trying it again, "Princess of Algol."

The name sounded right, but was it her name?

"Algolan Princess," she said, "Janesmith."

The first of the aliens said, "I heard you the first time, you elite product of generations of selective breeding."

The second of the aliens said, "But, your fabulous highness, I heard you first. It was I who responded to your graceful request for assistance, and I had the satisfaction of saving your perfect noble life."

"Shall we cut the coprolite, your patrician apexness? Are you really an upper-caste Algolan?"

"How dare you doubt me!" she said.

The two aliens scuttled away a few metres.

As they moved off, the dimensions of the huge chamber seemed to change, the spherical shape becoming distorted. Her own glowing shadow stretched and slid aside, as if trying to detach itself from her body.

The two aliens affected the light, she realised, the position of their bodies making everything brighter or darker. As the angles and intensity of the negative light altered, every perspective became optically warped.

They never changed, always remaining grey, but everything around them appeared to be changed by them. And in a universe where vision was all, appearance was everything.

"It has a voice of authority," one of them said, moving closer again. "A positive sign."

"That is the translation device talking, mucus mouth," the other said, also returning. "Your renowned potency must take no offence at my insistence, but your immaculate reflection does not match that of an Algolan."

She looked up. Although she could still make out nothing, the aliens must have been able to see an image in the random design of coloured lights which hung in the air.

"I am Princess Janesmith of Algol," she said. Again.

She realised she was trying to convince herself as well as the aliens. All she could remember was that she'd been somewhere else. Now she was here. On board an alien spaceship. They claimed to have rescued her. Now she needed to escape from them.

"You do not look like an Algolan," said one of the bloated aliens.

She stared up, but she still couldn't see anything pictured in the shimmering gleam.

"It is wearing a disguise, you trail of muck," said the other alien.

"No, you are wrong, you hideous sphincter. It is wearing garments."

"What are garments, you scraggy virus?"

"Synthetic skin that protects a vulnerable body against extremes of temperature; even the most unattractive ectomorph knows that."

"Remove your garments. Now."

The alien was talking to her, she realised. So was the other one, which said, "If you truly are an Algolan of royal birth, your dynamic worship, please remove your garments."

"I am not subject to your commands," she said.

"You are an alien. Probably, incorrectly, you see me as an alien. What do we have in common? We breathe," said one of the creatures.

"Without air, I cannot survive very long. How long can you survive, your asphyxiating dominance?" said the other creature.

The two of them shuffled slowly away from her, the dark light shifted, the shadows altered, the perspective stretched.

She inhaled. Deep. Deeper. Held her breath as long as possible. Let it out slow, slow, slow. When she breathed again, there was no more air.

Feeling dizzy, she staggered, but managed to stay upright. She was very light-headed, her mind even more confused than it had been.

They were suffocating her, she realised.

She had to obey, to get undressed, and she explored her body with her heavy hands. Her clothes seemed to have no fasteners. Because she wasn't wearing anything. How could she take off something that wasn't there? She ran her fingers over herself. This was her body. This was herself. This was her.

Whoever she was.

She tore at her flesh, ripping it apart with her bare hands. As the darkness shaded into black, her limbs became even heavier, her fingers cold and numb.

Then she fell, plunging into the midnight of a frozen winter, trapped in a world with nothing, not even air.

Time passed, and finally it became dawn, the dim light slowly returning until she could see the discarded symsuit lying on the floor next to her. She could also see herself, and she didn't like what she saw.

"Must go on a diet," she muttered.

She'd spoken, she realised. Which tended to indicate she was alive.

Her body had almost died, but because of the ordeal her mind had been resurrected.

She knew who she was. She was Kiru. She was from Earth.

Without her symsuit, she was horrified to notice how much weight she'd put on during the lifeboat trip. No wonder she felt so heavy and lethargic.

"Totally abhorrent," said one of the aliens, in apparent agreement. "Nothing but an ugly bag of bones."

"In a poised and elegant way, however, as one would expect from an enlightened dictator born to dictate enlightenedly over an empire."

Kiru stood up, or tried to, but it was very difficult because of her weight. No, she realised, that wasn't the reason. Her weight hadn't doubled, but the gravity was twice as much as she was used to.

She hauled herself to her feet and looked at the aliens. It seemed the galaxy was not full of people from Earth—or even people who could recognise people from Earth.

She was naked, but still had a slate, according to which this pair were Xyzians.

"Are you a princess?" asked one.

"Yes," said Kiru. She had to lie. Lie or die. "I am Princess Janesmith, heir to the throne of the Algolan empire. You'll both be very well rewarded for saving my royal hide."

"Reward me!"

"Reward me!"

Kiru watched the aliens as they swayed from side to side on their short grey legs. If a sphere could have corners, the Xyzians had her cornered. They were in what seemed to be a large chamber, but because the light depended on the aliens and their relative positions to one another, it was impossible to determine its exact size.

"Was I alone on my ship?" she asked. "Were there any other survivors?"

"Only the great despot which is your despotic greatness."

"I found no other living being."

What had happened to Eliot Ness? This was all his idea. He'd attempted to programme Kiru into believing she was an Algolan princess, and now he was gone. Kiru was alone again. As always.

She shivered. Because she was cold.

Under normal circumstances, being with two small, fat aliens would have seemed ridiculous. Nothing here was at all normal.

She shivered again. Cold and scared.

What did she have to be scared of? The worst they could do was kill her, which was what she was scared of.

"I was the victim of a dreadful spacewreck," she said. "It was such a tragic catastrophe. I was lucky to make it to the survival pod, but in the confusion I lost everything I own."

The best she could do was play for sympathy.

"You lost everything?"

"Everything you own?"

It didn't work.

Because if she had nothing, they were more likely to dump her overboard.

"I might seem naked," she said, "to have nothing, but that's only my physical appearance."

"Excuse me for this observation, your overwhelmingness, but your physical appearance is not blue."

"Algolans should be blue, it says here. Even royal Algolans."

"I've not been well," said Kiru.

"There is little similarity between the illustrations in the reference works and what I can see of your celebrated holiness."

"You do not even have a tail."

"No!" Kiru looked down over her shoulder. "Where's it gone?"

"Are you male, your ascendant princessness, or female?"

The question was completely different from any of the others, and Kiru didn't like its implications.

Eliot Ness had told her that the universe was binary. Most alien races had two of most things. Two lower limbs, two upper limbs. Two heads were seldom better than one, however, and most species only had one. There would probably only be one mouth, too, because of a single digestive tract. But there would be two eyes and two ears and two nostrils.

Most races had two sexes. More than that, and the survival of the species became complicated. Two was the optimum number, and these were usually referred to as "male" and "female"—which did not necessarily bear any resemblance to what a human meant by those terms.

Algolan society was dominated by females, Kiru knew, but as for the rest of the galaxy . . .

From her experience of Earth, and after, she could guess.

Kiru stood up as tall as she could and, in a deep voice, said, "I am male."

"I am male," said one of the Xyzians.

"I am female," said the other one.

"She is my husband."

"He is my wife."

"Oh," said Kiru.

"We do not see enough of each other, my treat."

"How can we? We have this entire ship to run."

"Work, work, work. We have to earn a crust, I know. But, my morsel, there should be time for play. Remember our games?"

"We are too old for games."

"You are not too old, my pudding, and you are just as gross and beautiful as when we first mated. We can still rekindle the flames of our barbecue."

"Can we, my succulent one? Or has the oven in our kitchen lost all its heat?"

"We need a different course on the menu, my sweet. An exotic new flavour neither of us has ever tasted."

As it spoke, the Xyzian looked up at Kiru.

And she realised there was something worse than being killed, perhaps even worse than Grawl taking over her mind and body: They were planning to eat her!

"You are a deviant," said the other one. "Am I not all you desire?"

"You are a banquet, my tasty one. Compared with you, this alien is less than a discarded crumb. But imagine it as an amusing appetiser."

Kiru was not amused. "No! I taste terrible. I'm an alien. If you eat me, I'll poison you!"

"Eat you? The idea makes my throat burn."

"My stomachs turn at such an unsavoury thought."

"To believe we would want to eat the deformed creature, such arrogance!"

"It must really be a princess, my laden dish, even if it is not an Algolan."

The aliens were bouncing up and down faster than ever, circling around and around, making Kiru dizzy.

She had to get away, to open a door and escape. But she could only open a door if there was one. And the Xyzians didn't seem to have invented doors.

"I do not care about any reward or salvage. The only reward I want is you, my staff of life."

"And all I want is to salvage our love, my feast, to devour and digest you forever and ever and ever."

"Exquisite ecstasy."

"Ecstatic exquisiteness."

They became still, although their torsos wobbled from side to side, up and down, then they shuffled closer to each other. Their obese grey bellies touched.

Kiru took a slow step sideways, hoping she could slip away while the aliens were so involved with one another. But it was an even slower step than she hoped, and in this gravity she stood no chance of running away.

The aliens noticed her first tentative step, and they began to bounce up and down again. The heavier gravity had no effect on them. This was their ship, the gravity the same as on their native world.

"I . . . I thought . . . that," said Kiru, as slowly as she had moved, "that at . . . at such an intimate . . . intimate time . . . you don't . . . don't want me around."

"We want you."

"We need you."

"What," she asked, "for?"

"Our sex slave."

She felt sick.

This was even worse than being eaten.

She started to retch.

Then she threw up.

All over the Xyzians.

Which was a serious mistake.

Because how was she to know that vomiting was their idea of foreplay?

Chapter Twenty-Seven

The lifeboat landed.

There was a bump, that was all. The ship was down. Intact. Then silence. The voyage had seemed silent, but now the silence was absolute. No engine sound. No vibration. Nothing.

"We made it!" said Wayne Norton, as he finally opened his eyes. "Isn't that great?"

Grawl was as silent as ever.

"Aren't you pleased? Nod. Just one little nod."

There was no hint of cranial movement.

After so long together, Norton thought he knew how far he could push Grawl. And this was far enough.

"How about breaking out the champagne?"

Norton poured two cups of water. Grawl allowed him to do this occasionally, although he kept the meals as his responsibility. The water was recycled, which Norton always tried to forget. Perhaps it wouldn't have been so bad if the lifeboat had had two recyling units. In fact, it had three—and he and Grawl were two of them, with whatever they produced then passing through the capsule's filtration system.

At least their food wasn't recycled. When Norton had first considered the idea, just thinking of what he might already have eaten led to him skipping numerous meals. That was the trouble with thinking; it gave you too many thoughts.

Fortunately, in spite of spending at least one or two minutes preparing each meal, Grawl never seemed to care whether Norton ate or not. In the end, he convinced himself the food wasn't produced via waste reprocessing. If it was, there would have been so many added flavours that it couldn't possibly taste as bad as it did.

He handed one of the cups to Grawl, who accepted the water but didn't drink.

Although he'd attempted to keep counting the days, Norton had lost track of time. If the voyage had gone on much longer, he would also have lost his mind. Then one day (or maybe one night, it was all the same) he noticed one of the stars visible on the viewscreen was slowly getting brighter, which meant it was getting nearer. The lifeboat was heading toward it.

That was when he realised the capsule was on autopilot. It would land on the nearest planet and they would be saved.

But not all planets were safe. Some worlds were too big, with an atmospheric pressure strong enough to crumple the lifeboat like a tin can. Assuming there was an atmosphere. And even if there was, it could be a lethal mixture of toxic gases.

For days, and nights, he had gazed out at the blackness, watching for an orbiting planet to come into view. Without success. It was the star which was pulling them closer, its gravity dragging them toward an inevitable fiery doom. But long before they were incinerated in the heart of the alien sun, the escape pod would become a stove and they'd be boiled alive.

Then at last he'd seen the planet, and it grew and grew as the capsule came nearer and nearer. It had to be habitable, or else the ship wouldn't be heading there. But was it inhabited? If not, Norton would be stranded on an alien world with only Grawl for company. Which was a vast improvement on being trapped inside a lifeboat with him. At least he could have half the globe to himself.

"Let's see where we are," said Norton.

He went to check the screen. It was blank. For a moment he wondered if it was damaged. But it was still operational, and there was nothing on it because there was nothing to see. The screen was dark, darker than it had ever been, because there were not even any stars.

"Must be night outside," he said.

Grawl shook his head.

Norton stared at him in amazement. This was almost the first positive response—okay, negative response, any response!—Grawl had made for weeks. Maybe even months.

"Shall we open the door?"

Grawl shook his head again.

"Is it too cold? Would we freeze out there?"

Again.

"Is it too hot? Would we fry out there?"

And again.

"Is the air poisonous?"

Again again.

"So why can't we leave?"

Grawl opened his mouth, closed it, opened it again, closed it again.

"I don't understand."

Grawl's mouth opened and closed in the same slow rhythm, but his lips didn't move.

He looked like a fish. Was Grawl playing charades? Why now? They could have done this weeks and weeks ago, to pass the time.

"A fish?" said Norton.

Grawl nodded his head. He was holding the cup in his right hand, and he started making circular movements with his left arm, rotating it over his head.

"Swimming?" said Norton. "A fish swimming?"

But what else did fish do except swim?

Grawl nodded again.

Norton kept looking at him, wondering what all this was supposed to mean. He shrugged his bewilderment.

Which was when Grawl threw the contents of his cup at him.

"Water?"

Again, Grawl nodded.

"Oh, yeah, water!"

Again again.

"We're in the water? No. On the water? No. You mean . . . *under* the water?"

The lifeboat hadn't landed. Not exactly. Because it wasn't on the land. It was in the sea. Beneath the sea.

Norton remembered shutting his eyes before the capsule came down. Grawl must have kept his open, which was how he knew they had fallen into the ocean.

"Can you swim?"

Grawl shook his head.

"Neither can I. How far down are we?"

Grawl shrugged.

"Ohhhhh," said Norton, "nohhhhh . . ."

But if they couldn't swim, it didn't matter how deep they were. They might as well still be out in space, a hundred parsecs from the planet. Norton had no idea how far a "parsec" was, it was just another unfathomable measurement. Unfathomable! How many fathoms beneath the surface was the lifeboat? He had no idea how far a fathom was, either.

"When I was a kid, my favourite movie was *20,000 Leagues under the Sea*. Did you ever see that? I don't suppose you did. Long before your time. Two-dimensional, non-interactive. Very primitive. A league can't be much. How deep is it to the bottom of the sea? Earth's deepest sea. Two or three miles? More? I don't know. Say it's as deep as Everest is high. Five and a half miles. Call it five. That's . . . what? . . . four thousand leagues to a mile. So a league can't be much more than a foot? About sixteen inches. Hardly anything. How many leagues deep are we? However many, it's too many. I wish I'd been born in California. On the coast. Southern California. I'd have grown up surfing. I'd have been able to swim. Could have swum out of here. Nevada? Middle of a desert. No chance. Did anyone learn to swim in the Hoover Dam? But I guess if I'd never been in Las Vegas my whole life would have been totally different and I wouldn't be here now and I wouldn't need to swim, would I?"

Grawl raised an index finger and put it to his lips.

Norton shut up.

Grawl started to move his finger away from his face, then paused, gazing at it. Then he touched his finger with his other hand. It was his right finger, it was his left hand, and both were gloved in the same strange fabric which covered the rest of his body, except for his face.

Norton was clad in exactly the same way, except that he didn't have a right index finger. His outfit fitted him better than any glove. A seamless overall, it was as comfortable as a second skin.

Having been in space before, Grawl knew the proper lifeboat drill, and it was he who had found the clothes. The things looked like paper bags at first, but Norton was glad of anything to cover his nudity.

The garment never needed washing, and neither did he. The water Grawl had thrown at him had already been absorbed into the colourless cloth. The material seemed to assimilate every drop of sweat, to neutralise every odour. The gloves prevented his fingernails from growing, and the hood kept his hair nice and short.

Because the lifeboat had no shaving facilities, Norton's stubble had started to grow. One morning there was a finger-shaped shaven patch on his cheek, and he guessed his finger had been pressed against his face while he slept. As an experiment, he held his palm against his chin for a long while. When he took it away, his skin was smooth. The glove had absorbed all the hair. After that, he was able to keep his face stubble-free.

Norton hadn't touched his own water yet, and Grawl grabbed the cup, thrusting his right index finger inside, swirling it around. Then he raised the gloved finger. It was dry.

Grawl nodded slowly, then looked up.

Norton also looked up, imagining all the water above the lifeboat.

Lifeboat! The word was a joke. A boat which had sunk to the bottom of an alien ocean.

Grawl walked toward the end of the capsule, the end where the hatch was.

"No!" yelled Norton.

Grawl reached for the controls.

Norton reached for Grawl.

"Don't!"

Grawl grabbed hold of Norton.

Then the hatch burst open.

And in flooded the water.

Water! The one thing Norton dreaded most in the world. In the universe. He hated water. He feared water. It was so . . . so *wet*. He'd always imagined this would be the worst way to die. Mouth and throat filling with liquid. Choking. Unable to breathe. Unable to resist. No air. Lungs saturated. Struggling, struggling, struggling. Drowning slowly. Slowly drowning.

Slowly dying.

"Ahhhhhhh!!!!"

Grawl's hand went over Norton's mouth, cutting off his scream of terror.

The capsule filled with water, totally engulfing them.

Norton waited to die.

CHAPTER TWENTY-EIGHT

"Time to come out," said the voice.

They knew where she was hiding.

Kiru felt her heart sink, and in the heavier gravity of the Xyzian spaceship it dropped even faster.

The aliens had been so entranced at the sight of her throwing up, so interested in what her half-digested food told them about her diet, that Kiru had seized the chance and fled through the bizarre contours of their spacecraft.

When she escaped, every step had seemed to be in slow motion. The aliens' legs had been faster than hers, but they were shorter, which was how she outdistanced them. But they knew the layout of their vessel, which she didn't, and they almost caught her, until she finally found a hiding place.

She moved several times, always looking for a safer lair, sliding through gaps which were too narrow for the spherical aliens, and hiding away in the deepest, darkest recesses.

It was warm within the ship, but some of the pipes which criss-crossed the wall panels were ice cold, which meant that water condensed on the surface and dripped into pools beneath. Without these, the heat and the water, she could not have survived.

As time slowly went by, the Xyzians tried to lure her out with promises of food. At first, this was easy to resist; but as her hunger grew, the bait seemed far more tempting. She tried convincing herself that whatever they offered would be inedible; but as more time passed by, her empty stomach began to win the argument over her almost equally empty brain.

She lay hidden, keeping still in case they could trace her movements. Her mind had become nearly as immobile as her body. There was nothing else to do but think, but her thoughts led her nowhere. She switched her brain to stand-by and spent most of her time sleeping. It was never a deep sleep, because she was always on edge, listening for the fat aliens. Even when she lay awake she was dreaming, hallucinating. It was better than calculating how long it would take to starve to death.

Now she listened, wondering if she'd imagined the voice.

"Come out, Kiru."

They knew where she was. They also knew who she was.

Although she'd tried to work out the geometry of the ship, she had lost all sense of direction during her escape. The voice was like a whisper, but it seemed to come from a distance, echoing through the depths of the vessel.

Then she thought of something: How did they know her real name?

"If you don't come out," said the voice, "I'll go without you."

She recognised the voice, but realised this could all be a trick. Cautiously, she slid her head out through the narrow oval opening where she lay.

The chamber was shaped like a cone which lying on its side, and Kiru was near the end, which tapered to nothing. The area was dimly lit, but the light was pure and undistorted, which she hoped meant the Xyzians were nowhere near. She peered all around, looked to either end, but saw no one.

"Ah," said the voice, "there you are."

She looked up.

Eliot Ness was standing upside-down, high above her.

"Come on," he said.

Kiru slid out of the tube, and it was as if she had been hibernating in there. Like an animal sleeping away the winter, her body had used up its reserves of fat and she was back to her normal weight. That was the only thing that was remotely normal, she realised, as she looked away from her grey body and up to the inverted figure of Eliot Ness.

"You're upside-down," she shouted.

"Don't shout," said Eliot Ness. "I can hear you."

"Can you?" said Kiru, in a lower voice, almost certain he wouldn't hear her. "You're so far away."

"We don't have time to discuss acoustics," said Eliot

Ness, who must have heard her perfectly. "And I won't be so far away when you join me."

"You're upside-down."

"You already said that. But you're upside-down. I'm downside-up."

"What?"

"Neither do we have time to discuss topography. We've got to go." Eliot Ness beckoned to her. "Follow me."

"I can't get up there."

"You can, Kiru. You walk. Remember how? One foot in front of the other."

He was wearing a symsuit, which must have been how he could hang upside-down. She was wearing nothing.

She looked up at him again. It was impossible.

"Do it!" Eliot Ness ordered.

Although Kiru had lost weight, her legs still felt heavy in the Xyzian gravity. She took one step forward, then another, and began climbing the curve of the cone.

After the first few, short, hesitant steps, she slid her soles across the surface, one by one, not wanting to raise her feet from the ground. She leaned forward for balance, but found herself being dragged in that direction—dragged upward. Instinctively, she put out her hands. Then she fell, fell upward, onto her hands and knees.

"If you can't walk," said Eliot Ness, "crawl!"

She crawled, sliding her hands and knees and toes along the curved wall, crawled upward, up and up, then upside-down, to where Eliot Ness stood waiting.

"You can stand up now," he told her.

Kiru looked up at him, then looked even higher up, which was also further down, to where she had been.

Eliot Ness reached down his hand to her; she took it, and he helped her up. His fingers were bare, without his symgloves. He'd also removed the hood of his symsuit. By not being completely covered, his metabolism was functioning at its normal human rate.

This was the first time they had ever touched, Kiru realised. Even within the narrow confines of the escape capsule, they had never so much as brushed against each other.

He was also grey. His symsuit, his black face, his white hair, his eyes. All had become shades of grey.

"Thanks," she said.

"As I said, it's time to go." He released his hand from hers, turned and walked away. In the heavier gravity, it was as if he was wading through water.

"Where are the Xyzians?" she asked, as she followed.

"The what?"

"The Xyzians. The aliens. The ones who answered the rescue signal. The ones whose ship this is."

"Xyzians? That's a generic slate translation for an unknown alien name. Zyxian, that's another. So is Yxzian."

"Say that again."

"Yxzian."

"That's what I thought you said."

They made their way along the top of the cone, or perhaps it was the bottom of the cone, to the end where the diameter was at its maximum. The wall facing them was convex, and at the intersection was an elliptical aperture, just high enough for an Xyzian, or whatever they were really called, to pass through. Eliot Ness and Kiru had to bend down to go underneath.

Ahead of them spiralled a narrow tunnel. Staying low, they walked along, around, up, over, upside-down, along, down, around, then did the same again, again, again.

"Where are they, the aliens?" asked Kiru.

"Trying to get their ship out of orbit," said Eliot Ness.

"It's in orbit?"

"Yes."

"Around a planet?"

"Yes."

"Is it, by any chance, the planet you wanted to reach?"

"Yes."

The tunnel twisted downward, turning into a vertical shaft. They walked down over the edge, and it became horizontal. After more slow walking, heads still bowed, the tunnel ballooned into a series of parallel tubes. Without hesitation, Eliot Ness entered one of these, Kiru followed, and they soon reached a flight of semicircular steps. This time, when they walked down, they really did go down.

At the bottom of the steps the tube funnelled wide to become an ovoid chamber, and below them lay their escape pod.

Either Kiru and Eliot Ness were upside-down or the lifeboat was. Eliot Ness walked down the steep curve of the wall and reached the capsule. Kiru followed. No longer needing to go on her hands and knees, she walked vertically down the wall.

This was the first time she had ever seen the lifeboat from the exterior. It was grey, of course, and because of its shape almost seemed an integral part of the Xyzian ship: The pod was oval, with a domed nose, curved fins and a rounded tail. When she had been inside, it was very small; now that she was outside, it seemed no bigger.

Eliot Ness gestured for her to climb on board.

"Is it safe?" Kiru asked, inspecting the hull for holes.

"We're not going far," said Eliot Ness.

Kiru went in through the hatch. Instead of joining her, Eliot Ness walked to the furthest side of the hull, knelt down, and studied the array of tubes and pipes, wheels and dials. After a minute, he began operating the controls.

He stood up, looked at what he'd done for a few seconds, then hurried as fast as he could to the lifeboat, clambering inside and closing the hatch behind him. Everything became dark for a moment until the internal lighting system kicked in.

The greyness was gone, the complete spectrum of colours had returned, and Kiru no longer had a shadow which was brighter than herself. It felt wonderful to be back in the tiny, cramped lifeboat.

Eliot Ness reached the far end of the capsule and began signalling at the screen.

"Thanks for waiting," Kiru said,

"I didn't," he said. "The ship wasn't in synchronous position." He was silent for half a minute, then added, "Until now."

Kiru felt a surge of movement as the lifeboat took off, dropping out of the alien ship and heading down to the planet below.

The positions of the alien ship and the planet it orbited were irrelevant. Eliot Ness had found her and led her back to the escape pod.

"Thanks," said Kiru. "Anyway."

Liberated at last from the alien gravity, she stretched, and it was almost as if her torso and limbs were growing longer, and she could feel her whole body becoming straighter.

Her priority was food. She was starving, and she opened one of the rations compartments, searching through for something which didn't need hydrating or flasheating. But there was nothing, and it would take ages before she could eat.

"You want something?" she asked, during the first few of the ninety long seconds she had to wait until her meal was ready.

"I'll wait till I get there," said Eliot Ness.

Kiru thought about what he'd just said—". . . till *I* get there . . ."

"Where," she asked, "are we going?" She tried not to emphasise the word "we."

Eliot Ness gestured toward the planet that filled the screen. "Caphmiaultrelvossmuaf," he said.

Kiru had heard the name once before.

"You changed the lifeboat course to here," she said.

"As a precaution. This should have been the nearest inhabited world."

"And while the Xyzians were chasing me, you navigated their ship here?"

"Yes."

After Eliot Ness had told her she would masquerade as Princess Janesmith, there was a gap in Kiru's memory. She couldn't remember anything about the escape pod being found and the aliens taking it on board their own ship.

"You made me forget who I was," she said.

"I was helping you with your role," said Eliot Ness. "As soon as they realised you weren't worth a ransom, you could have been dead. I didn't want you dead, Kiru, and I didn't want the aliens dead."

"You mean you could have killed them?"

"Yes."

"Why didn't you?"

"What for?"

"Because of what they did to me!"

"They didn't even touch you."

"Only because I was too fast for them."

"Good. It's all worked out perfectly."

"Perfectly?"

"Yes," said Eliot Ness. "We're alive. The aliens are alive.

We've almost reached our destination. After a minor detour, they'll eventually reach their destination."

Kiru slid the table from the bulkhead, collected her food and put it down, then pulled out a seat and sat herself down. Eliot Ness had said that their rations might have been basic, but they should be treated like a banquet. Instead of stuffing their mouths whenever they felt hungry, they had always dined together at regular intervals. Until now.

Eliot Ness said he wasn't going to eat, but he slid out another seat and sat opposite Kiru.

But she no longer felt hungry. She pushed her food away and folded her arms.

"Is something wrong?" asked Eliot Ness.

"No, nothing. I absolutely loved being chased by a pair of slimeball aliens who wanted to use me as a sex toy in their obscene games."

"You said it, Kiru. Games—they were only games."

"Food games? Sex games?"

"The most important things in any society. Food is essential for the survival of the body, sex is essential for the production of the next generation of bodies. It seems that the Xyzians, or Zxyians or Yxzians, evolved underground, where they were safe from hostile predators. Their primal courtship ritual involved food, which was very scarce on their world. Females fought their rivals over scavenged food, then left it as a gift for the males. When the male emerged from his lair, the female would pounce—and the male could only eat as a reward for sex. They evolved into the dominant species on their world, but their atavistic instincts are deeply rooted in their ancestral psyche and cannot be suppressed."

"And when that happens?" said Kiru. "They forget everything else?"

"Exactly."

"Such as checking the course of their ship."

"Exactly."

Kiru had been pursued throughout the alien ship; she'd been forced to hide; she'd thought she would starve to death—either that, or provide a meal for the Xyzians. All because Eliot Ness needed her as a decoy. She'd been used again, just as she had throughout her life.

Eliot Ness was looking at Kiru, but she didn't want to look at him or her food. She turned her head toward the screen and the planet that was displayed there. It was red, or half of it was. The rest of it was dark—the half of the world where it was night.

"This is where I was heading when I left Hideaway," said Eliot Ness. "Or where I thought the ship was heading."

He'd never spoken about this before. Perhaps he realised Kiru was upset, and that was why he felt he had to explain. She said nothing, not wanting to distract him. For a while, he also said nothing.

"But it was all a trick," Eliot Ness continued. "It was a death ship. With me as the victim. I didn't know I'd be the only person on board. Not that it happened like that, as you know. There was you, there was Grawl, there was—"

"Grawl!" said Kiru, and instinctively she glanced anxiously around. "I knew it! I knew it was a convict ship."

"It wasn't. It was my ship."

"Why was Grawl on board?"

"I guess he wanted to leave Hideaway. He was smart, heard about my ship, managed to get on board. Because he wasn't one of the pirates, he—"

"He was a pirate!" Kiru interrupted again.

"No. He was on Arazon, but he wasn't a space pirate. He was on their base when the Algolans attacked, so he was rounded up with the survivors and sent to Clink. He deserved to be there, of course, but for other reasons. Like I said, he was smart, smart enough to pretend he was a pirate. He hated them, but he knew his best chance of escaping from Arazon was to stick with them. And it worked. He escaped and took you with him when the pirates raided Hideaway."

"You know all this," said Kiru, "because you were one of the pirates?" That must have been why Eliot Ness had seemed so familiar when she first saw him; she already knew him on Arazon. "You took part in the raid, and that's why you had to escape from Hideaway?"

"I was there to do a bank robbery," said Eliot Ness. "A databank robbery. The pirate attack was a cover, a diversionary tactic. It all worked out perfectly. Until my ship was sabotaged." He paused. "I thought it must have been me they wanted to kill, but perhaps the ship was destroyed to kill Grawl."

Killing Grawl was a good enough reason to destroy a whole galaxy, thought Kiru.

Grawl had rescued her from Arazon only because he wanted something from her later. And what he wanted was everything, all of her.

Eliot Ness could have abandoned Kiru on the alien ship. It was only because of him that she had escaped. What price was he going to demand from her later?

"Or," continued Eliot Ness, "could it have been you? Who would have wanted you dead, Kiru?"

The whole universe, she thought.

"No," added Eliot Ness, shaking his head. "You were only there because of John Wayne."

"Who?"

"You've forgotten him already?"

"Forgotten who?"

Eliot Ness smiled.

"Forgotten who?" Kiru said again.

"John Wayne. You were with him when the reflexants captured him. The ghostly aliens. Remember?"

"I remember his name was James."

"He told me it was John Wayne."

Kiru shrugged. John or James had been lying to one of them. Or both of them. "He told me he was born three hundred years ago," she said, which was another of his lies.

"Yes, he was."

"Oh," said Kiru, and she wondered if Eliot Ness was also lying. "That explains why he seemed so . . ." She shrugged again.

"Old?"

"Different."

John or James, Kiru didn't care. Their time together had been very brief. She'd spent far, far more time with Eliot Ness; although she knew far, far less about him than she did about James.

But James was gone, dead, history, over, part of her past. She didn't ever think about him. Or hardly ever.

She had never mentioned James to Eliot Ness, but he was aware they had been together on Hideaway, then on the suicide ship.

"You met him on Hideaway?" she asked.

"No, on Earth. But it's because of me he went to Hideaway." Eliot Ness paused, thinking. "And it's because of him I'm going to Caphmiaultrelvossmuaf."

"James said you should go there?"

"No. I'm sure he'd never heard of the planet. Very few people have. Yet. He was working for me. In fact, he was working *as* me. That must be why the reflexants arrested him. They thought he was me, so they put him on the same ship to make doubly sure I was killed."

Kiru shook her head, not understanding.

"And me?" she asked because that was something she might understand.

"You were with him, with John, James, which made you an accessory. You were also with the pirates. They made doubly sure with you, too."

Kiru *did* understand, but it was the only thing she did.

"Want some more?" asked Eliot Ness, gesturing toward the table.

She looked down. All her food was gone. She'd eaten it without even noticing.

"No," she said.

"Clear this away," said Eliot Ness, as he stood up and slid his seat into the wall. "Strap yourself in and we'll go into zero gravity. Landing time is fifteen minutes."

First Earth, her native world; then Arazon, the prison planet; and now Kiru looked out across the surface of her third world, Caphmiaultrelvossmuaf.

Which was wet, as wet as could be. Almost the whole world was covered with water. It was also raining. The rain was pink, drizzling down from an orange sky into the sea. The red sea. The escape capsule had settled on a small atoll, and in the misty distance she could see several more islands. No, not islands, but buildings rising up above the waves.

Turning away from the hatch, Kiru glanced back into the capsule. After the brightness outside, it seemed dark within the cabin, and for a moment Eliot Ness was invisible. Then he stepped forward out of the gloom. He'd stripped off his symsuit and was wearing the same odd outfit in which she'd first seen him: loose dark trousers, long matching jacket, a white shirt, a narrow scarf around his neck. Presumably because of the rain, he was also wearing a hat with a brim. He carried a small black case, which was narrower at one end than the other and probably contained the proceeds of his robbery.

Kiru moved back so he could get by, and he climbed out of the hatch, his shiny black and white shoes touching down on to the red surface of the planet. Without a backward glance, he walked forward until he reached the edge of the water. Fully dressed, with his case in one hand, he stepped into the sea.

"What about me?" said Kiru.

"What about you?" asked Eliot Ness.

"I haven't got a thing to wear."

"It's warm. You don't need anything. You're not a native, no one will notice. You'll get by."

Kiru watched him wade away through the shallows between the scarlet reefs.

She had come into her own world naked, and now she had arrived naked on an alien world.

Naked and alone. Again.

"Come on," said Eliot Ness, beckoning to her.

"Me?"

"No, not you. All the hundreds of others in the capsule. Are you coming? Stay there if you want. This isn't Arazon, Kiru. You're not a convict here. You're a free woman."

If she was free, she didn't have to do what Eliot Ness said. She could do exactly as she wanted. There were no more orders to obey. She was her own boss.

"Coming," she said, and she jumped out through the exit.

The ground was soft and damp, and she flexed her toes, luxuriating in the feel of the non-earth. She inhaled deeply, breathing in the fresh, unrecycled air. The rain was so heavy that in under a minute she was soaking wet. She ran forward, enjoying the gentle pull of normal gravity, and dashed into the alien water. It was warm and wet, and who cared that it was red?

Kiru kicked and splashed, slipped and fell, sinking completely under the surface. When she sat up, spitting out a stream of salty water and shaking the drops from her hair, she almost laughed. Almost.

"Good to be alive, isn't it?" said Eliot Ness.

He'd stopped and turned to face her. The sea was above his knees, but his trousers didn't look wet, and the rain seemed to have no effect on his hat or his jacket.

"Yes," said Kiru, "it is."

"Then make the most of it." Eliot Ness glanced toward the horizon. "It might not last."

CHAPTER TWENTY-NINE

There was water everywhere.

Water in his mouth, his eyes, his ears, his nose. All over his body. It was horrible. All over his head. It was terrible. All over his hair. It was awful. All over his face. It was—gone . . .

If it was gone, it meant his head must be above the surface. Wayne Norton spat, coughing up a spluttering stream. His mouth was open, but no more lethal liquid forced its way in. Only air. He breathed in, in, deep, then coughed again, his throat knotting as he spewed up another torrent of water.

He gasped for air, breathed again, and was alive once more.

His eyes were stinging, but he opened them—and discovered he was covered with blood. He may have been alive, but not for long. Blood everywhere. All over him. All around him.

He was in an ocean of blood. Blood was dripping down on to him. It was raining blood. The whole world was red, from the palest of pink to the deepest crimson.

Norton was on his back, gazing up at the sky. The alien sky. The orange alien sky. From which the rain poured down like a shower of orange juice.

He was floating. But he couldn't swim. His overall was keeping him afloat. He lay totally still, not daring to move in case he lost his equilibrium and slipped back down into the depths where the lifeboat had become a sunken wreck.

The overall had saved his life.

And Grawl had saved his life.

It hadn't seemed like that at the time. The hand over Norton's mouth hadn't been to stop the scream getting out

but to stop the water getting in. Then Grawl had pushed
him through the hatch, and he'd shot up to the surface.

But where was Grawl?

"Grawl! Grawl!"

Norton turned his head, looking from side to side. The
water was relatively calm, but he couldn't see very far because he was so low down. At sea level.

"Grawl! Make a noise if you can hear me!"

Norton raised one arm above the surface, then brought
it down with a splash. He closed his eyes and mouth as he
did so, in case the ocean washed over his face. It didn't, and
so he lifted his arm even higher to make a louder splash.

"Like this!"

He watched the pink drops of water drip down his arm.
His arm. His skin. Not the overall. He could see his bare
arm. His outfit was gone. It must have dissolved in the
water.

So what was keeping him afloat . . . ?

Nothing.

As he slowly, carefully began to lower his right arm, he
also pushed down with his left to balance himself. His hand
sank below the surface, followed by his arm, then the rest
of him—and he rolled over.

"Ahh . . . gug . . . gug . . . gug . . ."

Norton's mouth filled with water again. This time he
couldn't spit it out because his head was under the surface.
There was nothing but water, miles and miles of red water
below him. He'd instinctively closed his eyes and was glad
he couldn't see it.

In a blind panic, he kicked his legs, thrashed his arms,
desperately trying to stay afloat. But he was floating, he
suddenly realised. He wasn't sinking because he couldn't
sink. The alien water was very buoyant, and it was keeping
him afloat.

Afloat but upside down.

By twisting his neck, he turned his face halfway above
the waterline. He still couldn't breathe because his mouth
and nose were full of water, and he couldn't spew it out
because his neck was bent. Instead of coming up, the water
went down his throat. He swallowed, coughed, swallowed,
choked, sucked in a single gasp of air, then a wave broke
over his face and his mouth was full of more water.

As he kicked and struggled, his head became submerged again. He wriggled and writhed, twisted and turned, and when he bobbed back up above the surface again his face was upward.

He lay without moving, eyes shut, doing nothing except breathing.

If there was one thing he'd always hated, it was water. Water and everything in it. Even seeing a goldfish swimming around and around and around in a bowl gave him the shivers. He would never eat fish. Once, when he was a kid, he'd started to eat a piece of fish and found himself chewing a mouthful of bones, tiny and sharp, which impaled themselves in his gums and tongue and throat.

Norton kept breathing, breathing and thinking.

He shouldn't have moved, shouldn't have splashed, shouldn't have shouted for Grawl. Sound travelled faster under water than on land, and who knew what alien creatures inhabited the deeps beneath? A school of deadly fish could be swimming a yard below him at this very moment.

Was that what had happened to Grawl? Had he been swallowed by an alien whale?

Was this to be Norton's own fate? He'd been born over three centuries ago, crossed half the galaxy, and his ultimate destiny was to become fish food?

No, of course nothing was going to eat him. Even if a whole college of piranha sharks swam by, Norton was equally as alien to them. Alien and inedible. But they wouldn't find out how bad he tasted until they'd sampled a few bites.

How far was he from land? How long until the tide cast him ashore? Was there any land?

He could be adrift on an endless ocean, a sea which covered the whole planet. (What was the difference between a sea and an ocean?) Or maybe it was just a lake, although that could make it the size of Lake Superior. Or perhaps this might only be a pond. (And when did a pond become a lake?)

It made no difference. He couldn't swim, so he could float here forever. There was water all around him, but none to drink. It was far too saline, and already he was thirsty because of the liquid he'd accidentally swallowed.

He opened his mouth and put his tongue out to catch

the drops of rain. It was fresh water. He gazed at the orange sky, and the rain was cool and soothing on his sore eyes, but it would take a long time to quench his thirst. That was all Wayne Norton had: time.

How much time? The water was lukewarm, so he wasn't going to die of cold. Which meant he'd die of something else.

While he was considering the possibilities, he felt something beneath the surface brush against his leg.

"Ahhhhh!"

He yelled out in surprise and fear, then became silent, not wanting whatever it was to hear him.

But it was too late. Only a few feet away from him, the water bubbled, and an ugly red head surfaced above the waves.

Norton gasped in horror as a pair of huge crimson eyes gazed at him. The creature's mouth opened, wide, and orange water dripped from its sharpened teeth. Norton's heart stopped.

"Good afternoon, sir or madam," said the hideous sea monster. "Isn't it a lovely day?"

A talking fish. A talking alien fish.

Norton's heart resumed its beat, but it had lost all sense of rhythm and hammered away at double time.

"Let's hope the rain lasts," added the talking fish.

"Yeah," Norton managed to say. "Yeah."

"I came as soon as your ship was observed, sir or madam," the aquatic alien continued. "I do hope I haven't kept you waiting too long."

"Er . . . no," said Norton, as he stared at it. "You . . . you're speaking English!"

"I'm sorry, sir or madam," said the creature, "I don't know that word."

Norton didn't have a slate, and he was sure the fish wasn't using one. With a slate, the original sound could always be heard in the background, with a louder translation superimposed. Here, the alien's lips were synchronised with what Norton actually heard. This meant it was speaking English, or the twenty-third century fastspeak variant. Away from their planet, Earth people were known as Terrans. So was their language.

But if this sea creature could speak Terran, did that mean

Norton was back on Earth? Was that how a lifeboat functioned? It returned its occupants to their native world?

All Norton could see of the piscine beast was its head and neck, both of which were covered in red scales. Water cascaded down the ridges of its skull, there were fins where it should have had ears, and on either side of its throat was a series of gills.

He studied the alien, wondering if perhaps it wasn't one. Could it be some kind of mutant, a cross between a human and an animal? Dolphins were supposed to be smart. Was this a biomodified dolphin?

"What's the name of this world?" asked Norton.

"Caphmiaultrelvossmuaf, sir or madam."

"Do you have twenty-four hours in a day, three hundred and sixty-five days to a year?"

"No, sir or madam, this is a very backward planet. We don't have days on Caphmiaultrelvossmuaf. Not yet."

"Does everyone here speak . . . er . . . speak the language you are now speaking?"

"No, sir or madam, not yet. My learning has been fast-tracked so I can greet visitors. And you are my first visitor, sir or madam."

"Forget the 'madam,' just call me 'sir.' Okay?"

"Sir, okay."

"You're here to greet me?"

"Yes, sir, I already told you that. As soon as your ship was seen, I was assigned to you."

"You mean you're here to take me to dry land?"

"No, sir. I'm only here to greet you. Oh dear. Silly me. I forgot."

The alien vanished, its head sinking beneath the waves. A second or two later it was back, streams of water pouring from its cranial crevasses.

"Welcome to Caphmiaultrelvossmuaf, sir," said the alien. "The owners and management hope you have an enjoyable and profitable vacation, and may I add my own sincere personal welcome as a statistically typical inhabitant of this warm and friendly global paradise."

"Yeah, er, thanks."

"If you have any questions, sir, please don't hesitate to ask."

"You're here because my ship was seen landing? No, not

landing, but . . ." Norton shook his head, trying to think of an appropriate word, then wished he hadn't. More salty water sloshed all over his face as his head moved, and he spat out yet another mouthful.

"Yes, sir," agreed the alien.

"Have you found anyone else in the water?"

"No, sir. Is there another guest?"

Norton thought of his ex-shipmate. Perhaps he was still trapped in the lifeboat. If so, it was too late. Grawl would certainly have drowned by now.

"No, no," said Norton. "I was just wondering how many guests arrive the way I did."

"You're my first guest, sir. Have you any other questions?"

The alien kept watching him. Norton glanced around, looking for a topic of conversation. But there was only water, red water.

"Why is everything red?" he asked.

"I'm no expert, sir," said the scaled tour guide, "but I believe it's partly because of a spectral anomaly in the axial coefficient of light refraction, partly because of the very high aqueous distribution ratio, and partly because of a unique mineral oxide which is held in suspension in every drop of water on the planet."

"Yeah," said Norton, "that's what I thought."

"I couldn't help noticing, sir . . ."

"Noticing what?"

"And I do hope you won't mind if I mention the fact, sir, but . . ."

"Mention what?"

"I'm aware, sir, that the most considerate guest will try to fit in with the customs and habits of the planet he or she is visiting, and obviously this is what you believe your good self to be doing."

This was a fish. There was no reason why he should have understood it, but Norton had to ask, "What are you talking about?"

"You're not wearing any clothes, sir. We on Caphmiaul-trelvossmuaf may not be very advanced by your standards, but we're quickly becoming more civilised. May I demonstrate, sir?"

"Er . . . yeah, sure," said Norton.

The alien suddenly leapt up from the water, its upper half rising above the surface for the first time. Norton had expected a fish shape. Instead, the creature had a torso and arms, two of them, each with webbed fingers. It was humanoid.

And it was wearing a bra.

It was a mermaid, Norton realised.

He watched as the creature plunged head first into the red water, arching itself over. Then its lower half flipped above the surface. Instead of a fish's tail, the mermaid had two long, red legs with webbed feet. It was also wearing yellow briefs.

Bright yellow bra, matching briefs. This had to be the Caphmiaultrelvossmuaf version of a bikini.

The alien's head reappeared. "It was a giant dive forward, sir, when we learned to wear clothes," it said, or *she* said. "Imagine, sir, clothes to wear in the water! The sheer sophistication of a such a concept is almost overwhelming. We're so proud, sir, that our little puddle of a planet is to be admitted to the great commonwealth of culture."

"This puddle of yours," said Norton, "is it a lake or an ocean?"

"It is the sea, sir, the sea of life. Without the sea there can be no life on Caphmiaultrelvossmuaf."

"Yeah, yeah, but how far does this particular stretch of water . . . er . . . stretch?"

"It covers the world, sir."

"The world? The whole world?"

"We have some land, sir. We're not primitive savages."

"I know," said Norton, quickly. "I know. It's just that I'd like to see this land of yours. It is *dry* land, isn't it?"

"How can it be dry, sir? It rains on the land as well as the sea."

The amber rain kept beating down, adding to the vermilion sea, and Wayne Norton tried again not to wonder how many watery leagues lay beneath him.

Although the surface was fairly calm, riding up and down on the gentle swell was making him feel queasy. His neck ached from trying to hold his face above the surface.

He gradually became aware of something different. There was a sound in the distance. Water kept washing in and out of his ears, so it was difficult to be certain. He listened.

"Do you hear that?" he said.

"Yes, sir, I do," said the alien in the yellow bikini.

The noise was growing louder, coming closer.

"What is it?"

"It's for you, sir."

Norton couldn't work out from which direction the unknown sound was coming. He raised his head as high as he could, trying to see whatever it was. The noise was like a soft wind at first, but now it was blowing louder, rising toward gale force.

"I hope my services have been satisfactory, sir," said the alien.

"What?"

The creature raised its voice. "I hope my services have been satisfactory, sir."

"Yeah, but—"

"It's been a privilege to have been of assistance, sir. Thank you for honouring me with your conversation."

A webbed hand touched its wrinkled forehead in salute, and the bikini-clad alien sank beneath the waves.

By now the wind howled all around Norton, as if he was in the eye of a storm. Then it suddenly stopped. All was silent. He turned his head and saw a boat looming directly above, about to run him down.

"Noooooo . . . !"

The boat went right over him. It wasn't floating on the water, but above it, skimming the surface a foot above the waves, but only two or three inches above his face.

The craft was slowing rapidly, and for a few awful moments it seemed it was going to settle down on top of him. But the hull kept gliding above the surface and its height never dropped. Norton was in darkness, shadowed from the light, but also sheltered from the rain.

Finally, it passed completely over him and started to drift away. More of a raft than a boat, its hull rippled like the waves it rode above. It was red, of course, pale red. About fifteen feet long, half that across.

With someone on board, someone standing near the edge, someone with a lethal weapon aimed directly at him.

The someone with the gun had red hair. But this was a

different kind of red from all those he'd seen on this planet, as if it belonged to another spectrum, to another world.

A different kind of red. And a different kind of shape. Human shape. Female shape.

"Kiru!" said Norton.

CHAPTER THIRTY

"Who are you?" demanded Kiru, looking down from the skimmer, her gun aimed at him.

Floating on his back in the water a few metres away, he looked like James, but looks weren't everything. Appearances could be very deceptive.

"It's me," said James, or maybe John. John Wayne, that was the name he'd told Eliot Ness. (Or the name that Eliot Ness had told Kiru he'd told him.) "You know who I am. You must remember."

"Who are you?" she repeated. "What's your real name?"

"It's James," he said. "You know that, Kiru."

"You're not called John Wayne?"

"No."

"Have you ever been called John Wayne?"

"No." He hesitated, staring at the weapon pointing down at him. "Yes. But how do you know?"

"What's your real name? Is it James?"

"Yes." He kept looking at her gun. "No. My name is Wayne Norton. Really. It is. Honest."

Whatever he was called didn't matter. His true identity was far more important than his name, and Kiru had to be certain who he was.

"Where did we meet?" she asked.

"On Hideaway," said Wayne, or John, or James.

"How did we meet?"

"You came into my room."

"What was I wearing?"

"Nothing."

"What was I carrying?"

"A gun." He forced a laugh. "It was almost like this, wasn't it? I was naked then, I am now. You had a gun then, and you have one now. The only difference is, you're not naked. This is the first time I've ever seen you with anything on, Kiru. I almost didn't recognise you." He forced another laugh.

Caphmiaultrelvossmuaf was warm, but it was wet. Despite the canopy over the skimmer, Kiru's bodysuit was slick with rain, and her hair was soaked.

"Then what happened?" she asked.

"You know what happened."

"Remind me. What did we do?"

"Well . . . er . . . you know."

"Yes, I do know. But I don't know if you know. What did we do together?"

"I can't talk about that."

"Why not?"

"Because it's too . . . er . . . personal."

"But I was there," said Kiru. James/Wayne/John was slowly drifting away. She kept the gun aimed at him. "Tell me something only you and I know, or I'll have to assume you're an impostor."

"What do you want to know?" he asked.

"Everything," she said. "In exact detail."

"Okay, okay," he said. "You climbed on top of me, and . . ."

"And?"

He told her. Everything. In exact detail.

She was amazed how much he remembered, far more than she did, but his graphic account soon brought back her own memories. It didn't take very long until she was certain this was him. James. Or Wayne. Or someone. But she was enjoying his version of their time together too much to make him stop.

". . . and then the spaceship blew up," he concluded.

"I believe you," said Kiru. She had kept the skimmer close to where he was floating, and now she reached down to pull him up. Their hands touched, fingers interlocking. She hauled him on board. "Welcome to Caphmiaultrelvossmuaf, James."

"My name is Wayne," he said.

As they looked at one another, Kiru realised he was almost a stranger. They had only known each other for a few hours, and it all seemed a long time ago. She wondered what to say to him.

"It's good to see you," she said.

"Good?" said Wayne. "It's fabulous! It's tremendous! It's magnificent! Isn't it?"

Kiru nodded. "I suppose so."

"What's wrong with your face?"

"My face?" She reached up to touch herself. Had she been hideously disfigured by cosmic radiation, or scarred by acids in the alien water?

"Yeah. You're . . . I hate to say this, Kiru, but you're . . . *smiling.*"

Smiling? Was she? She wondered why.

"Am I?" she said.

"Yeah!"

Wayne laughed, and Kiru realised he was right. She was smiling. Perhaps it was because she was—what was the word?—*happy.*

They kept looking at each other.

Suddenly, they were in each other's arms, kissing and caressing, then tumbling down on to the deck of the skimmer. Kiru's clothes were soon gone, as if melted by the incessant rain. Together again, naked again, they continued where they had left off. It was as if they had never been apart.

"You didn't seem surprised to see me," said Wayne.

"It's a small galaxy," said Kiru.

Limbs entwined, they lay staring up through the canopy at the alien sky. Scarlet rain showered down from the orange clouds.

"You knew I was coming," said Wayne.

"I knew an escape capsule was coming," said Kiru. "And I knew it was probably from the ship we'd been on. All I could do was hope it was you on board."

"Who else could it have been?"

"Grawl."

"Er . . . who?"

"Grawl. The guy who tried to wipe my mind and steal my body. The one I escaped from on Hideaway, just before we met. I told you about him."

"Er . . . yeah, yeah. You mean . . . he was on board that ship with us?"

"Yes. And I thought he might have been in that escape pod."

"That's why you aimed the gun at me?" said Wayne. "You thought I might have been him?"

"Yes." Kiru looked at him. "I'm still not totally convinced."

"What?" Wayne stared at her.

"Convince me again," said Kiru, and she smiled.

The skimmer drifted over the vermilion sea. Although the hull rippled with the waves, the deck remained level. But even if there had been a hurricane, Kiru and Wayne wouldn't have noticed. It was nothing compared to the tempest they created between them.

"What makes you think Grawl was on that spaceship?" asked Wayne, during a lull in their typhoon.

"Eliot Ness told me," said Kiru.

"Eliot Ness? The Untouchable?"

"I never touched him."

"Who is he?"

"You don't know? He knows you. Or, maybe I should say, he knows John Wayne."

"What's he look like?"

Kiru told him.

"That's not Eliot Ness," said Wayne, "that's Colonel Travis."

Kiru shrugged. "You can talk about all your different names when you see him."

"He's here?"

"We escaped in the same lifeboat, came to Caphmiaultrelvossmuaf together."

"Tell me about it," said Wayne, and so Kiru told him about her voyage in the escape capsule and gave him Eliot Ness's most recent version of recent history.

It was hard to say how long since the two of them had arrived on Caphmiaultrelvossmuaf because this was a world where there was no day and night. Instead, there was day or night. In this hemisphere, it was always daylight; in the other half of the world, it was always dark.

Without day or night, it was almost like being back in the escape pod. Except there was a lot more room. It was also much wetter. As well as being redder. And she didn't only have Eliot Ness for company.

Since reaching the watery world, things had gone better than Eliot Ness had feared. He hadn't been killed.

His rivals had attempted to stop him reaching the planet by destroying the ship he'd been travelling on. Once he arrived, he'd wondered if their next move would be to annihilate the whole globe. Kiru had thought that a little excessive, but Eliot Ness told her that his death (and hers) would merely be a by-product. The main reason for deconstructing Caphmiaultrelvossmuaf would be to eliminate a new competitor, a planet that could soon eclipse Hideaway as the galaxy's premier pleasure world.

Caphmiaultrelvossmuaf was relatively near the famous leisure satellite. (The closest habitable world, in fact, which was why the two escape pods from the doomed ship had made it their goal.) Because Caphmiaultrelvossmuaf was far larger than Hideaway, its potential for profit was even greater.

Built long, long ago by an unknown race, Hideaway had finally been occupied by galactic brigands as a base from which to raid starships. Then the pirates had discovered a far more profitable and less risky way of making money: by marketing the artifical asteroid as the ultimate paradise, a world where every secret desire, every forbidden thrill, every sensual delight, every hedonistic wish, could be satisfied—at a price.

The pirates' new venture had been a tremendous success until they dared to defy the most feared and fearless organisation of all, a syndicate which operated under a multitude of names, all with the same parasitic purpose: to leech the lifeblood from every person, human or alien, on every world.

When the ex-buccaneers neglected to pay their tax assessment and failed to negotiate the narrow temporal window allowed for appeal, the Galactic Tax Authority took possession of Hideaway in lieu of payment. The pirates were evicted and returned to stealing and looting, until their new base was discovered and destroyed by an Algolan war fleet, after which the survivors were imprisoned on Arazon.

"Why are you talking like that?" asked Wayne.

"Like what?" said Kiru.

"Like a door-to-door insurance salesman who's learned everything from a correspondence course."

"Like what?" she said, again.

"Forget it."

Kiru ignored it. She also ignored the part of her journey that had been on board the Xyzian spaceship because that was something she *did* want to forget.

"So we ended up here," she concluded. "And now I'm Eliot Ness's personal assistant."

"What does that mean?" said Wayne. "You drive a boat?"

"Amongst other things, yes. It's an essential skill on Caphmiaultrelvossmuaf."

"But not for the natives."

"No," agreed Kiru. "But for you and me, Wayne, a skimmer is a good idea." She snuggled up closer to him. "A very good idea. What about you? How did you get here?"

"Same as you. Except I was on my own, of course. I managed to get into a lifeboat, but it was the wrong one. Not the one with you in. Stayed in there forever, all alone, then finally came down here. And there you were, waiting for me. It was worth the wait."

They kissed.

"Where are we?" said Wayne. "Caff-what?"

"Caphmiaultrelvossmuaf."

"Everything's very . . ."

"Wet?"

". . . red," said Wayne.

"Like your eyes."

He blinked for a few seconds. His eyes no longer felt so sore.

"Ninety-nine percent of the surface is water," said Kiru. "The Caphafers have evolved from creatures that lived in the sea. Like humans did."

"Except they still live in the sea."

"Mostly, because most of the planet is water. They're amphibious. They can go on land. Not that there's much on the land. That's why this world is ripe for development."

"Development?" said Wayne. "You mean like . . . boats?"

"People have to get around."

"The locals don't need boats. They don't need bikinis, either."

"Bikinis?" said Kiru. "What's a bikini?"

"I was asked that once before, back on Earth. By Colonel Travis. Or Eliot Ness. Or maybe it was his daughter."

"And what's the answer?"

"You sent that native to meet me, to greet me?"

"The Caphafer, yes. We knew the capsule was coming down, and I wanted to be there, but the natives can swim much faster than a skimmer can go."

"Yeah, okay. A bikini is what the alien was wearing. A two-piece swimsuit. Designed for a female. A human female."

"If the Caphafers are going to work here," said Kiru, "they mustn't offend the tourists. They have to be covered for the sake of modesty. They've got these big, ugly, dangly things down there." She gestured wildly. "And the males are even worse." She burst out laughing.

Wayne just looked at her, and he shook his head. "You're different, Kiru."

"Don't you like me?"

"No," he said. "But I love you."

They kissed. Again.

"This is wonderful, Kiru."

"I know."

"You're wonderful."

"I know."

"You're so lovely, so attractive, so beautiful, so glamorous, so exotic, so perfect, so everything."

"Stop it, Wayne. You're making me blush."

"In this light, I can't tell." Wayne sighed. "Is this real? Are we really together again? I must be dreaming. I've thought of you every day, every hour, every minute, since we were forced apart."

"Me, too," said Kiru. "Of course."

"Stand up," said Wayne. He rose to his feet, pulling Kiru up. Once she was standing on the deck, he knelt down in front of her. "I mean it. I love you, Kiru."

"And I . . . I like you, whoever you are."

"I love you, Kiru. Not just now, not this minute, but forever. Will you marry me?"

"Marry?"

"There is still such a thing as marriage, isn't there?"

"You're offering me a nuptial contract?"

"Yeah, could be. Doesn't sound very romantic."

But this was very romantic, Kiru realised, as she gazed down at Wayne before looking beyond him at the alien world where they had found themselves, watching the red rain falling from the red sky into the red ocean.

Wayne said, "This is what I promised I'd do if we ever met again. If? No, *when*. I swore that we'd be wed, Kiru. Because nothing can stop a love like ours. The universe exists because of us, for us. Time is no barrier. This is why I've lived so long. The years couldn't keep us apart, Kiru. Neither could the light years." He reached for her, turning her face back toward his. She looked down at him. He looked up at her.

"You must be wondering about my prospects," he continued, "my career opportunities. So am I. All I know is my future will be your future. *Our* future. We'll have forever, Kiru. What do you say?"

She said nothing.

"Will you marry me?" Wayne said again.

She didn't know what to say.

"You don't have to say 'yeah,' not yet. But please don't say 'no'. You're not smiling anymore, my love. I know what you're thinking."

"You do?" said Kiru. She was so stunned she couldn't think of anything. "What?"

"You're remembering your life before me. Whatever you did, Kiru, it doesn't matter. I forgive you."

"You forgive me?"

"I do, yeah."

"For what?"

"Because of your past. Because I wasn't the first man you ever . . . er . . . ever . . ."

"My past! You've got far more past than I have, or so you say. Three hundred years of it!"

"Yeah, but I was flat on my back most of the time."

So was I, thought Kiru, but she kept the thought to herself. In Wayne's original time, it seemed, when a couple had sex it meant mating for life. How primitive.

But that was one of the things she liked about him, how he was so innocent yet also so savage. And he had a great body. As for his mind, what went on inside his head? What made him think she'd ever want to marry him?

In time, maybe, but it was far too early to make a decision.

How long had they been together? An hour on Caphmiaul-trelvossmuaf? Two on Hideaway? Three on the spaceship?

Probably the best few hours of her life.

"Get up, Wayne," she said, pulling at his arm.

"Not until you give me an answer," he said.

"I can't be rushed into such an important decision, but I promise you one thing: If I'm going to marry anyone, Wayne, it will be you."

"Great!" Wayne stood up and kissed her cheek. "So we can consider ourselves engaged?"

"What's that?"

"It means we won't date anyone else."

"What's that?"

Wayne shook his head. "Give me a smile, Kiru. You're a supernova lighting up my whole universe."

"Wayne, you don't have to lie to me. I can always tell when someone's lying."

"How?"

"Because they open their mouths. My whole life has been shaped by lies. I don't want your eternal love and devotion, Wayne. Just be honest and true with me."

"If everyone was honest and true, the whole galaxy would fall apart."

Kiru and Wayne both turned their heads, glancing over the side of the skimmer, toward the voice.

Without either of them realising, the airboat had piloted itself back to the land and had settled down on the shoreline. The Caphafers spent most of their lives in the sea, and the hundreds of small islands that dotted the globe were usually barren and rocky.

This was the island where Eliot Ness had established his headquarters, where the first development was taking place. The new buildings were like giant sandcastles, spiralling upward, every successive level becoming narrower as it became taller. They were growing at an amazing rate. The sea-bed was dredged up to provide the raw, red material for this vertical development and also for horizontal expansion. The island was speading, its natural shape sculpted and redesigned by the addition of piers and marinas, lagoons and swimming pools, criss-crossed by bridges and aqueducts.

Kiru stared at the person who had spoken. She thought

she knew all the humans on Caphmiaultrelvossmuaf. This must have been a newcomer, although she seemed familiar. She was standing near the edge of the water, wearing an outfit similar to the one Eliot Ness always wore.

"Diana!" said Wayne.

"Get dressed, Sergeant," said the woman.

"How can I?" said Wayne. "You're wearing my suit."

"You know her?" said Kiru, who began pulling on her clothes.

"Yeah," said Wayne. "This is Major Diana Travis, Colonel Travis's daughter. Diana, this is Kiru."

"I know," said Diana.

"You!" said Kiru, suddenly recognising the woman. Her hair was covered by a hat, her features half in shadow, but Kiru would never forget her face. "You're dead!" she yelled, and reached down for the gun.

"No!" said Wayne, putting his foot on the weapon.

Kiru elbowed him in the stomach. He grunted in pain and doubled up. She grabbed for the gun, but Wayne's foot was still pinning it down, and now he also held it with one hand. Kiru turned and rushed toward the edge of the skimmer. Before she could leap off, Wayne seized her.

"What's going on?" he said.

"Let me go!" Kiru demanded, trying to shake him off. "Let me kill her!"

But Wayne held her even tighter, his arms encircling her elbows and waist, and Kiru could do nothing except glare at the woman responsible for her ending up on Arazon.

Back on Earth, cold and hungry, Kiru had used her talent to open a door. It turned out to be the door of a police base. If a male officer had been inside, there would have been little problem; an arrangement could have been made. Instead, there was a female. This female. Who had arrested her. And Kiru had been exiled to Clink.

"Relax," said Diana. "Be calm. Think. You hate me. You think you hate me. Because you got a rough deal and were deported to Arazon. But if you hadn't gone there, you'd never have reached Hideaway, never have met . . . him."

Kiru glanced over her shoulder at Wayne.

"You think he was worth any of that?" she said.

"What man's worth anything?" said Diana.

"I'm worth it," said Wayne. "Aren't I?"

Kiru and Diana both looked at him, then looked at each other. They both shrugged.

"What are you doing here?" asked Wayne. "Where's Colonel Travis?"

"I am Colonel Travis," said Diana.

"Promoted, huh? Okay, but where's the other Colonel Travis? You know, your father?"

"That's me," said Diana. "I'm him."

"Where's Eliot Ness?" asked Kiru.

"That's me," said Diana, again. "I'm Eliot Ness."

CHAPTER THIRTY-ONE

It wasn't raining.

That was the third thing Wayne Norton had noticed on reaching the island.

The first was Diana.

The second was what she was wearing: his suit, the one he'd designed and ordered on Hideaway from Xenbashka Bashka Ka, alias Princess Janesmith of Algol.

Norton had to make do with what looked like a sleeveless undershirt and a pair of long-johns. Short long-johns, which only reached his knees. Red, of course. The only alternative seemed to be a bikini, which was the standard uniform for the Caphafer construction workers who were transforming their own world.

It wasn't really a bikini. The upper half was more like a scarf, the same width all around, while the lower half resembled a pair of shorts. Norton wasn't sure what purpose the top served because all the Caphafers were flat-chested; as for the second part, he was prepared to accept Kiru's word.

These garments provided almost the only variation in colour on Caphmiaultrelvossmuaf. Everything else was some shade of red, even Kiru's skintight outfit. Apart from Diana's gangster suit.

Or Colonel Travis's gangster suit.

Or Eliot Ness's gangster suit.

One thing was certain: It wasn't Wayne Norton's gangster suit.

Diana had said she'd arrived on Caphmiaultrelvossmuaf with Kiru. Kiru had said she hadn't, that she herself had arrived in an escape pod with Eliot Ness. Diana had claimed she was Eliot Ness. Kiru's description of the person named Ness matched that of the man who'd told Norton his name was Colonel Travis. Eliot Ness and Colonel Travis were one and the same, Norton could accept that, but Diana also claimed she was Colonel Travis.

"But you're father and daughter," said Norton.

"Exactly," said Diana. "I'm both father and daughter. There's male and female in all of us."

"Not in me," said Norton. "Not in my time."

"Eliot Ness is older than you," said Kiru, who was sitting with arms folded, staring at Diana, trying to kill her with her eyes.

They were at a three-sided table in a plaza at the centre of the island. Norton realised this was the first time he'd been on solid ground since leaving Earth, the first time he could see further than the wall of a spaceship or satellite or lifeboat. All around them loomed red conical towers. None of them had windows, Norton noticed.

"We're the same age," said Diana. "I'm the same age. I've had a rejuve. In my role as a senior male authority figure, it's better to look older, more distinguished. As a female, it's always better to be young and attractive." She studied Kiru for a few seconds, then took off her hat.

For a moment, Norton thought he could hear faint music. He glanced at Diana's hat before looking around as she shook her hair free. The style was different again. Her hair was long, jet black, in a single plait.

"You can't be Travis," said Norton. "I was with him when I first met you. You were both there at the same time."

"What's the point of being two people if you can't both be in the same place at the same time?" said Diana.

"But you aren't two people," said Norton. "You're one."

Diana shrugged. "Who's counting?"

She'd claimed that, in her male guise, she had reached Caphmiaultrelvossmuaf in the same escape capsule as Kiru. But Norton remained silent about his own travelling companion. He didn't want to mention Grawl because it would scare Kiru if she knew; and as Diana hadn't referred to another survivor, which she surely would have done if Grawl had been found, it seemed safe to assume he had drowned. Norton had to admit he wasn't sorry.

"What was my secret mission?" he asked. "Why was I sent to Hideaway?"

"You were there as me," said Diana.

"But you were there."

"I was there as Diana. You were there as Travis. That was why you were attacked on the ship: They wanted to stop Travis getting to Hideaway. Understand?"

"Er . . . yeah."

"You were using him as a decoy," said Kiru, "just like you used the pirate attack on Hideaway as a diversion."

Diana looked at her. "Who told you that?"

"I worked it out."

"I haven't worked it out," said Norton. "Will someone tell me?"

"When the escaped convicts from Arazon invaded Hideaway," Diana told him, "it was to divert attention from Eliot Ness's more subtle assault on the asteroid."

"You mean your assault?" said Norton.

"Depends which way you look at it."

Norton preferred to look the other way, and he glanced around the plaza. Construction work was so rapid, he was sure the nearest buildings had grown since he'd last looked.

"What were you doing while the pirates attacked Hideaway?" asked Kiru.

"Every guest there is guaranteed absolute anonymity and complete confidentiality," said Diana, "although naturally all their details are recorded. During the raid, I was copying the data on Hideaway's biggest-spending clients."

"So you could invite them here?" said Norton. "Never-to-be-repeated opening offers for pre-selected lucky customers."

"Who told you that?" said Diana.

"I worked it out," he said. "A mailing list? This was all about getting hold of a mailing list? I hope it was worth it."

Diana didn't answer. "Shall we order?" she suggested. "Or shall I do it for you?"

"Yes," said Norton.

"No," said Kiru.

The were sitting at the only table in the only restaurant on the planet.

"I recommend the fish," said Diana, and she smiled.

"I hate fish," said Norton.

"Too bad," said Kiru. "That's all there is. Seaweed and fish." She also smiled.

The table was a proper table, with legs. The chairs also had legs. There was an open umbrella above the table, which must have been essential on Caphmiaultrelvossmuaf. It wasn't raining, however. In fact, not a single drop had fallen on the island in the short while since Norton had reached land.

The sky above was thick with pink and orange clouds. There must have been a huge invisible umbrella in the sky, so that construction work wasn't halted by the incessant rain.

But nothing seemed to halt the building. Norton had glimpsed a number of off-worlders, humans and various aliens, who must have been supervising the island's transformation. There were gangs of Caphafers all looking very busy, although they didn't seem to play any actual part in the construction process. Nor were there any girders, cranes, concrete mixers, prefabricated slabs. Everything was very quiet. It was almost as if the towers built themselves, silently spiralling ever upward.

When Norton first met Diana, he'd thought she was a waitress. Here, the waitress was a mermaid. He was a long way from home, and he was getting used to it. Being served by a red amphibian with webbed hands and feet, wearing a blue bikini, seemed relatively normal.

The first Caphafer Norton had seen was wearing a yellow bikini. Those who were watching the buildings go up were in green, while the restaurant staff were clad in blue.

Why bikinis? There was something very familiar about this, but Norton wasn't sure what it was.

"The natives eat the fish raw, complete with the heads, fins, scales, guts," said Diana. "You can have yours cooked any way you want, Wayne." She paused. "Should I call you 'Wayne,' or would you prefer 'Sergeant'?"

"I wasn't a sergeant. Call me Wayne, it's my real name. Is yours 'Diana?' "

"Of course not."

"Or Travis?"

"No."

"Eliot Ness?" said Kiru.

"No," said Norton. "The real Eliot Ness was a gang-buster, not a gangster. Is that why you're wearing my suit?"

"Your suit?" said Diana, frowning.

"Yeah. I ordered two of those on Hideaway, from that shop run by the Algolan princess. Is the other in the violin case?" He gestured to the case by Diana's feet. "I designed that as well as the suit."

"Did you?" said Diana, reaching down for the case and putting it on the table. She opened the lid to reveal a dataset and comscreen. The inside of the lid was mirrored. Diana leaned close and inspected her face. The case also contained a bag of makeup, and she brushed her eyebrows. "It's ideal."

"Can we get some food?" said Kiru.

This was to be the first meal for the first guests in the new restaurant, a trial run. Probably the only kind of trial Diana would ever have to face, thought Norton. "On the house, naturally," she'd said. It had to be. He didn't have any money, and he guessed that neither did Kiru.

"I'll order the wine," said Diana. "Red?"

"White," said Norton. That was the only thing he knew about wine: red with meat, white with fish.

Diana summoned the mermaid. Although the Caphafer was wearing a bikini, Norton knew that didn't mean it was female. Not that he cared anything about the sex of an alien, of course. What bothered him was Diana's gender. She'd kissed him. They'd shared the same bed. Nothing had happened, and now he was very grateful.

"I arrived on Hideaway as a woman," said Diana, looking at Norton. "I left as a man," she added, looking at Kiru. "In between, I needed a change of clothes. I found this wonderful emporium run by a fugitive princess, and she had exactly what I needed." She ran her fingers over her jacket lapels. "And it looks good on me now, don't you think?"

"Perfect," said Norton. "You're a gangster, so you should wear a gangster suit."

"Are you trying to tell me something, Wayne?"

"Yeah. You're mixed up with the space pirates, which means—"

Diana held up her hand to interrupt him. "Space pirates," she said, "that's such an outdated term. These are businessmen, galactic entrepreneurs."

"They're criminals," said Norton, "and you're a criminal. I thought you and Travis . . . er . . . both of you, either of you, I thought you were a police officer. You told me I was working for GalactiCop. Instead, you used me as a cover for criminal purposes. You've made me into a gangster."

"Is that why you wanted the suit?"

"No!"

"What's the matter, Wayne?" said Kiru. "Everyone knows that cops are criminals."

"Why did you check into Hideaway under the name 'Robin Hood?'" asked Diana. "A hood who robs people. Did criminals once wear hoods, is that where the name comes from?".

"No. It's short for 'hoodlum.' Robin Hood was . . ." Norton shook his head. "It doesn't matter. What matters is, you lied to me."

Diana laughed. Kiru laughed. After a few seconds, Norton also laughed. He shrugged. What did it matter now? What did anything matter?

The alien in the blue bikini brought out a tray with a decanter of wine and three glasses, started to pour the wine, but spilled most of it. Diana took over instead.

"New to the job," she explained, as she filled the glasses. "Cheers." It was a toast Norton had taught her when they were spacebus stewards. She clinked her glass against his.

"Here's to crime," he said.

Diana looked at Kiru. Kiru brought her glass against Diana's, perhaps too hard, as if maybe trying to break it. Nothing broke.

"In your century, Wayne," said Diana, "there wasn't much co-operation between the police and criminals. Because there was so little communication, it meant conflict and an inefficient use of resources. It's much better for everyone if the two sides can work together."

"Organised crime, you mean?" said Norton.

"Exactly!" Diana clinked her glass against his again. "We had to merge, amalgamate. And now that Earth is pulling out of the Crash, we have to think galactically, not just globally. We're competing against the universe."

Kiru was watching her. "You talked about being in two places at once," she said. "Does that include Arazon? Did I first meet you there? Were you the pirate boss who led the decoy attack on Hideaway?"

"No."

"Who was he? Where is he now?"

"No idea."

"You must know something," said Kiru. "Your arrival on Hideaway and the timing of the pirate raid were co-ordinated."

"Not my area of responsibility," said Diana. She sipped at her drink. "What do you think of the wine?"

"A bit salty," said Norton.

"Yes, we'll have to do something about that. It's made from kelp."

Norton pulled a face, then remembered the origins of the water he'd had to drink on board the escape pod. He much preferred something made from wholesome seaweed.

"Keep it salty," he said. "People will get thirsty, drink more of it, get even thirstier, buy even more."

"What a great idea," said Diana.

"It's an old idea. If there are free salted nuts in a bar, people get thirstier, buy more drinks. In Las Vegas, they gave away free drinks. If you give away something for free, people will spend more on everything else."

"Great," said Diana. She smiled and poured three more glasses of wine. "Great."

"When are you going to tell him?" said Kiru.

Norton looked at her, looked at Diana. "Tell me what?"

"Where was the place you came from?" said Kiru.

"Vegas," said Norton.

"This," said Kiru, gesturing beyond the red buildings going up all around them, "is going to be Vegas World. And it's all because of you, Wayne."

"Not all," said Diana.

"Vegas World?" said Norton. "That's a lot easier to say than Caff . . . what is it?"

"Caphmiaultrelvossmuaf," Diana and Kiru said together.

"Yeah, Café World."

"What did you say?" said Diana.

"Café World," Norton repeated.

"Café," said Diana. "Café." She nodded. "Café World. I like it. I love it. What's it mean?"

"It means . . . er, it's a French word. French? No? From France? An extinct language. Café. A coffee house. Café is French, was French, for coffee. You've never heard of

France? They invented kissing." Norton looked at Kiru. "French kissing, you know?"

"No," said Kiru.

"You do. Remind me to remind you."

"Café World," Diana said. Again. "It has a certain . . ."

"Panache?" said Norton.

"You know, Wayne," said Diana, "I'm glad you're here, glad you're still alive."

"Thanks. So am I." Norton looked at Kiru again. "How about you?"

"I'm not sure yet," said Kiru. She sipped at her wine to stop herself smiling, then glanced at Diana. "Tell him why we're here."

"Remember back on Earth," said Diana, "when we talked about Lost Vegas?"

"Kind of," said Norton.

"You said Vegas could have been improved if it was by the sea, but gambling couldn't happen outside because the sun would go down and people would be aware of time going by."

Norton nodded. Las Vegas was a twenty-four-hour city. Day or night made no difference.

"The sun never goes down here," said Kiru.

Norton glanced up. Although Caphmiaultrelvossmuaf's star was forever hidden behind the swirling orange clouds, it was always very warm. If the sun ever broke through, the temperature would make Nevada seem like the Arctic.

"The sea," said Norton, beginning to remember. "The sun." He looked up into the red sky. "It shouldn't be raining."

"It's not," said Diana, "not on this island. We're starting here. In time, we'll expand to other islands. We'll fix the rain as we go."

"You chose this planet," said Norton, slowly, as he began to realise the magnitude of the idea, "because of what I said?"

"We had a number of options," said Diana, "but your expertise helped with our final decision."

"Sea, sun, sand, bikini girls," said Norton, remembering it all. "Is that why you've got aliens in bikinis?" He shook his head in amazement, then finished his wine in a single gulp. "I'll be damned."

Las Vegas in space. Planet Vegas.

"Ready to eat?" asked Diana, as she signalled the Caphafer in the blue bikini.

"Yes," said Kiru, and Norton nodded.

It was the first food he had eaten since being in the escape capsule, and he didn't even care that it was fish. His head was spinning. Because of an apparently casual conversation, a whole world was being transformed into a casino planet. The concept was mind-blowing. Or maybe it was just the salty wine, which was scrambling his brain.

While they ate, Diana pointed out all the new landmarks—enviroscapes, dreamzones, skytels—and talked about the future of Café World.

"Café World?" said Kiru. "Are you going to pay Wayne a consultancy fee?"

"That's just a provisional name," said Diana. "I'll have to discuss it with my fellow partners."

"The galactic thieving bastards?" said Kiru. "Although you probably call them 'entrepreneurs.'"

"You were right the first time," said Diana. "I'm talking about the new partners. Hideaway's top people are arriving here in less than fifty hours, when the partnership details will be finalised."

As Kiru and Norton both stared at her, Diana shrugged.

"They tried to kill us," said Kiru. "Wayne, me, even you."

Diana shrugged again. "After what we did, who can blame them?"

"What *we* did?" said Norton. "What *you* did!"

"It's sound business sense," said Diana. "By operating together, Hideaway and Café World will be far more profitable. Instead of competing, we'll complement each other. Hideaway can concentrate on serving the elite of the galaxy, and with their professional expertise we can soon develop a planet-sized version to provide entertainment and vacations for the mass-market."

"But you thought Hideaway was going to annihilate Caphmiaultrelvossmuaf," said Kiru.

"That was just a negotiating tactic. They would never have destroyed a valuable asset like this." Diana toyed with the stem of her wine glass. "Because if they had, Hideaway would have been vaporized as a reprisal."

"That's good," said Kiru. "At least the whole Caphafer race wouldn't have died in vain."

"Mutually destructive business plans are very short-sighted," said Diana.

"So now you're working for the tax men," said Norton. "Or tax aliens."

"Don't we all?" said Diana. "They started on one world, but they thought big, which is how they became the largest organisation in the galaxy. The Galactic Tax Authority owns whole planets, entire solar systems, and every person who lives there is in debt to them—although they don't even know it."

"And they're coming here for the big pow-wow," said Norton.

"What?" said Diana, and Kiru said, "What?"

"You're going to smoke the pipe of peace."

"What?" said Kiru, and Diana said, "What?"

"Another reason for choosing this planet," said Norton, gazing up at the sky, "was the colour, yeah? It's the ideal world for Red Indians."

"I see what you mean," said Diana, and Kiru said, "I don't."

"We're talking about Red Indians," said Norton.

"What's a Red Indian?" asked Kiru.

"You are," he said.

Kiru ran her fingers through her red hair. "Am I?"

"We all are," said Norton. "Or so I've been told."

Kiru shrugged, sipped at her wine, then resumed eating. She shifted in her seat and glanced around, making it evident she found her surroundings far more interesting than her companions.

"Will your partners become blood brothers?" Norton continued. "Or sisters?"

"There'll be no mixing of bodily fluids," said Diana. "This is strictly a business arrangement, although there'll be an appropriate celebration after the contracts have been signed and witnessed. After that, if anyone wants to become involved in a personal liaison, it's up to them."

"A personal liaison?" said Norton, looking at Kiru.

A skimmer slid off the ocean and went by thirty yards away, and Kiru waved. The three on deck waved back. It was hard to tell if they were all human, but they definitely weren't Caphafers. Instead of bikinis, they were wearing dark suits—as designed by Wayne Norton.

The skimmer disappeared as silently as it had arrived, and Norton realised the restaurant must have been within a sonic screen. That was why the building work seemed so quiet, because sound beyond the plaza was reflected back out.

"Who were they?" asked Norton. "Fellow convicts?"

"No idea," said Kiru.

"Some of my colleagues," said Diana. "Gino, Rico and Pedro."

"Pedro?" said Norton.

"You know her?"

Norton shook his head.

"When Hideaway was under different management, she was called Jack. Gino was Deuce and Rico was Ace." Diana paused. "They're a trio."

"Is that where the music was coming from?" said Norton.

"Music? They're not musicians."

"I heard music earlier. You said they were a trio."

"They are," said Diana. "A sexual trio."

"Oh." Norton nodded, as if understanding. "Three of them? Is that . . . er . . . ?"

"Two men, one woman," said Diana. "That's the best arithmetic. Or geometry."

"You mean . . . they have sex? All three of them? With each other? At the same time?"

"I presume so. Why else get married? Go and ask them."

"They're married? All of them? To each other?" Norton drank some more wine. "One attraction of Vegas I never mentioned," he added, "was that people went there to get married."

"Because it wasn't legal anywhere else?" said Diana.

"No. Because they could get married immediately. There was no license restriction in Las Vegas."

"People had to have a license to get married?"

"Yeah."

"You're talking about a formal conjugal agreement?"

"Probably." Norton glanced at Kiru, who was still looking away. "I thought that . . . er, maybe, you know . . . you could hold wedding ceremonies here."

"Why? What for?"

"Does Hideaway provide weddings?"

"I doubt it. There isn't much demand for that kind of thing."

"I'm only a cop, but isn't the whole idea of business to advertise and create a demand? People used to spend a fortune on weddings."

"Did they?" Diana began to get interested.

"Yeah. Getting married was every girl's ambition, the biggest day of her life."

"That's pathetic," said Kiru.

"How did they spend a fortune?" asked Diana.

"On the clothes," said Norton. "On the wedding presents. On the reception, which was a meal and party after the ceremony. On the honeymoon, which was when the bride and groom went on a luxury holiday together after the wedding." He gestured with his wine glass, encompassing the whole planet. "If couples came here to get married, they'd also have their honeymoons here."

Diana nodded thoughtfully. "This could work. I'm going to suggest it to the board of directors." She paused and studied Norton. "You're not on a percentage, so why are you telling me this?"

"Because," said Norton, "I want to be the first person to get married here."

"The first?" said Diana. "As far as I understand it, marriage is not a solo event. So who's going to be equal first?"

She was looking at him in an odd way. Surely she didn't think Norton meant her! She who was sometimes a he . . .

Norton looked at Kiru. Diana looked at Kiru. Kiru looked at Norton.

"No," she said.

"In fifty hours plus," said Diana, "it's the official opening. There won't be any paying guests, not for a while. But the gaming halls will take their first bets. The first pleasure dome will begin to revolve. Everything will begin to happen. Maybe this restaurant will be serving edible food by then."

Norton glanced at her meal, noticing that she'd hardly had anything. He'd eaten everything, as had Kiru.

"It's going to be a spectacular occasion," Diana continued. "I've been trying to think of something unique, something so very absolutely different, to generate extra publicity. Now

I know what it is. We're going to hold our first wedding. Your wedding, Wayne."

"But not mine," said Kiru.

"He's getting married," Diana told her. "If not to you, then someone else."

"Who?" said Norton.

"I don't know," said Diana. "Anyone. Pedro, for example. As well as Rico and Gino, of course. But don't get your hopes up. All three of them would have to accept you. Quartets are very rare. They never last. Maybe you could marry one of the natives. That would make a great story."

"What?" said Norton.

"No," said Kiru. "He's mine."

"Am I?" said Norton, and he stretched his hand across the table toward her.

Kiru shrugged. His hand touched hers. She didn't move it away. His fingers squeezed hers. Her eyes wouldn't meet his.

"Kiru," said Norton, "you've made me the happiest man in the whole galaxy, and I promise I'm going to make you the happiest girl in the entire universe."

"Okay, okay."

"Enough of this," said Diana. "What should happen during a wedding, a really expensive wedding?"

Norton told her. Diana listened intently to every word, nodding her head, while Kiru sank lower and lower into her chair, shaking her head.

"Now I'm in a real dilemma," said Diana. She stood up and began to circle, or triangle, the table. "Will I go as your best man, Wayne? Or should I be your bridesmaid, Kiru?"

"Why not both?" said Kiru.

"That's a possibility," said Diana, "although the most important role seems to be the person in charge. She has the most dialogue, far more than the bride and groom."

"She?" said Norton. "It's usually 'he.'"

"Not on Café World," said Diana. "Kiru must promise to love, honour and obey, you said?"

"Yeah," said Norton. He couldn't remember very many of the lines. What was the groom meant to say?

"Honour and obey?" said Kiru. She hid her face in her hands. "Were women treated like slaves in your era?"

"No, well . . . er, yeah, I guess . . . slightly . . . er, in a way."

Kiru opened her fingers to peer at Diana. "If you're doing weddings here, will you also do divorces?"

"No," said Norton. "It's 'until death do us part.' "

"Yes, master," said Kiru, and she yawned. "Of course, master. To hear is to obey, master."

"Divorce and marriage?" Diana nodded. "Can't have one without the other."

"Good," said Kiru.

"You want to officiate at our wedding?" Norton said to Diana. "Will that be legal?"

"Definitely," Diana replied. She sat down at the table, reached for the violin case, opened the lid and thumb-coded her dataset. "I'll enact a law to it make it legal."

CHAPTER INFINITY

The bride wore white.

A white bikini.

The smallest bikini on Caphmiaultrelvossmuaf. And probably, thought Wayne Norton, the smallest in the history of the universe.

Kiru looked terrific, absolutely fantastic. He was so glad they were getting married, that she was to be his forever. She was dressed in the ideal outfit—for their wedding night.

But with all the other people around, human and alien, he wished she was wearing, well, *more*.

It wasn't just the people, it was the cameras. The official opening of Café World was being transmitted to the whole galaxy. Autocams zoomed about everywhere, recording all the festivities and the premiere of every new dream palace on the island.

Norton had to bite his lip, forcing himself not to say a word about what Kiru was almost wearing. If he'd objected, his bride might simply have walked out on him.

That wouldn't have been the worst of it.

The wedding was scheduled as one of the highlights of the opening ceremony. If Kiru had changed her mind, then Norton would have had to marry someone else. Pedro. And her husbands. Or a Caphafer. Or Major Diana Travis . . . alias Colonel Travis.

Diana had remained in her female guise and was dressed as a Red Indian chief. Or her version of what one looked like. She wore a feathered head-dress, which hung halfway down her back, but the feathers were metallic and kept changing colour, as if they had a kaleidoscope of lightbulbs inside. The fringes on her buckskin jacket and pants were of similar construction and illumination. At least her moccasins didn't flash on and off with every step she took, even if they did have five-inch soles and ten-inch heels.

The bride was meant to be the centre of attention at her own wedding, but it seemed Diana was trying to steal the show. Norton was pleased, because it meant fewer eyes would be gazing at his wife-to-be.

He had to admit, however, that although he was convinced Kiru was the ultimate wonder of the galaxy, the non-humans on Caphmiaultrelvossmuaf were unlikely to spare her more than a passing glance.

Soon after their spaceship entered orbit, the Galactic Tax Authority representatives arrived to begin final negotiations with Diana and her associates. Norton wished he'd asked for his missing finger to be brought from Hideaway, so he could be reunited with it.

Discussions must have been successful, because later the same vessel disgorged hundreds of guests to visit the countless different attractions on what its owners hoped would become the new vacation capital of the universe.

In the past fifty hours, the island seemed to have doubled in size, with four times as many soaring red buildings. During that time, Norton was busy arranging his own wedding. The hardest part was coming up with a form of words Kiru would agree to. "Obey" had to go, as did "honour," and she wasn't even very enthusiastic about "love."

Then Diana told him, "Keep it very short. After the banquet, our new partners will be eager to sample what they've bought for their money."

"I can't imagine them being eager about anything," said Norton. "You made a deal?"

"We came to a mutually advantageous conclusion," said Diana.

They were in the plaza where the first restaurant had stood. By now, there was another on each corner. In the centre of the square was a ring of tables, and Caphafers in blue bikinis were covering them with red cloths.

Negotiations had taken place inside the building nearest the sea. Although it was of exactly the same shade of red, this construction was smaller than most of the others. It was a steep pyramid, and it was also the only building with any windows. These were crescent-shaped, dropping down each angled side in a single row from the apex.

The entrance was arched, and outside were the seven delegates from the Galactic Tax Authority. They stood in a neat line. Instead of gazing up at the impressive sights of Café World, their heads were bowed.

"Miserable bunch," said Norton. "Do we have to invite them to the wedding?"

"It's more a case of them inviting you to their banquet," said Diana. "We eat first, then come all the speeches, and—"

"Yeah, I've written out my speech."

Diana glanced at him. "Your speech?"

"Yeah." Norton nodded. "The groom always makes a speech, I told you that."

"You also said the bride's father makes a speech. I liked Kiru's idea of repeating the last thing her father ever said to her. What was it exactly? Yes, I remember. It was, *Ahhhhhhhhhhhh . . . !*" Diana stared up, all around, then over at the alien tax collectors. "The speeches will be about the future of Café World. We have the banquet, the speeches, then the wedding. A fast wedding."

Instead of being a highlight of the festivities, the marriage had been rescheduled as after-dinner entertainment. Norton said nothing. There was no point. If he protested, it might be cancelled. All that mattered was that he and Kiru would be wed, their lives entwined for as long as they lived.

"Where's your knife and tomahawk?" he said, studying Diana's outfit. She wasn't dressed up for the wedding, he realised, but for her high-powered business conference.

"There are no armaments on the whole island," said Diana. "Carrying weapons to peace talks sends the wrong signals."

Norton thought of making some remark about smoke signals, but said instead, "What about the warpaint?"

Diana opened her violin case, checking her face in the mirror. Blue and white and red lines were daubed across her cheeks and forehead.

"They don't know it's warpaint," she said. "Not that it is. We're partners now, allies."

"Colleagues?" said Norton. "Friends?"

"Who could be friends with a taxperson?" said Diana,

watching them. "I've spent hours with them, and I don't even know their names."

The aliens were all small and slender, almost entirely clad in black. They wore black gloves over their hands, each of which had two thumbs and five fingers. Only their heads were uncovered, although their eyes were protected by black goggles.

"Palefaces," said Norton.

Diana nodded. "That's a good name for them. They're all identical, all anonymous, all apparently of equal rank. The location of their native planet is a secret, probably because they're scared of reprisals. From all the evidence— the way they cover their eyes, their translucent skin—their race is nocturnal, maybe from a planet where it's always dark."

"So you've brought them to a world where it's always light, and you're making them sit outside for a banquet?"

"Yes," said Diana. "Ah, here's your bride. Right on time."

Barefoot, long red hair cascading down to her white bikini top, Kiru walked across from the other side of the plaza. Norton couldn't keep his eyes off her, and he wasn't the only one. An autocam swooped down to encircle her. Kiru noticed Norton watching, and she slipped one of the straps off her shoulder, pouted and blew a kiss to the camera.

When she reached Norton, he leaned forward to kiss her. She sprang aside, laughing.

"Wait till we're married," she said.

"You look fantastic," he said.

"I know."

He'd never seen her hair like this, so glossy, and in long ringlets. Her lips were redder than ever before, her eyelashes darker. She'd also painted her fingernails. White. Her toenails were the same. To match her bikini, he realised.

In her other role as Colonel Travis, Diana had worn white nail varnish. Kiru must have borrowed it. For the first time since Norton had known her, she had access to makeup.

"And me?" said Norton, gesturing to his own clothes. He was finally wearing the suit he'd designed on Hide-

away, and he wished Princess Janesmith could have been
the seamstress. His outfit had been fabricated on Caphmiaultrelvossmuaf, and although it looked right, almost, it
simply didn't feel right. He guessed the suit was made from
fish skins. Whatever the case, it was the least worst thing
he'd worn since his resurrection.

Kiru looked at him, shook her head, sighed, shrugged,
then scanned the plaza. "Where is everyone?"

"Enjoying themselves," said Diana. "Neuroscapes, sex
salons, mindlay. All for free."

"And your new partners?" said Norton.

"They're enjoying themselves most of all. Those guys
really know how to party."

The seven tax delegates were still standing in line. They
hadn't moved, not a muscle.

Diana continued, "We don't expect our invited guests to
give up all the other pleasures on the planet for the banquet, but each place will be filled by members of our
corporation."

"Pirates," said Kiru.

"Architects, builders, consultants, every letter of the al-
phabet," said Diana.

"Arsonists, burglars, conmen," said Kiru.

Before she could continue, Norton said, "We don't get
married until the very end."

"Might as well go for a swim while I'm waiting," Kiru
said, and she took a few steps toward the sea.

She'd spent several of the past fifty hours in the sea and
had tried to entice Norton into the water, telling him that
Caphmiaultrelvossmuaf was the ideal place to learn to
swim. He hadn't been persuaded.

"If you don't take your seat," said Diana, "someone
else will."

"Stay," said Norton, who was very worried about who
that someone else might be.

Kiru turned back.

Diana raised her right arm and snapped her fingers.
Within a few seconds of her signal, a group of people appeared from around one corner, another from the opposite
direction. Human and various humanoid aliens, they took
their places around the tables. Diana walked across to col-

lect her new partners, and a Caphafer approached Kiru and Norton.

"Have I the privilege, madam and sir, of addressing the bride and groom?" said the native.

"Er . . . yeah," said Norton.

"Please follow me to your table."

The red amphibian led Kiru and Norton to their seats. They shared a table with eight others: Diana and the seven alien tax officials.

It was the longest meal Norton had ever sat through in his long life. Literally, figuratively and gastronomically.

However brief the meal, it would have seemed to last ages because he was so anxious about the wedding ceremony.

And it did take ages, because there were so many different courses.

Norton hardly ate a thing; he was far too nervous. Even so, he ate more than the enigmatic aliens. That wasn't difficult. They ate nothing, they drank nothing, they said nothing.

Diana tried to get them to speak. To pass the time, Kiru also did her best to entice out a single word, just a slate-induced "yes" or "no," or some kind of gesture. All they did was stare down at the table, eyes hidden behind the black goggles which almost appeared to be grafted onto their pale faces. Norton had other things on his mind, and he didn't bother trying to start a conversation.

Every now and then, he sipped at his salty wine, careful not to empty the glass. He didn't want to get drunk, didn't want to fluff the few words he was being allowed at his wedding.

There were speeches, but he paid little attention. Diana gave the opening address, welcoming the organisation's new partners. One of the tax collectors at the table stood up, as if about to reply. Instead, the alien simply bowed in acknowledgment. Someone else gave a speech, then someone else, and so on. Then Diana was on her feet again, giving another speech about a wonderful new marketing enterprise, a special tourist attraction on Café World which was bound to be a fabulous success. Norton realised she was referring to weddings.

"One of the ancient marriage traditions of my native

planet," Diana was saying, "is that a magnificent confection is baked for the wedding feast, a piece of which is given to every guest. To mark the first wedding to be celebrated here, our master chef has recreated an original Terran recipe. The owners and management of Café World are pleased to present this as their wedding gift to Mr. and Mrs. Norton."

"Mrs. Norton?" said Kiru. "Who? Is that me?"

Diana began to applaud. Taking this as their cue, most of the others at the banquet did the same. Despite their extra thumbs, the palefaces didn't join in the clapping.

Norton watched as two Caphafers wheeled a large trolley toward their table. Whatever was on it was covered by a red cloth. They slid the contents of the trolley onto the table, then withdrew. Diana whisked the cloth away, revealing an enormous wedding cake.

Covered in white icing, consisting of several tiers, each laid directly on top of each other, the whole thing was at least five feet high, with the base about two feet in diameter. As the elaborate cake became taller, the tiers became smaller, and on the very top stood two small figurines, one in a white bikini, one in a gangster suit.

"Wow," said Norton.

"My own personal gift, Wayne," Diana said, quietly.

"Thanks," he said.

"No," said Diana. "Thank you."

"Everything he's done for you," said Kiru, "and all he gets is one lousy cake!"

Norton kept looking at the cake. It was amazing. He could hardly believe it.

"Shhh," said Norton. "Wow. Looks too good to eat."

"Too good?" said Kiru. "Seaweed and fish."

"Can I please have your attention for another minute?" said Diana. "I'm proud to say that you're all about to witness our first Café World wedding. Before long, this planet will become the galactic marriage centre, the chosen destination of every sophisticated couple or triple who wishes to make a legal nuptial agreement. Kiru and Wayne, stand up."

Norton rose to his feet. Kiru drained her glass and did the same. Norton removed his hat.

"Kiru," said Diana, "do you take this man to be your legal husband?"

"Lawful wedded," whispered Norton. "Lawful wedded husband."

"Yes," said Kiru.

"No," said Norton. "You've got to say, 'I do.' "

"Wayne," said Diana, "do you take this woman to be your legal wife?"

"Lawful," Norton said again. "Wedded," he repeated. Then he gave up. "Yeah, okay. I mean 'I do.' Yeah, I do."

"As the judicial authority on Café World," said Diana, "I affirm you—"

"No!" said Norton. "Not yet, not yet." He'd just remembered one of the key lines: *With this ring I thee wed.*

He also remembered he didn't have a ring. Carrying the ring was the best man's job. He also didn't have a best man.

"What's the matter now?" said Diana.

Norton gazed around anxiously, up, then down, not knowing what he was looking for. The ground was surfaced with tiles, making it smooth and regular, but already sand and loose pebbles had been kicked up from the beach. Something caught his eye. He went over, picked it up, examined it.

"Okay," he said, "go ahead."

Diana repeated, "As the judicial authority on Café World . . ."

Norton reached out for Kiru's left hand and slipped what he'd found onto her third finger. It slid across her fingernail, past the first knuckle. With a slight push, it went over the second knuckle. A perfect fit.

". . . I affirm you are now wife and husband," Diana concluded.

Kiru was staring down at her finger, at her wedding ring. A broken seashell, forged by the elements into a polished circle, it glinted in the light, ruby and amber, like a gemstone.

"It's . . ." Kiru kept gazing at the shell, lost for words.

"We'll get a real ring later," said Norton, "a gold one."

". . . the most wonderful thing anyone's ever given me," said Kiru. She looked at Norton, and she smiled. "Not that anyone's ever given me anything."

"You can share the wedding cake," said Norton.

A soft voice said, "Under the circumstances, we are also prepared to make an endowment to these two humans."

Norton looked around. One of the seven aliens was standing up and speaking.

"This announcement is in no way to be regarded as establishing a precedent," the tax delegate continued, "but as of the start of the next financial year, the tax liability of these two humans is to be reduced to the minimum applicable category on whatever world the specified humans are domiciled for assessment purposes. This applies exclusively to personal taxation of every description, but not corporate taxation. This allowance will be terminated immediately in the event of divorce or separation of the specified humans or upon the death of the first of them, whichever is the sooner."

"That's the most astonishing thing I've heard in my life," said Diana. "In either life. I think I'll get married."

A paleface with goggled eyes turned toward her. "To repeat my earlier statement, this announcement is in no way to be regarded as establishing a precedent," said the alien.

"Er . . . thanks," said Norton.

"Yes," said Kiru.

The tax assessor bowed, then sat down.

Norton wasn't aware he had to pay tax. How could he, if he had no job, no salary? He was reasonably sure Kiru had no regular income. Under the circumstances, reduction of tax liability didn't seem much of a wedding present. Still, the thought was there.

"Can I kiss the bride?" asked Norton.

"Why not?" said Kiru.

The bride and the groom kissed and kissed and kissed.

Then they headed for the top of the tallest skytel on the island, where they spent the first few hundred hours of their marriage in the new honeymoon suite.

Because Kiru and Norton never did divorce or separate, their privileged revenue status enabled them to save enough for a rejuve (tax free) each. Although this extended their lives by approximately fifty percent, finally they died.

In cosmic terms, even considering Norton's extended lifespan, their existence was less than a nanosecond; but to them, the only relevant era was that brief moment of galactic history when they were alive.

During that time, Kiru and Wayne Norton lived happily together.

Which, for them, was forever.

AN END

Norton reached out for Kiru's left hand and slipped what he'd found onto her third finger. It slid across her fingernail, past the first knuckle. With a slight push, it went over the second knuckle. A perfect fit.

". . . I affirm you are now wife and husband," Diana concluded.

Kiru was staring down at her finger, at her wedding ring. A broken seashell, forged by the elements into a polished circle, it glinted in the light, ruby and amber, like a gemstone.

"It's . . ." Kiru kept gazing at the shell, lost for words.

"We'll get a real ring later," said Norton, "a gold one."

". . . the most wonderful thing anyone's ever given me," said Kiru. She looked at Norton, and she smiled. "Not that anyone's ever given me anything."

"You can share the wedding cake," said Norton.

"The cake isn't for either of you," said Diana.

"But you said—" began Norton.

He heard a crash behind him and he spun around. One of the autocams had dropped out of the air. There was another crash, then another, as all the cameras smashed to the ground.

Something else caught his eye. The wedding cake. It had moved. Then it suddenly burst open. A small, wide shape sprang up from inside.

"Grawl!" screamed Kiru, and she grabbed hold of Norton, clinging on tight.

Grawl was wearing a gangster suit. Instead of a tie, the heart-shaped silver amulet hung around his neck. The crown of the cake was balanced on top of his hat, the two tiny figures twisting and tilting as he turned around. Cradled in his arms was a gun.

The alien tax delegates gazed up at him. Grawl knocked the hat off his bald cranium, then looked across at Diana.

"I'm dissolving the partnership," she said.

Standing on the table, Grawl took aim.

Diana nodded.

The killing began.

Grawl fired. The first alien died, toppling over, thudding to the ground. None of the others made any attempt to escape. They only moved when they were hit, when they fell, after which they didn't move anymore.

One by one, shot by shot, Grawl executed them all.

Everything was still, everything was silent.

All the other banquet guests must have known what to expect. They had already left the scene, or else they were sheltering under the tables.

Norton began slowly backing away, pulling Kiru with him. Her whole body was limp, and she was staring in horror at Grawl.

"You can't have her," said Diana, who was standing above the seven corpses.

"She's my wife," said Norton.

"Ha!" said Diana, as she picked up her violin case, opened the lid, took out a gun, aimed it at Norton. "Like I said, it's ideal."

Norton continued retreating, pushing Kiru ahead of him, keeping himself between her and Diana.

"You can go, Wayne," said Diana. "Leave Kiru. She belongs to Grawl now."

Grawl was still standing on the table, within the demolished ruins of the wedding cake. He held the gun loosely in his right hand, stroking the silver pendant with his left.

"It's over for her, Wayne," said Diana. "And it will be for you unless you step aside. Is this what you want? To end your life here? For what? For her? She's nothing to you."

Norton stopped and turned to face Kiru. They looked at each other then joined hands: two hands, four thumbs, fifteen fingers.

He didn't want to end his life here. But Kiru was his life. She was everything to him.

"I won't give you up," he whispered. "You're mine."

"No," said Kiru, squeezing his hands, "you're mine."

Norton glanced over his shoulder. Now Grawl's gun was also aimed directly at him.

"I love you," said Kiru. She kissed Norton lightly on the lips. Catching him off balance, she suddenly twisted him behind her.

There was a blast of blue lightning.

Kiru was hit. She dropped.

"Kiru!" yelled Norton, sinking to his knees and clutching her body.

No one could have her now.

"She's dead?" said Diana, and she sounded surprised. "Why did he use lethal?"

Jumping down from the table, Grawl made his way over to where Kiru lay. Norton stared up at him, his eyes full of tears and hate.

Grawl put the barrel of his gun against Norton's forehead.

Wayne Norton closed his eyes.

The universe ended.

ANOTHER END

Norton reached out for Kiru's left hand and slipped what he'd found onto her third finger. It slid across her fingernail, past the first knuckle. With a slight push, it went over the second knuckle. A perfect fit.

". . . I affirm you are now wife and husband," Diana concluded.

Kiru was staring down at her finger, at her wedding ring. A broken seashell, forged by the elements into a polished circle, it glinted in the light, ruby and amber, like a gemstone.

"It's . . ." Kiru kept gazing at the shell, lost for words.

"We'll get a real ring later," said Norton, "a gold one."

". . . the most wonderful thing anyone's ever given me," said Kiru. She looked at Norton, and she smiled. "Not that anyone's ever given me anything."

"Duke Wayne?" said a voice behind them.

Norton turned, looking at the creature standing on one leg. Tall, plump, small-beaked face craning forward, dark eyes at either side of its head, enormous wings folded across its back, the grey-feathered alien held its other clawed leg forward, offering a package.

"Who are you?" demanded Diana. "How did you get here?"

"Delivery for Duke Wayne," said the courier.

"Is that you?" said Kiru.

"Well, yeah," said Norton, trying to remember. "I used that name. Once." He looked at the box. "What is it?"

"Don't know, pal," said the alien, its head bobbing backward and forward. "If you want my professional opinion, I'd say a bouquet. If you want my professional advice, I'd say open it. Sign here."

Norton wondered why he was being sent a bouquet. Because it was a mistake, he assumed. It should have been for the bride.

"Just there," said the avian courier. "First-digit print. Ah. No first digit. Never mind the receipt, pal."

The creature gave the package to Norton, waddled away, spread its wings, flapped them, then took off, soaring upward.

Norton was about a hundred yards from the edge of the water, and he heard a distant splash. He turned, but his view was blocked by the conference pyramid. Although the courier had already vanished amongst the orange clouds, Norton glimpsed a trace of light high in the red sky—in the opposite direction. He kept watching the heavens, kept listening, but he saw nothing else, heard nothing more.

"What is that?" said Diana, gesturing toward the package.

Norton shook the box. It was light, didn't rattle. He handed it to Kiru.

"Now you've had two things," he said.

"Must be my lucky day," said Kiru, as she started unwrapping it. "In spite of getting married. It's not a bouquet. Ow!"

Instead of a bunch of flowers, Kiru was holding a bundle of thorns and nettles. She put a finger to her mouth, sucking at the blood where she'd been pricked.

"Did you hear that?" said Norton, inclining his head toward the sea.

"No," said Kiru. "What?"

He thought he'd heard another far-away splash in the ocean, and he stared up into the sky. When he looked back, he realised most of the banquet guests had already left. Almost the only ones still seated were the strange seven from the Galactic Tax Authority. Diana stood on the far side of the table, opposite where Norton and Kiru were standing.

That seemed to be it. The wedding was over without the cake being cut. Norton didn't care. The best was yet to come. It was time for the honeymoon.

He heard a crash behind him and he spun around. One of the autocams had dropped out of the air. There was another crash, then another, as all the cameras smashed to the ground.

Something else caught his eye. The wedding cake. It had moved. Then it suddenly burst open. A small, wide shape sprang up from inside.

"Grawl!" screamed Kiru, and she grabbed hold of Norton, clinging on tight.

Grawl was wearing a gangster suit. Instead of a tie, the heart-shaped silver amulet hung around his neck. The crown of the cake was balanced on top of his hat, the two tiny figures twisting and tilting as he turned around. Cradled in his arms was a gun.

The alien tax delegates gazed up at him. Grawl knocked the hat off his bald cranium, then looked across at Diana.

"I'm dissolving the partnership," she said.

Standing on the table, Grawl took aim.

"Nobody move!" shouted a voice which echoed around the plaza. "Drop that gun!"

Grawl's dark suit became speckled with bright white spots, the targeting beams from a score of weapons focused on him.

"Drop that gun! Now!"

Grawl obeyed, letting his weapon fall to the table.

The square was surrounded by an army of small, broad figures, all heavily armoured and heavily armed. They looked familiar.

"What are they?" said Kiru.

"What are they?" said Norton.

"Algolan hailstorm troopers," said Diana.

"They've come to kill me!" gasped Kiru.

She was still holding onto Norton, and now she held him even tighter. Kiru had been terrified of Grawl, but that was nothing compared to her fear of the Algolan soldiers.

"Why?" said Norton.

"Because they think Janesmith is here," said Kiru.

"So?" said Norton

"They think I'm Janesmith," said Kiru.

"Why?" said Norton.

"Because Travis made me say I was." Kiru looked at Diana. "It's his fault. Her fault."

The troopers marched nearer, closing the noose on those who remained in the plaza: Kiru and Norton, Grawl and Diana, the seven alien tax assessors.

"Is that how you treat our gifts of affection, Duke Wayne?"

Norton spun around. One of the Algolans had stepped within the ring of bronze-plated armour. Taller and slimmer, this had to be the commander. Clad in black battle armour, instead of a ridged helmet the figure wore a circle of barbed spikes on her head.

Her hair was white, her ears were pointed, her face was oval, her skin was blue, her feline features dominated by her huge, sloping eyes.

"Who's that?" said Kiru.

"Janesmith," said Norton. "The real Janesmith."

Kiru clutched him even tighter. "She's here because I pretended to be her."

"Silence!" ordered Janesmith, gesturing at Kiru with a gauntleted fist. "Pick those flowers up. Give them to Duke Wayne."

"Do it," Norton whispered, "and move away."

Kiru bent down for the nettles and thorns. "Ow!"

Janesmith glared at her.

Kiru handed the bouquet to Norton, then slowly stepped back.

Janesmith kept looking at Kiru, before her gaze took in the seven seated figures, then Diana, until she finally gazed at Grawl. She growled with pleasure. Grawl was still standing on the table, and he stared down at his spats, not meeting the Algolan's huge, sloping eyes.

"This is a nice surprise, Princess," said Norton. "What brings you here? Just passing by?"

"Our imperial warfleet brought us here," she said. "But your information is obsolete. We are not a princess. Our sister Marysmith is dead and the throne is ours. We are the Empress of Algol."

That explained the black spikes; it was her imperial crown. Norton wondered what the usual protocol was. What did one say to an empress?

"Er . . . congratulations."

Janesmith halted in front of Norton, staring at him.

"Turn around," she ordered. "This deserves a long painful death."

"What!" said Norton, and he spun back to face her.

"Who's your tailor?" said Empress Janesmith, gazing at

Norton's suit. "The fabric makes a mockery of the classic design."

"Er . . . yeah," Norton agreed.

"Nobody move!" yelled the echoing voice again. "That means you! Or you will be nobody!"

Diana must have tried to make a discreet exit, because she was now in a different position. She froze instantly.

"You are not of noble blood, we understand," said Janesmith, looking away from Norton so she didn't have to see his outfit. "You attempted to deceive us."

"No," he said. "Never. Not at all. It was a misunderstanding."

"It's of no consequence," said Janesmith.

Norton heard another distant splash and turned his head, guessing what it must have been. An Algolan hailstormer had dropped out of the sky and into the ocean, immediately sinking below the surface because of the weight of his armour.

"Your soldiers are drowning," he said.

"They live only to die in our service. Would you not willingly die for us, John Wayne?"

"You know who I am?"

"Yes. You are why we are here."

Norton said nothing, slowly considering what the Algolan had said. He was the reason she was here; she had come for him.

The new Empress of Algol had travelled across the galaxy to find him.

"But," he asked, "why . . . ?"

"We are the Empress," she said. "We need an Emperor."

The universe dissolved. Every planet and every atom was shattered. Wayne Norton was left totally alone, shivering in ultimate zero.

Emperor of Algol . . . ?

"That was the idea," said the Empress of Algol. "An alien Emperor. A virgin Emperor." Her gaze travelled to Kiru. "But we've changed our mind. We don't need you, what we need is—"

She paused, turned, pointed a chain-mailed finger.

"—Grawl!"

"Grawl?" said Norton. "You know Grawl?"

"We have had the honour of knowing the most hand-some being of all," said Janesmith, gazing up at Grawl.

Grawl was still standing on the table, within the demol-ished ruins of the wedding cake, his arms raised in surren-der. Janesmith glanced away as if dazzled by his radiance.

Norton suddenly realised why the Algolan troops seemed so familiar. Small and squat, they were like armoured ver-sions of Grawl. Janesmith had claimed that she was ugly and that Norton was deformed, but Grawl must have matched the Algolan ideal of the perfect male.

"Grawl," said Kiru, hesitantly, "is going to be Emperor of Algol?"

The Empress growled, and Kiru stepped back.

"Show us your genitals," Janesmith said to Grawl.

And Grawl cowered down. A look of total horror, of ultimate fear, contorted his face. It was an expression he had never shown before, a feeling he had never known before.

"Let's go, our love," said Janesmith.

Grawl jumped from the table. He grabbed his gun—and turned it on himself. Before he could fire, he was rushed by a group of Algolan troops. They dived on him to prevent his suicide, then carried him away.

"You shouldn't have left," Empress Janesmith said to Norton. "You don't know what you missed."

Norton was glad he didn't know. He remembered what he'd seen, briefly, when Janesmith had been naked. What-ever lay ahead of him, for Grawl it was a destiny worse than death.

Janesmith gestured contemptuously, dismissing Norton. Her eyes passed over Kiru, ignoring her. She stared at the palefaces for a few seconds, then focused her attention on Diana.

"You are someone of importance on this world?" she said.

"Yes, yes, I'm—"

"We will establish a diplomatic embassy here," said Janesmith.

"Great, great," said Diana. "I look forward to a lasting and cordial relationship."

"You will be our puppet. This world will become part of our empire."

Then the Empress of Algol turned. Escorted by the rest of the bronze hailstormers, she strode imperially away, vanishing between the spiralling red buildings on the far side of the plaza.

Norton sighed with relief, threw away the bouquet of brambles, took Kiru's hand, and led her to one of the tables. They sat down, and he poured two overflowing glasses of wine.

"That was Grawl," said Kiru, swallowing half her wine in a single gulp.

"I know," said Norton, swallowing three-quarters of his. "We came here in the same escape pod."

"You were with him all that time?" said Kiru. "Why didn't you kill him? You knew what he tried to do to me."

"He saved my life," said Norton, and he downed the other quarter.

"What kind of pathetic excuse is that? Why didn't you tell me he was on Caphmiaultrelvossmuaf?"

"I thought he was dead. I didn't want to upset you."

"Upset me? Upset me!" Kiru finished her wine.

"He's gone now," said Norton, refilling both glasses. "He must have liked you."

"Liked me! What? He wanted to kill me!"

"No. Not exactly. He didn't want you dead."

"He wanted my soul to be dead. He wanted to replace it with the . . . the essence, the being, of someone else."

"Yeah," said Norton. "Someone important to him. And he chose you, chose you to hold the most important person in his life."

"I should be grateful?"

"I wonder who it was? Someone who loved him."

"Who could love him?" said Kiru.

"Janesmith," said Norton. He gazed up, imagining the Algolan warfleet encircling the planet. "How do they know each other?"

"It's a small galaxy."

"You're not curious about whose spirit was in Grawl's silver pendant?"

"No! I don't want to think about it."

"Who would love him?" said Norton. "His mother?"

"Grawl never had a mother," said Kiru.

There was movement at the next table, the table where

Kiru and Norton had originally sat, and where the Galactic Tax Authority representatives were still seated. At exactly the same instant, they all stood up.

"Considering your recent behaviour," one of them said to Diana, "we may have to renegotiate the terms of our partnership."

It seemed Diana hadn't thawed out since being ordered not to move. She was standing in the same place, as if stunned by everything that had happened. All she could do was watch as the seven palefaces started to leave, following each other in a neat line.

But then she opened her violin case and pulled out a gun. As the aliens filed away, Diana took aim.

Watching in disbelief, Norton realised she wasn't going to give them a warning or tell them to stop. One by one, she was about to shoot them in the back.

Norton leapt to his feet, dashed forward, yelling out an instinctive warcry.

"Geronimo-o-o-o-o!"

Diana's head turned, then her gun followed.

But she was too late; Norton was on her, deflecting the barrel, grappling with her. She was strong, very strong. He couldn't hit a woman. Except she wasn't a woman. Not all the time. He was Colonel Travis. And Norton socked him on the jaw, knocking him to the ground.

Kiru picked up the gun, jerked out the ammo charge, threw the weapon back down.

"Tough stuff, Wayne," she said, admiringly.

"That's me," said Norton. He opened his right fist, wiggling the thumb and three fingers. "I'm just a Stone Age man."

He watched the delegation from Hideaway. They hadn't glanced back, hadn't missed a single step. They disappeared out of the plaza.

"What was that you shouted?" asked Kiru.

"Geronimo," said Norton. "Not to be confused with Gino and Rico and Pedro." He looked down at Diana, at Travis. "Does this mean we can't use the honeymoon suite?"

Diana/Travis rubbed her/his jaw.

"What are you all staring at?" she/he said. "Get everything neat and tidy and put away."

Norton glanced around, seeing the Caphafer restaurant workers behind him.

"Clean this mess up," ordered Diana/Travis.

"No," said one of them.

"No," said another, then another, then all of them.

"No, no, no, no, no," they chorused.

Norton felt a drop of water on his head. When he peered up, another drop hit his face. It was beginning to rain. Red rain was again starting to fall on the island.

The Caphafers tore off their blue bikinis, throwing them down at Diana/Travis.

Remembering Kiru's earlier words, Norton glanced away, not wanting to discover what the natives had under the lower halves of their bikinis.

As the amphibious aliens turned and headed for the sea, Kiru watched them and she smiled.

"Are they going on strike?" asked Norton.

"Permanently," said Kiru. "They're the Caphmiaultrelvossmuafan Liberation Army. Or maybe Navy. It's their world. They want it back. Come on." She reached out and took his hand, leading him away from the square.

"How do you know all this?" asked Norton.

"I've made friends with them while I've been swimming."

"Where are we going?"

Norton was becoming suspicious. He slowed down. The route they were taking led only to the ocean.

"Where else can we go?" said Kiru.

By the time they reached the shoreline, it was raining heavily on land as well as sea. Kiru swiftly peeled off her white bikini.

"What are you doing?" Norton asked.

"You can see what I'm doing. This thing isn't designed for the water, and neither is your suit. Take it off."

"I'm not going in the water!"

"Wayne, listen to me: Where else are you going to go?"

"Ah . . ." Norton looked back toward the island, guessing that it might not be such a good idea to return. ". . . yeah."

As he gazed at the red ocean, the waves, imagining the unknown depths beneath, Kiru undid his tie, slipped off his jacket, removed his vest, unbuttoned his shirt.

"I can't go in the sea," he said. "I can't swim."

"You can float, you know that," Kiru told him. She unfastened his shoes. "There are other islands out there, caverns that can only be reached from under the water, places where we'll be safe. We'll be okay. We've got friends." She took off his pants. "I've got friends. It's lucky Diana didn't thank you in her speech for helping them choose this planet, not that the Caphafers would have known who you were. We all look the same to them."

Norton stared at the red alien ocean, noticing all the red aliens waiting out there. Waiting for them.

Friends? He hoped so.

Kiru held up her left hand, showing Norton her wedding ring.

"That's all I need," she said, taking his right hand in her left.

"You're all I need," said Norton, and they kissed.

Countless aeons ago, on a far-away planet, their distant ancestors had crawled out of the primeval sea in their quest for a new life.

Now it was time to return.

As naked as when they were born, Kiru and Wayne Norton waded out into the alien ocean, away from the land and toward the unknown horizon.

NOT ANOTHER END . . .

. . . but a new beginning

PENGUIN PUTNAM INC.
Online

Your Internet gateway to a virtual environment with hundreds of entertaining and enlightening books from Penguin Putnam Inc.

While you're there, get the latest buzz on the best authors and books around—

Tom Clancy, Patricia Cornwell, W.E.B. Griffin, Nora Roberts, William Gibson, Robin Cook, Brian Jacques, Catherine Coulter, Stephen King, Ken Follett, Terry McMillan, and many more!

**Penguin Putnam Online is located at
http://www.penguinputnam.com**

PENGUIN PUTNAM NEWS

Every month you'll get an inside look at our upcoming books and new features on our site. This is an ongoing effort to provide you with the most up-to-date information about our books and authors.

Subscribe to Penguin Putnam News at
http://www.penguinputnam.com/newsletters